Birthday Girl

Minnesota Ice, Volume 3

Lily Kate

Published by Lily Kate, 2017.

This is a work of fiction. Similarities to real people, places, or events are entirely coincidental.

BIRTHDAY GIRL

First edition. September 26, 2017.

Written by Lily Kate.

Also by Lily Kate

Minnesota Ice
Boss Girl
Birthday Girl

The Girls
Hangry Girl

To my other half.

Interested in receiving *Love Letters from Lily*?
Sign up for her new-release newsletter at: LilyKateAuthor.com!

Acknowledgments

W.A. for being the other half of my brain.

Virginia for your sharp proofreading eyes.

Perfect Pear Creations for the fabulous cover design.

All of you, **readers**—beta readers, ARC readers, bloggers, and the entire book community—each and every one of you are fabulous!

And, of course, to the very **best of friends**... you know who you are!

Synopsis

Good things come in extra-large, smoking hot birthday suits.

Bad boy **Cohen James** has screwed up yet again. Star forward of Minnesota's pro hockey team, Cohen's made a name for himself—and not in a good way. So, at the insistence of his agent, he's stuck volunteering at the local YMCA teaching introductory adult swim lessons for ten weeks. Ten weeks of torture.

What he doesn't expect is *her*.

Annie Plymouth, star pupil.

Her ruffled green bathing suit might be the most ridiculous thing he's ever seen, but after a few heated breaststroke lessons and some intense mouth to mouth, Cohen's ready to get her out of the water and into her birthday suit... except *she* has a different game plan.

Is the pair destined to sink... or can they swim?

Chapter 1

Annie

"Are you *sure* you can't get married on firm ground? Absolutely *positive*?" I face my mother and cinch the fluffy towel closer to my body. "I'll bribe you. Name your price; I'll do anything."

"Annie, please. Claude loves the ocean." Ellie Plymouth tucks a freshly highlighted bang behind her ear and issues a smile brimming with sympathy. The sympathy doesn't matter much, however, since she's clearly not budging on her decision. "It's just a ten-week class. Once per week, and then you'll be a swimming guru."

"Saturday *mornings*. Ten weeks." I turn and face the mirror. "For what? I'm not going swimming on the cruise. I'm not going to throw myself overboard or flip around with the dolphins."

"You promised you'd learn before your birthday, dear."

"That's the other thing! You didn't have to get re-married on my birthday."

"Seven is Claude's lucky number."

"So why not the seventh of June? How about August? It just *had* to be July?" I frown at my reflection in the mirror. There's no possible way I can pass for a normal human being in this outfit. "Green, mom? At least you could've gone with black. It's slimming."

"You're plenty slim. And you look *great*. Now shower off because your instructor won't wait for you all day."

4

I survey my body—and the swimsuit on it—and decide there's no hope for me. I'm wearing a one-piece bathing suit made from a shade of green that resembles alien vomit. There are ruffles on every available surface. So many ruffles. Probably enough extra ruffles to make a dress from the excess material.

It's my fault, really. I'd made my mother a stupid promise. When she'd gotten engaged to Claude, she'd begged me to learn how to swim before my twenty-third birthday. Because ironically, that is the same day as their wedding.

The wedding will take place on a cruise ship, and therein lies the problem.

I hate water.

Now, this *hate* is not a casual dislike of lakes, or even a modest mistrust of the ocean. It's not even a slight hesitation to go swimming without a life jacket. No, my fear is all consuming. I am utterly, undeniably terrified of large bodies of water.

I've managed to get by so far in life without learning the art of the front crawl—it's always "that time of the month" during pool parties. My gym teacher probably thought I had a chronic case of the flu thanks to my spectacular acting performances to avoid swim class. At home, I generally avoid taking baths because I'm terrified of falling asleep and drowning in my own tub, but showers work just fine.

My mother once tried to enroll me in swim lessons through the local community center, but I cried so hard that my teacher begged my mother to reconsider. Now that I'm twenty-two, she thinks enough time has passed to try again.

I'm as equally unenthusiastic as I was the first time around. The only difference is that this time, I can't sob my way out of it.

"Dear, you need to face your fears," my mother says again as I drag my feet into the locker room, dreading whatever the next hour will bring. "It's for your safety."

"Yeah, right."

"What do you mean by that?" she snaps. "It *is*! I don't want you to fall overboard after you've had one too many margaritas and *die*, Annie. Not on my wedding cruise. You're the maid of honor for crying out loud."

"Right, and it'd be really inconvenient to plan a funeral from your honeymoon."

"We *love* you," she says. "Claude and I care for your safety."

"Claude calls me Amanda. He doesn't care about my survival."

She huffs, but doesn't reply. She's run out of arguments, I guess, which is just fine with me since I don't want to discuss this any longer. I'm angry enough standing here at eight a.m. on a Saturday morning, in the middle of a late February snowstorm, freezing my ass off in a lime-green bathing suit.

My mother's lucky that I can't stand it when she cries. When the tears started flowing at Thanksgiving, I broke down and agreed to swimming lessons as part of her wedding gift. Not a day later, she'd signed me up, paid for the class, and told me she'd supply the swimsuit. I am regretting all of it, especially the swimsuit.

It's too late to come up with an excuse, however, which leaves me stuck here with two choices: wear the stupid ruffles, or scale down to my birthday suit, and *nobody* wants to see that. I mean... it's February. I'm whiter than Frosty the Snowman. People will need sunglasses to look at my butt.

"There you are!" Gran putters into the showers with a huge smile on her face. "Did your mother tell you we were all coming together today? She said you might be nervous. That's why I'm here. I've got moral support coming out the wazoo."

The spray of water splutters over my shoulders as I swipe a hand across my eyes and peek at my grandmother. "No, I didn't know you'd be here until you showed up at my apartment this morning. I could've come by myself."

I glance at her festive attire. It's a testament to how upset I'd been earlier this morning that I hadn't even noticed my Gran's clothes until now. I'd been too annoyed at my mother to speak at all on the ride over. I couldn't be mad at Gran, though. She'd just come along for the ride.

"It's really not necessary. None of this is necessary."

Gran follows my gaze down to her tube socks straight out of *That Seventies Show*. One sock says "Go!" and the other says "Annie!"

My name is Annie Plymouth. Everyone will be able to see that quite clearly, thanks to Gran. There are also pom poms in her hands, and I cringe as she begins to wave them around.

"Annie, Annie, go... Bananie!" She does a high kick, but the floor is a little slippery, and she grasps onto a towel rod for balance. The whole thing clatters to the floor, a cacophony of metal on tile as Gran screeches for help.

I leap for her just as she's starting to topple with it, cradling her in my arms, praying she doesn't dislocate a hip. I needn't have worried. Within seconds, she's popped right back into her cheer.

"G-O Annie Bananie!" Gran finishes. "Rah, rah, rah!"

"No cheerleading in the bathroom," I tell her as I do my best to reattach the towel rod to its mount. "You're a liability."

Carefully, I lean the pole against the wall after determining the entire thing is ruined. I can't chastise her too much, though, since she's newly widowed. My grandfather died last year, and it's been rough on her. I'm just happy to see Gran waving pom poms again. "What are you really doing here?"

"Besides cheering for my favorite granddaughter?"

"Yes."

"Well, I have synchronized swimming lessons right after you." Gran bats her eyelashes at me and offers up a brilliant smile. "I've moped around long enough. I loved your grandfather dearly—still do, but I need to meet some new friends and get some social interaction. I'm going crazy in my house all alone, day after day."

"Aw, Gran, but I come to visit."

"Only three times a week."

"Mom lives there."

"Yeah, but sometimes she's boring. Plus, she's busy with work and *Claude*." Gran winks in my direction. Then, her eyes cross slightly as she appears to notice my bathing suit. Giving a low whistle, she shakes her head in appreciation. "That suit is gorgeous, Annie Banana. You think they have one in my size?"

"I'll tell you what—I'll give you this one. Just as soon as I get a new one. Like, in an hour. As soon as possible."

"What are the kids saying these days? *You rock*?" Gran extends a hand and gives me a fist bump. "I'll gladly adopt your bathing suit."

"Annie, it's time!" My mother yells from outside of the showers. "Hurry! If you don't get a spot in this class, I am not going to be happy! I called months ago to reserve you a seat."

I shuffle out of the showers with a towel the size of a comforter wrapped around my body. Stepping in front of my mother, I stop and exhale a sigh. "Look, mom. I'm doing this for you. As a favor. I hate the water, you know that, and I have no desire to learn how to swim—"

"—but it's for your safety!"

"Mom!" I take in her brows, furrowed in confusion, and lower my voice. "Please. I'm doing this to make you happy. So can we please cut the crap with the cheerleading squad? I told you not to show up today... but you didn't even trust me to drive myself, and you brought Gran?"

"I had to bring you the suit," my mother says, crossing her arms. "I also happen to know how stubborn my daughter is, and if I hadn't shown up, I'm willing to bet *you* wouldn't have attended class at all."

My lips are a tight line, and I don't have anything to say because she's right. Until about ten minutes ago, I'd planned to show up, slip the teacher twenty bucks in exchange for whatever stupid certificate I need to pass the class, and skedaddle.

It'd never been my intention to actually go through with the entire lesson. For crying out loud, I'm twenty-two. If I haven't learned how to swim by now, I can probably manage for the rest of my life.

Plenty of other people don't have skills. Some people never learn how to ride a bike, or roller blade, or ice skate. It's not *that* weird, but clearly, my mother disagrees.

"We have got to make a deal," I tell her, my voice a low hiss. "I'll show up for ten weeks, but you *must* keep Gran and her socks away. Including today."

"But she has synchronized swimming lessons—"

"Away!" I move past her, trying not to wimp out. I can't help but add a polite, "Please."

My mother and I never fight. She's odd sometimes, and makes choices that I don't approve of (*Claude*), but we're friends. My snappish attitude is probably coming from the fact that I'm steps away from facing my worst fear: big, open pools of water.

"Honey." My mom's hand catches my arm before I get much further. She waits until I turn to face her, the sparkling hazel eyes mirror images of my own. "Thank you. It's going to be okay—really, I promise. This is a good thing."

I take a deep breath. "I hope so."

"I'll buy Gran an ice cream cone," my mom says, her lips lilting upward in a smile. "That should give you a good head start. Who knows? Maybe we'll wind up in Target for an hour and she'll miss your lesson."

I offer my mom a half smile and a wave. This is our version of a truce, and I'm glad we've reached it because it's just her and me—it always has been, and it always will be.

Except for Claude, but he doesn't really count. We've had men come and go over the last few years, but none of that matters much because we've always had each other. I'm an only child, and my mom is my best friend, and the only horrible thing in the world right now is getting into that stupid pool.

Until everything gets worse.

Chapter 2

Annie

I step outside of the locker room, and of course, I find my answer. It *can* be worse.

There's a room full of supermodels—or, what I would classify as soccer moms of the Beverly Hills variety—waiting to get in the pool. I inch onto the deck, scan the crowd of women there, and freeze.

I double back to read the sign on the door to make sure I'm in the right spot. Sure enough, there it is in big, bold letters: **Adult Beginner Swim Lessons**.

I slide back into the crowd, glancing around for another kindred spirit. Someone who doesn't have Botox in their forehead or a slinky bikini that wouldn't hold half my boob. I'm not fat by any means, but I'm not athletic either—I'm just sort of average, and I'd be popping out of those flimsy triangles the Model-Moms are sporting.

Finally, I spy another woman who looks just as confused as I feel. She's also wearing a one-piece, which means we're probably on the same team, a team called *I don't want to be here*. Sidling over, I assess her briefly and offer a polite smile. She's Asian, probably ten years older than me, with a quick grin and a pleasant expression.

"Hi," I say once we're shoulder to shoulder. "Are you here for swimming lessons?"

Her brown eyes flick toward me, warm and bright with a hidden smile behind them. "I thought so, but I'm starting to feel like I stumbled into the Miss Universe pageant."

"You and me both," I say. "What is going on here? I thought this was just a stupid YMCA class."

"Me too!" She laughs and extends a hand. "I'm Leigh. I'm only here because my kids made me sign up. I'm making my oldest register for swim lessons, and he's too smart for his own good. Asked why he needed to learn how to swim if his mother didn't know how."

"So you're practicing what you preach?"

She exhales. "Kids."

"Well, I'm here because of my mom."

Leigh gives me a look. "Did she pick out the suit?"

"Unfortunately. She also picked out the fiancé who wants to get married on a stupid boat."

"And she's terrified you'll drown when you get drunk at the reception and salsa dance off the plank."

"Something like that."

"Planning a funeral so soon after a wedding wouldn't be a great start to a marriage," she says with a tinkling laugh. "As a fellow mother, I understand where she's coming from."

I'm grinning too. I like Leigh, even if she's siding with my mother. "She's well-intentioned."

"You'll understand when you have kids of your own," Leigh says. "Unless you have them already?"

I'm about to tell her that there's no way I can take care of anyone else at this stage of my life. I'm a senior in college, graduating after this semester with plans to continue to law school. I'm lucky if I can feed myself most of the time, let alone a child.

However, before I can tell her all this, I'm silenced by a collective gasp from the supermodel moms.

"I guess this is it?" Leigh whispers, straining on tiptoes to see over the crowd. "The moment we've all been waiting for. You're taller than me. Can you see anything?"

"No, nothing..."

Nothing except for a sea of fake chests that'd been blown up by talented plastic surgeons, and multiple sets of lips that'd seen the same fate. There's even a man who's shiny all over, as if he's waxed and bathed in oil, wearing nothing but a Speedo.

"I mean, there's lots of skin to see," I clarify. "But nothing else."

Leigh snickers next to me. "I have to confess, I almost tried to pay off the swimming teacher for a certificate that said I passed. But I figure my kid would smell a lie."

"Me too! Except, minus the kid and add my mother," I say, and we bond with another smile. "She's actually upstairs with my Gran right now. They have a—"

Leigh taps my arm. "Look! There. Can you see anything?"

I stop mid-sentence and raise onto my toes. I'm about to tell Leigh that the only thing I've spotted is a bad bikini wax on the woman to the left when my eyes lock on the target of everyone else's attention.

It's not a thing, so much as it's a *him*. But *him* isn't a term that does the man walking toward us justice. He's an impressive specimen, sculpted like an athlete. From what I can see of his body, it's gorgeous, more deity-like than man—although, when he turns his face upward, it's not beautiful in the traditional sense.

He's rugged, almost dangerous with a scar that cuts across his eyebrow and a mess of black hair combed back from his face. One strand has broken loose and hangs a little low over his eyebrow, and it's just enough to give him a burst of humanity that has my stomach twisting in knots.

His eyes rake over the crowd, and if I'm not mistaken, he looks pissed. He stands still, tall, which causes his torso to show off the lean muscle he's sculpted from years of... something. I'm not sure if the man works out or if he was gifted that body from God, but something is working. There are lines that I never knew existed across his abs.

Then, there are his arms. One arm is a complete sleeve of tattoos—shoulder to wrist. I've never been a tattoo sort of girl. I'm pretty vanilla when it comes to guys, if I'm honest. Maybe because those are the only ones I seem to attract. I can count the number of boyfriends I've had on one finger—my middle one—and he *definitely* didn't look like the guy before us.

"I'm guessing by the stars in your eyes that you're single?" Leigh's grinning at me as I glance her way. "That's the look of insta-lust."

I realize my mouth is slightly open. "No, of course not. He's not my type."

"I figured. He's *their* type." Leigh nods toward the group before us. "I can see that hiring Cohen on to be the swim lesson instructor brought in serious cash for the Y. Not a bad idea for a fundraiser."

"You know him?"

She gives me a dumbfounded stare. "Of course. They gave us a slip of paper about it when we signed up for the class."

I close my eyes and massage my forehead with a hand. "Of course they did."

"Your mom didn't tell you?"

"Not a word."

"Cohen James plays for the Minnesota Stars. The *only* reason I know this is because my son asked me to get his autograph."

"Stars... that's hockey?"

"So they say. I was never a sports girl until I had kids, and now it's all I hear about. My son says he can't read a book, but he has no trouble reading and pronouncing the name on every sports card he can find. I'm telling you—too smart."

"So what's the deal with this class? Shouldn't he be... I don't know, skating around or whatever?"

Leigh smirks. "He should be. But according to the papers, our buddy Cohen doesn't often do what he should be doing."

"Troublemaker?"

"To put it lightly. That's what landed him here. At least, that's what the rumors say. Of course, the papers are saying that he's doing it as a charity event to help the YMCA out, but... I can't believe that's true."

"What do you mean?"

"I'm betting his agent told him to clean up his act, otherwise he's not going to be lacing up his skates next season," Leigh says, her voice a whisper now. "He's been in trouble on more than one occasion this season alone. His last team traded him—the LA Lightening—because of behavior issues. I think."

"Yikes."

"Yep. And I'm betting his coach—or someone—told him to give up the late nights, the parties, the excess, and do something wholesome or he's off the team."

"So he picked swimming lessons?"

"It may not have been *his* pick. Good press opportunity, though. Who knows. If we ever get started with this class, maybe we can ask."

Mr. James quiets the room by raising a hand. My eyes lock on his tattoos, follow the marks up past his sculpted shoulder to a face that's darkened with a wry smile, to eyes that are fixed... *Oh, no.* Please, no.

His eyes are fixed on me, and it's not hard to guess why. My swimming suit is blinding in all of its lime-green glory.

"Annie Plymouth?" he calls in a gravelly, world-worn sort of voice. From the slight lilt, I'm guessing it's not the first time he's said my name, and he's scanning the crowd for a sign of recognition. "Is there an Annie here?"

Unfortunately, I can't seem to find my voice. It appears to have gone missing the second Cohen said my name. Thankfully, Leigh puts the pieces together and clasps her thin hand around my wrist, raising it high.

"Here!" she squeaks for me.

I nod vigorously, ignoring the stares from the rest of the women. They've got this sort of oddly-fascinated look on their faces as they watch me, scan my suit, and shake their heads. It's an expression of pity, as if I'm so out of their league that I'm not even considered competition.

Which is true, I guess. I'm not competing for anything.

One of the women murmurs to her friend while staring in my direction, and I can make out something about my suit. Specifically, words that sound like *toxic waste*.

My face blooms a bright red, and I lower my hand, stepping behind a taller woman who is more than happy to block my face. It doesn't, however, block the sound of Cohen's voice booming through the pool room.

"Love the attire, Annie. It suits you."

I look at him, a blank expression on my face. "Suits me?"

He grins, and it's a sexy, lopsided smile that boils my insides. "I like it. Now, is there a Leigh here?"

As my newfound friend raises her hand, I'm left to ponder what the hell Cohen meant when he said my attire *suits* me. I mean, toxic waste and alien vomit are the two things this suit brings to mind, and neither are great comparisons.

I'm still debating whether or not I should be offended when I catch a glimpse of the woman who'd been bad-mouthing my ruffles. She's glaring at me now, and it gives me an odd sense of satisfaction.

The lady's suit is black and boring, like really thick floss tied together across her chest. I smile back blandly, forgiving my mother somewhat for the horrid color of this thing.

My smile disappears the next second, however, when Cohen James calls for everyone to get into the water.

All thoughts of sexy men, tattoos, and surgically enhanced body parts leave my mind. I'm frozen stiff, and I can't bring myself to take one more step into the pool area.

The rest of the group seems more than happy to take flying leaps off the edge of the wall. There are women swan-diving and cannon-balling and dipping one dainty toe into the water all seductive and smooth. Meanwhile, I'm stuck like a snowman on the ledge, trying not to melt into a puddle.

"Annie, is it?" The instructor's soft voice breaks through my fog of uncertainty. "I'm Cohen. Nice to meet you."

I nod at him. Completely mute.

"It's okay," he says, his voice like a rocky beach—rough at times, but also smooth, cool and steady. "If you're not ready to get in, that's okay. I need help with the first exercise, anyway. Can you come over here with me?"

I follow him like a robot, slipping a little on the wet deck. He holds out a hand and links his arm around mine. As we stroll, I catch a glimpse of the same woman who'd been talking smack about my suit. If she looked annoyed before, she's murderous now. I'm too terrified of slipping into the pool to find any satisfaction in it at all.

My breath comes in short spurts while my heart is speeding a million miles an hour. It's all I can do to make it to the side of the pool as Cohen calls out for the group to give him their best five-hundred-yard swim—in any style the group prefers. He'll select the winners for a prize after.

"What's the prize?" I ask, when he turns to me. "Also, I think I'm in the wrong place. I thought this was for newbies. Adults who don't know how to swim."

We turn together and watch rows of swimmers flying up and down the lanes. Only one or two of them look like they're struggling at all. One of them is Leigh, and I give her an encouraging thumbs up.

"Just you wait, sweetheart."

We both freeze as he uses the nickname. Me, because it's the last thing I expect to hear from him.

"Shit. I should be more professional." He runs a hand through his hair, looking frustrated. "Any chance we can forget I called you sweetheart?"

"Sure thing, baby," I say. Then I clap a hand over my mouth. I have no idea where that came from. It was filled with sarcasm, but I'm not that girl—I'm not the girl who flirts with her gorgeous instructor. I'm the girl who's drowning and blinking water out of her eyes. "Sorry, I didn't mean to say that."

He's smiling when I brave a glance at him. It's a quirky smile. His nose is a little too big, and there's a small bump there, as if he'd been clocked hard with a hockey puck. But his features come together in a way that makes me stare longer, falling a little deeper into those glittering pools of green.

"I knew I liked you the second you walked in, *sweetheart*," he says. "Now, let's get to the fun stuff."

Chapter 3

Cohen

I run my eyes over the crowd of ladies and, yes, even a gent, who showed up for beginners swim lessons, and do my best not to roll my eyes.

I might have made plenty of idiotic choices in my life, but I'm not a moron. These people can swim. With the exception of about four adults here, everyone is fully capable of holding their head above water.

Taking special attention to look at my watch, I time the group as they complete their five-hundred-yard swim. It's a pretty big request for a class of beginners—like asking an infant to read me a bedtime story. It's just not realistic.

A few of the faster ladies finish quickly, panting, looking up at me with an expression that, had I seen it in a bar, would've been quite welcome. I'm not opposed to older women, so long as they're unattached.

But this is one of the *only* times and places where I'm not allowed to look at a woman's ass, let alone take her to bed, and it's driving me nuts. I'm required to be professional.

It's not the cougars who showed up to my class that have me on edge, though. It's the frigging adorable girl standing too close to me on the pool deck—so close I can smell her perfume—that's got my blood pumping.

She's sweet and sugary, her scented perfume bright—just like her eyes. Then, there's the suit. I have my theories on why she's wearing a ruffle machine, but I'll have to hold my tongue. I already slipped and called her sweetheart, and I can't screw this up.

Thankfully, she seems to brush it off. She also doesn't seem the least bit interested in giving me the once over that I'd been seeing from the rest of the women here. I have to admit, a part of me is annoyed. Did she not know what she'd signed up for? She couldn't really be here to learn how to *swim*, could she?

"What am I supposed to be watching for?" she asks, turning those big, hazel eyes on me, an innocent question reflected there. "You told me to pay attention, but... I don't know what I'm looking at."

"Forget it," I growl.

I can't even remember what I was talking about when I told her to watch the group for me. She'd been looking up, eyes full of fear as she slipped on the deck, and it was all I could do not to tuck her under my arm, pull her against me, and taste those full lips.

She's a complete stranger. I shouldn't care if she can swim like a freaking fish, or if she's petrified of the water; it's inconsequential to me. I'm here for one reason, and one reason only: Public Relations. A fundraiser, some photo opportunities—that's it.

My coach stuck some overachieving young PR lady on me after my latest screw up which, if I was being honest, wasn't entirely my fault. Sure, I'd been caught outside Ryan Pierce's window, drunk and serenading him next-to-naked, but I'd done it for a good cause.

Team spirit. Otherwise known as hazing for the new guy.

Okay, *maybe* it was my fault that I'd ended up here, in a swimsuit, on a freezing Saturday morning. I'd made a few stupid choices that led to a certain amount of messes for my new team, the Minnesota

Stars. One of my problems was picking an argument with the captain of the squad, a Ryan Pierce, and ending up on his shit list.

Up until today, the idea of teaching a group of adults to swim was less appealing than poison, but seeing as the only thing in this world I've ever loved—and will ever love—is hockey, I'm sucking up the punishment and teaching this damn class.

The twist? The appearance of one ugly-ass bathing suit and the hottie inside of it. My mind has been changed. A little. Ten weeks of this crap and maybe my coach won't want to put my balls through the blender. Unlikely, but worth a shot.

"I think they're done."

I startle as Annie whispers. She's leaning so close her words leap off my shoulder, and I jump back as if she's breathing fire. "I can see that, thanks."

"Sorry."

Now I feel like dirt. It's not her fault she's got me on edge—it's her body. Despite her choice in clothing, it's impossible to miss the curvy figure underneath the swimsuit.

The thin straps sit over pale white skin, teasing anyone who has an ounce of testosterone in their blood. The fabric cinches tight against her hips and rides just a little too high on her ass. Yes, I checked. Sue me, I'm a man.

"You ready for this?" I mutter as I walk by her, tapping my clipboard and pretending to be important. I haven't even tried to put faces with the names on here—most of them will be scratched off in the next thirty seconds. "Nice job, everyone. So, if you've finished your five hundred, I'm going to need you to come into this lane. You're getting an upgrade."

As predicted, ninety-nine percent of the class shifts one lane over. The only people left are Annie, Leigh, and an older gentleman wearing a shitty excuse for a Speedo. I'll have to talk to him about covering his genitalia if he wants to stay in my class.

"Great," I say, once I've marked down everyone who's shifted over. "You all are excellent swimmers."

Several of the women preen under the compliment, and the younger man in the group gives me a look that is probably meant to be seductive, if I were into that sort of thing. Which I am definitely not, no offense. If I had to pick a "thing" to be into, it would look suspiciously like Annie friggin' Plymouth.

"Upgrade?" one of the woman asks. "Like personal, one-on-one lessons?"

When I find her name on the sheet, it's Lydia. She's the one who made fun of Annie's outfit. I take extra pride in giving her my most genuine smile.

"Even better," I tell her. I scan the rest of the pool area which, for a YMCA, is quite large. I spot a man nearing his nineties in a saggy bathing suit. He's got goggles on his head the size of a scuba mask. "You all get to spend some time with my friend, Duke."

Duke doesn't look up—probably because that's not his name. I've never met the guy. However, I suspect most of the group only showed up to get my attention. The problem is that I'm not here to sign autographs; I'm here to teach a stupid lesson. I'm a slacker by nature, and I'm not teaching forty ladies to backstroke if I can teach three. Especially if one of those three is Annie.

"What?" Lydia asks. "You can't be serious."

"Of course I am." My smile widens at the sight of Annie, who's hiding a laugh behind her hand. I can tell she knows I'm making this stuff up as I go. "Duke charges a lot more than I do for his lessons, so you're really getting a deal. Free upgrade—no extra cost to you. If you'll just wait here, I'll go get your new instructor..."

There's a mass exodus from the pool. I'm hearing every excuse from blisters to the stomach flu to deadly cramps. The room is silent and evacuated within twenty seconds.

"So…" I walk back to the remaining three folks. "Leigh, Annie, and Jason. Welcome to the class."

Chapter 4

Annie

The lesson passes quickly. Far too quickly for my taste.

It's only a forty-five minute class, but the first forty minutes fly by like lightning. For being a little bit of a cocky hockey star, Cohen is surprisingly attentive when it comes to lessons.

To Leigh, at least, and Jason. He mostly ignores me, but that's okay because I don't want much to do with him, either. It takes enough concentration for me to kick my legs and swing my arms and generally keep myself from drowning, so I worry that if he paid me any attention at all, I'd probably die a watery death from distraction.

When the five-minute countdown hits, trouble comes with it.

"Let's head to the deep end," Cohen says. He's standing on the edge of the pool, giving us a spectacular view of his abs. "Best to face our fears right away. Come on, it'll only take a second."

"Nah," I say, waving a hand, attempting nonchalance. "I think I'll sit this one out."

"Come on," Leigh says. "I'll be right next to you."

"*Nah*," I say again. "I've already swallowed enough chlorine to set off a drug test. That's clearly a sign I'm not ready for the deep end."

"Go on," Cohen tells the others. "I'll convince her."

Leigh and Jason make their way slowly down to the other side, alternating between a splashy doggy paddle and a simple fingertip drag along the wall.

Meanwhile, Cohen lowers himself so that his feet dangle in the water and our faces are inches apart. Closer than we've been all day, ever since we watched the others compete like marathoners at the beginning of class, and I'd accidentally touched his arm.

"You're doing great," he says, watching me through a jungle of green eyes. "Let's try it. Come with me, and I promise that I won't let anything happen to you."

There's an aspect of wild in his gaze. I can see it—the sort of wild that has my imagination running. Before I can control my thoughts, I'm wondering who he is, why he's here, what his hands would feel like against my bare skin.

Also, there in his eyes, is a glint of protectiveness. The combination has me wanting to prove I'm not a total wimp. Just half a wimp.

"Do I get a life vest?" I ask. "I need something floaty."

"I'll be right there. What's got you so nervous about the deep end?"

I give him a blank stare. "Uh... the fact that I can't swim?"

"You are so close! You almost had it about five minutes ago."

"Really? I'm surprised you noticed. You were doing *such* a great job ignoring me."

"Annie." My name sounds fluid on his tongue, like a whitecap on the ocean—turbulent and strikingly beautiful. "You know *exactly* why I ignored you."

"Is that right? Because it sure felt like you—"

"Wanted to take you into the back office... alone?" He leans in so close his breath dances across my ear, tantalizing in its spicy freshness. "*That's* the reason I stayed far away from you."

"But—"

"If I weren't here to clean up my act, sweetheart, I might have a different game plan."

"Oh."

"Unfortunately, you're safe from my charms."

"I am?"

"Yes." He grins a playful smile. "I have to behave."

My heart is pounding, an inexplicable rush pulsing through my veins. The scent of him is intoxicating, raw, and it makes me giggle like I've sucked in a gallon of helium. "Safe from *what* charms?"

He winks. "Just you wait."

"I'm going to switch classes. See if Duke's got availability."

Cohen ignores me, extending a hand instead. "Let me help you."

I cross my arms. "Give me something floaty, and we've got a deal."

It's his turn to smile. He watches me for a long second, then gives a shake of his head. "You win this time, sweetheart."

I hate that his little nickname, the wayward touches of his hand against mine, the subtle glances my way, make me sizzle with happiness. He probably calls three different girls *sweetheart* on any given night, hoping one will fall hook, line, and sinker into his bed. I can see it in the way he carries himself, in his confidence. He's not used to being turned down.

Luckily for both of us, he's not interested—and neither am I. There's too much on the line to risk getting involved with someone like Cohen—I'm waiting to hear back on my law school applications, and until I'm officially accepted into one of them, I can't let my grades slide. Getting involved with someone like Cohen James would most *certainly* count as a distraction.

Not to mention, I've made a pact with myself not to date until I'm done with grad school. This, here, is exactly why. One second I show up for swimming lessons, and the next I'm staring into my instructor's bright green peepers and wondering what it'd be like if I let him kiss me.

I push away my wayward thoughts as Cohen hands me a thin pole that has floatation devices on either end. It's like a barbell made of Styrofoam. I'd much rather have a huge life jacket that hugs my body, but I'm done whining to Cohen. So, I stick the floaty out in front of me and kick toward the deep end.

I feel his eyes on me, watching from a safe distance on the pool ledge as I clumsily flop down the lane. At first, I think he's watching me out of concern. You know, for my safety. Making sure that I don't drown. However, when I slide a glance in his direction, I'm proven desperately wrong.

"Hey," I hiss in annoyance. "Get your eyes off my butt."

"What?" His attention snaps to my face, and he has the grace to give a sheepish shrug of his shoulder when he sees my glare. "It's my job; I need to watch your form."

I roll my eyes and continue onward, faster. I'm halfway there, and with each kick my stomach is wrapping itself into knots. The water against my stomach grows colder with each inch the floor drops away, and I can feel the emptiness below my body. If I put my feet down, I won't be able to touch anymore.

I take a moment to glance between my arms, seeing nothing but the deep, clear blue of the nine-foot pool. It's everything I can do not to hyperventilate. I can't tell if Cohen is staring at my face, my legs, or my chest-—and I don't care.

I can hardly remember Leigh's name as she reaches for me. She must sense the panic in my eyes, the short, raspy breaths echoing against the walls. The fear freezing my body.

When our fingers connect, I latch onto her as if she's my guardian angel, as if I can't ever let her go. She stills my floundering, offers a word of encouragement, and guides me toward the wall.

Finally, once I'm stabilized and my breathing doesn't sound like a cat with a hairball, I offer Leigh a smile. "Well, thank you for saving my life."

Leigh laughs and waves a hand. "Nothing you wouldn't do for me. Well, you know... once you can swim."

I focus on peeling a few fingers back from the wall. Then, I focus on pretending Cohen doesn't exist. *How embarrassing.* I'm a grown woman, and I just freaked out in the middle of a very safe pool.

Meanwhile, Jason and Leigh have already made huge strides; both are treading water without the help of floaties and without the fear of dying at any given moment. While I'm happy for them, it only makes things worse for me.

Thankfully, Cohen, after peering at me for a long moment, brushes past the whole incident. "You all are doing great," he says, glancing down at his clipboard. "To pass this level, you're going to have to tread water for sixty seconds. We'll work on five seconds for now and build up a little each week. Sound good?"

Leigh and Jason nod.

"No," I gasp, re-tightening my fingers against the wall. "You might as well fail me now. I'll never be able to do that."

"Sure you will." Cohen sounds completely confident as he flicks a glance over me. "We'll start with five seconds."

"Nah," I say. "I'd rather not."

"You can do it. . Just stay close to the wall."

"Not interested."

"I *know* you can manage five seconds. Your kick is strong enough to keep your head above water. Your arms need some work, but we'll get there."

"*Your* arms need work," I mutter back. When I'm frightened, apparently I revert back to first grade retorts. "Please don't make me."

"Fine." Cohen glances at the other two. "We'll start with you—five seconds, beginning now."

I watch the others complete it successfully. I even scoot a little away from the wall, with my floatie of course, to offer a high-five to

Leigh after she brushes water out of her eyes. They've both done it. In fact, Jason's still going with no signs of stopping.

"Try it with me," Leigh says brightly. "If I can do it, you can do it."

I begin to shake my head, but that's when I feel the floatation device slipping from my grasp. I clutch at it, holding on tight. Then, I realize, it's not slipping away... it's being *stolen* from me. By freaking Cohen James.

With one hand, he's guiding the floatie out from under my arms while reaching for me with his other hand. Except, he doesn't catch me before the *freak-out* begins. The flailing happens, my arms waving every which way as I slip below the surface, sinking like a bag of coal.

I use my kick, scissoring my legs hard, but it only pokes my head through the surface long enough to screech for help before I'm plunged back underneath, water licking into my lungs. I catch a flash of panic in Cohen's eyes as he reaches, still further, for me, and misses once again.

It's too late, I think, turning as paralyzed now as I did back then. The first time I knew that I hated water. A day of ice skating on the lake that went horribly wrong.

Six years old. That's how old I'd been when it happened. Others had been out before me that winter, skating, playing hockey, driving cars across the lakes. However, I drew the short straw that day, apparently, and hit the thin patch of ice. Without any warning, I'd plunged straight through to the frigid waters below.

When I tried to come up for air, I'd hit nothing but sheer frozen water. Trapped under layers of ice, lungs grasping for air, I had thought I would die.

I didn't die, of course; I didn't even go unconscious. My friends pulled me out and warmed me up, and I was fine. But nothing, absolutely nothing, could bleach the memory of utter silence from my mind. From the intense claustrophobia of seeing the sunlight, watching rays filter through a layer of crystals, only to be trapped underneath in the darkness.

The same panic is back now, my heart racing. My ears are full, as if there's no space for sound of any kind and the world is blanketed in stillness. My throat burns, eyes stinging when I at last force them open.

There's a flash of legs, a glimpse of flesh, and then I'm sinking, sinking toward the bottom, but my feet have yet to touch. I can't push off from below, and I can't reach the top.

The images come back strong from that day.

Lungs burning, fists pounding against the ice, distant cries yelling my name. The frigid cold, the soul-crushing temperatures struggling to steal my breath, take every wisp of energy—of humanity—as the darkness set in.

Then I'm back, the images are gone, and I'm hacking up water against the edge of the pool. Someone's hands are on me, warm against my skin.

Cohen.

I know this before I turn to look.

"I am so sorry," he's saying. "I didn't realize... I'm so sorry, Annie."

My gaze lands on him, no doubt rimmed by terror, that terror rapidly making way for anger. If there's one thing we, as humans, don't enjoy, it's having our soft sides exposed for all to see—for others to leer at, to pity, to watch with a keen interest because it's not *them* hurting. It's equal parts curiosity and sympathy.

Judging by the look in his eyes, I don't need to explain how I'm feeling. There's relief and fear there, and a mix of other things I don't bother to explore. I'm too frustrated, now that I know I'm not dead. Because I definitely don't want to die wearing this stupid swimsuit.

I pull myself to my feet, ignoring his gaze. I could get mad at him, yell, or ream him out for stealing my noodle, but I don't. It's not worth my breath.

Instead I pull myself out of the pool area and, without a word, wrap a towel around my body at the door. I make my way toward the showers, leaving him and the rest of the class behind me.

I step under the steam of the shower and let the water cascade down my back. The goose bumps wash away, as does the rush of adrenaline. Eventually, the nightmarish memories wash down the drain, too—at least for now.

Surprisingly, the only thing that doesn't fade is the memory of Cohen's hands around my waist. His fingers just a little too low, a little too close to my core. When he held me it was nice; it was strong, protective even, as if he'd never let me get hurt. This makes me even *more* annoyed because it's the last thing I should be thinking about right now.

I stay under the water until another woman enters and decides it's her time to shine in the karaoke spotlight that is the women's locker room. She begins belting out a little ditty from *Night at the Roxbury*, and I decide it's time for me to leave before my eardrums turn in their resignation letters.

I towel off, change, and return to watch my grandmother's synchronized swimming class once I've calmed down. If I didn't absolutely have to stay, I'd already be gone. Unfortunately, Gran's my ride home. Well, my mother is, technically, and she won't let me leave Gran here, so I have no choice but to wait.

As I enter the pool area, the last thing I expect to see is Cohen James, asshole extraordinaire, holding a baby. And looking sexy as hell doing it.

Before my ovaries combust, I turn away from where he's teaching something that looks like a toddler swim class and face a bunch of women in their eighties attempting handstands and dance moves in the water. The change in scenery from Cohen James to retired synchronized swimming is not ideal, but it'll have to work.

Because the way Cohen's gaze met mine just now, across the open pool, a look of apology waiting specifically for me—the whole thing nearly wiped away my entire grudge against him. His eyes have an almost magnetic pull to them, as if begging me to run across the deck and jump into his arms.

That's out of the question, however, since I'm still pissed at him.

Maybe, someday, I'll forgive him.

Then, maybe, I'll let him kiss me.

Chapter 5

Annie

"Hey, are you okay?"

I turn on the bleachers from where I've parked myself to watch Gran, surprised to find Leigh sitting next to me. She's dressed in jeans and a sweatshirt, her hair wrapped into a bun on top of her head, her face free of makeup.

She's likely older than me by a good ten years, but dressed like she is now, she's got the fresh face of a college student and the bright eyes of a child.

"I didn't hear you sneak up," I say, scooting over to make room. "Are you also watching your grandma try to do the splits underwater? If so, I'll spare you the details; it's not pretty."

She laughs. "I'd love to be like your grandma when I'm eighty. Out there doing stuff that I was too scared to do in my twenties. Which one is she?"

"Can you guess?" I gesture to the six ladies in the water. Only one of them is flopping around like a fish. It's my grandmother.

Leigh guesses correctly.

"I guess we flop in the same style, huh?" I give her a wry smile. "Like grandmother, like granddaughter."

"No, you have a lot more grace to your flopping."

I laugh. "Sorry I sort of just stormed off like that. I just get nervous in the water."

"I understand." Her smile fades a bit, and she focuses her attention forward. "I just wanted to make sure you were okay."

"I'm fine. Really," I say. "But I appreciate you checking on me. Thank you."

She waves a hand and together we watch the ladies twirl to the tune of an eighties beat. I have to give them credit; none of them are moving all dainty and careful, as if they might bust a hip at any moment. They are attacking the water like masters of karate.

"He felt really bad," Leigh says after the women have completed their routine. "I could tell."

"Who, Cohen? Well, good. It wasn't a very nice thing for him to do."

"No, it wasn't, but still..." Her voice trails off, and so does her gaze. She glances over her shoulder, watching the other, shallower pool. "I don't think he realized how much it would upset you."

"I told him *no*, and that should have been enough. I'm paying money—er, my mom is paying money—so I can learn how to swim, not so that he can drown me. He's my instructor, not my drill sergeant. What does he care if I pass or not? He gets paid and his stupid photo taken for his PR lady either way."

"That's the thing. I think he does care. He was just misguided. A mistake. He was trying to push you to succeed, and he took it too far."

"Then why did he try to kill me?"

"I know it was scary, but I just thought I should give you my opinion." Leigh pats my leg and gives a bland smile. "And I think you should give him another chance. I'll bet he apologizes before the day is over."

"Oh yeah? What makes you say that?"

"The fact that he looks over at you every chance he gets."

I find myself glancing over my shoulder before I realize I'm doing it. I can't help it. I also can't stop the iceberg I've built between him and I from melting a little bit as I watch him guiding a happily screeching toddler through the water, the pair of them laughing as they chase a toy boat.

"He's dumb," I say, for lack of something better.

Leigh laughs, not fooled by my halfhearted attempt to stay angry. "He looks good with a baby though, doesn't he?"

I raise my eyebrows at her. "I'm not interested!"

"I didn't say you were, girlfriend! I'm just stating facts. If he weren't ten years my junior, I'd consider it."

"You're..."

"Divorced."

"Oh, sorry."

"It's a good thing, don't worry." Leigh turns her smile back on me, though it's a tiny bit dimmer this time around. "I have to pick my son up from his sleepover now, so I'm going to head out. You sure you're okay?"

I nod. "Yeah, thanks, Leigh."

"It was mostly selfish," she says, standing to face me in front of the bleachers, taking a long, luxurious stare at Cohen. "If he tries to apologize, let him, will you?"

"Why?"

"Because I didn't get his autograph yet, which means I'm stuck coming back for another week of lessons. Jason's nice and all, but I'm pretty sure he ate garlic for lunch, and I can smell it coming from his pores. I need you in class with me or I'll be all alone with him and Cohen."

"You're lucky! I'm feeling generous."

"See you next week." With a wink, she's gone.

I watch her leave, surprised by how quickly I'd decided that I liked the woman. Usually it takes me some time to warm up to a person, but something about Leigh—her independence, her fierce love for her son, her ability to laugh despite what must be a tough gig as a single, working mom, required an instant boost of admiration for her.

Another week, I thought, chancing one more glance over my shoulder at Cohen. Maybe I could suffer through one more week of coughing my way up and down the lap pool, but only for Leigh.

If I show up at class again, it's absolutely not because I want to see Cohen James.

Chapter 6

Annie

The rest of Gran's lesson flies by. Thankfully, from what I could tell, none of the women sustained injuries of any sort from their leaping and bouncing through the pool.

Now, I'm leaning against the edge of the front counter, waiting for someone—either my mother or Gran—to arrive. Gran's in the shower, mom's grabbing the car, and I'm stuck somewhere in between, loitering around the front door like a high school hoodlum.

Okay, it's not the waiting at the front door that has me feeling like a hoodlum, it's the shifty eyes I've got going on, half expecting to see Cohen at any second. I'm sneaking glimpses down the stairs like I'm waiting for a getaway driver.

But I have a plan—at the first sight of him, I'm bolting outside, rain or not.

Ten minutes pass, my mom's nowhere to be seen, and Gran's still singing in the shower. The lady at the front counter won't stop staring at me, so I shift into the seated area a floor above. It's a balcony-style lounge, so I can see the front door, the desk, and the coming and going of everyone including Gran... and Cohen. It's a safe place.

There's a pot of coffee gurgling in the corner, and I approach it carefully, with a little bit of caution, like I might approach a lion. Turns out it doesn't smell half bad, so I pour myself a cup.

And nearly gag. It's thick mud, sludgy in color and peppered with the dregs of the pot. I frown, watching as a few men Gran's age play chess and sip the concoction. I can barely hide a shudder.

In fact, I'm mid-shiver when a hand lands on my back, startling me. My half-full cup tips straight into the trash can as I stifle a *yelp* of surprise.

"Sorry," Cohen says, wincing as I turn to face him. "Seems I have the habit of surprising you today."

"*Surprising* me?" I wipe the coffee remains off my hand with a napkin from the coffee station. "Sure, if that's what you want to call it."

"Annie, I..." He stalls, running a hand through his hair as his eyes come to rest on me. He's changed into jeans and a sweatshirt, and he looks comfy and perfect. "I came to apologize for what happened in the pool."

"It's fine."

"No, it's not. I shouldn't have surprised you like that."

"Correct," I huff. "I'm glad we agree on something."

"I would have *never* let anything happen to you, I hope you know that."

I raise my eyebrow, watching his colorful eyes as they dart across my face. He holds my gaze, waiting for a response. "Fine," I say. "I believe you."

"Good," he exhales. "We agree on two things."

"I still think you're an asshole."

"Join the club."

"I guess I owe you a thank you, too," I say grudgingly. When he looks surprised, I cross my arms. "For sticking up for my bathing suit."

He laughs, a contagious sound. A few of the older gentlemen turn around and watch the pair of us until Cohen puts his arm around me and guides me into the hallway around the corner.

"It wasn't the suit that did the trick," he says. "I think it's the woman who makes the suit."

My thank you has completely and utterly backfired. Heat's rushing to my face, and there's a slight tremble in my step as I move away from him.

"Don't worry," he says, raising his hands in surrender. "It's just a fact. I already told you that I can't hit on you."

"That's great," I say. "Because you're not my type, anyway."

"Ouch."

I shrug, pretending I'm not affected by the way his eyes flicker over my body. There's not much to see now: a winter coat, yoga pants, little-to-no makeup. The traditional Saturday college attire. "It's true. People like you and people like me aren't a good fit."

"Tell me, what's your type?"

"Does it matter?"

He flings his keys in a circle around his finger, catching them as he gives me a wry look. "So, are you coming back next week?"

"Depends. Are you planning to steal my noodle?"

"I won't take your noodle if you don't wear that horrible bathing suit."

"No promises," I tell him, fighting back a smile. "I don't own a bikini."

"Shame."

I furrow my brow. "What's it to you, anyway?"

He leans in, so close I can smell his freshly shampooed hair, the expensive gel he probably used to lather every inch of his lean, beautiful body. "I'm a man, sweetheart. I'd have to be dead not to appreciate you."

"Cohen!"

He waits a moment, but I don't have a follow up, so he gives me a wink and heads down the stairs, taking them two at a time.

My eyes are drawn toward him, watching him jog through the front doors, wave to the receptionist, and then turn forward. He even opens doors like an athlete, smooth and confident, with full control over his limbs. Unlike my wild flailing in the water.

I'm in the middle of coming up with a great, witty-but-belated retort to yell after him when he pauses to hold open the door for a young mother from the Baby-and-Me class.

As she passes by, he gives the baby a smile, and the kid laughs. It's adorable. I watch the whole thing as if Cohen's performing magic tricks. It's ridiculous. *I'm* ridiculous.

Then, Cohen says goodbye and finishes his exit. He climbs straight into some fancy-looking Porsche. Straight into the *passenger's* side because there's a girl behind the wheel, and she's gorgeous.

That's when the spell breaks, and all fantasies I might've *ever* entertained about Cohen James are shattered. He leans across the seat, gives her a not-so-chaste smooch on the lips, and then slams the door shut.

"*Asshole*," I murmur under my breath.

"Whoa, Nelly. Now, I love the language, but your mother won't," Gran says, appearing at my shoulder. "How about that class though? Boy, do I feel limber. You really should join us, dear."

"No, thanks." I'm unusually gruff in my retort. "Ready to head out?"

"What got your undies in a twist?" Gran sidles up next to me, looping her arm through mine. Then she follows my gaze to where Cohen is getting whisked away in a shiny sports car. "Oh, I see. Men."

"Idiots, more like."

"He is handsome, isn't he?"

"I don't know, I can't tell," I lie. "I'm not interested."

"Sure you're not," Gran says. "How about we go shopping? I think we need to find you a swimsuit that doesn't look like something my great aunt should be wearing. She's dead. Have I told you about Frannie? She had nine cats."

"Fine," I agree. "Shopping it is."

Chapter 7

Cohen

"Hey, good lookin'," Erica greets me. "How'd it go?"

"Mind if I drive?" I ask, even though she's already pulled onto the main street. Still, she's moving like a turtle, and I suddenly need to get far away from that YMCA.

"Oooh, you want to take me for a ride?" Erica purrs, then giggles. "The car, I mean."

"Sure," I say, but only because it'll get her to agree faster. "Let's pull into the Starbucks up here."

"Oh, I love coffee. Spontaneous coffee date? *Your* treat?"

I give a shake of my head as she parks. "I've gotta get somewhere, sorry."

"Aw bummer! I was hoping we could spend some time together."

I look across the seat at Erica and raise my eyebrow. At least, I think it's Erica. It might be Erin, but I can't say for sure—it was dark last night, and the bar was loud when we met. She only told me her name once, and I'd feel like a tool asking for her to repeat it after all this time.

Last night had started out innocently enough. After the bar, a group of my buddies ended up at an apartment with a group of girls—friends of friends. Turns out the apartment belonged to Erica. Erin? Whatever.

The group of us played a round of Cards Against Humanity until five in the morning and, instead of trying to drive home at that hour, I found myself asking to stay on her couch.

Erin-slash-Erica had readily agreed, inviting me straight into her bed. Judging by the fact that she'd had her hand on my knee and her ass halfway on my leg the entire night, I had a good idea what she had in mind. Even so, I'd turned her down.

I've been there, done that, earned the puck bunny t-shirt. I love women, don't get me wrong, but this one is a bonafide Stage-Ten clinger, and I just do *not* have the time, patience, or energy for someone like her at this point in my life.

A few years back... *maybe.* I *might've* taken her up on her offer for a single night of fun, but I'm too old to deal with the aftermath of it, now. Does that mean I'm finally becoming an adult? I sure as hell hope not. I'm not a fan of responsibility.

I glance over toward Erica who's inching her fingers up my thigh even before we've left the Starbucks parking lot. I've changed over to the driver's seat after handing over her nonfat skinny latte, and I realize that maybe... becoming an adult isn't *so* bad. If I'd have slept with her last night, I'd feel guilty *and* annoyed. Right now, I'm just annoyed. I feel like I deserve a fucking pat on the back.

But she *did* drive me to my first day of volunteer work, so I should probably take a chill pill and throw her a bone. So, I flash her a smile which earns me a tittering giggle in return.

If *only* I'd woken up early enough to make the mile trek back to my place, I wouldn't be in this position. However, because I'd slept through five of my alarms, I'd had to choose between showing up on time or driving my own car, and I'd chosen the former.

"Bad day, huh?" she asks. "I sense a cranky panda over here."

She shifts toward me, her full lips forming a pout that should've made my pants just a little too tight. Right now, though, there's *nothing* happening down there. I think even my penis is annoyed.

"Day was fine," I mumble.

"Let me give you a little kiss to make things better."

I dodge her lips which, now that I'm seeing more clearly in the light of day, look like they've been enhanced by a jug of helium. My eyes wander down to her chest, and sure enough, my suspicions are confirmed. That woman could back float with only the help of the balloons strapped in by her shirt.

That is, if the swatch of fabric over her body could be called a shirt. There's a 'v' in the neckline that dips so low I can probably see her belly button if I look hard enough. I'm simply not interested.

For a moment, I wonder if it's because my mind is busy imagining the curves—the real, homegrown variety—underneath Annie Plymouth's ruffled bathing suit. There's nothing fake about her, that's for sure. She can't even pretend to enjoy my company.

"Babe, I'm talking to you." Erin/Erica frowns deeper. "Bad morning or what? Why don't you drive us to my place and I'll distract you for the next hour. Then I've gotta get to work, okay?"

I don't respond, instead using the moment to calculate the time it'll take me to get to my car. Fifteen minutes if I fly. Cranking the vehicle onto the highway, I press my foot to the floor and ease the car as fast as I can legally go onto the on ramp.

Then, I come to a screeching halt.

Thanks to a stalled out car, the drive to Uptown takes forty-five minutes. During this time, I find out that Erica's real name is not Erin, but Jill. Who would've thought?

She finally tires of talking about her cosmetology class and tries again to sneak her manicured fingers down my pants. Against all logical thought, I find myself moving those fingers back onto her lap with the excuse of needing to focus on the road.

Jill frowns, then looks in the mirror to check her makeup. She stops frowning immediately, mutters about wrinkles on her skin, and then settles into a vacant glare that has me wondering if I should buy her a Big Mac. She looks hungry. And she's skinny.

"Hamburger?" I mouth as we pass a fast food place. "Shake?"

She wrinkles her nose and shakes her head. "Gross."

"Great." Less time that we have to spend together.

When I arrive at my house, Jill looks around, confused. "This isn't my house."

"Yeah, sorry. I really have to get going." Ironically, we missed the turn for her house about ten blocks back and she never even noticed. "I'm not feeling great."

"Aww, poor baby. Come home and let mama cook you some soup."

I look at her. "You cook?"

"No, asshole, we can order it from the Japanese place across the street."

"Sorry, Jill. Maybe another time."

"My name's Julie."

"Oh. Shit."

I should apologize, but I'm finding it difficult to do so. After all, the only reason she wants to 'cook' for me is because of my name. She basically told me so last night after quizzing me about Los Angeles, celebrities, and other random crap that is *not* part of a hockey player's lifestyle. Her vision is far more glamorous than the real deal.

After all, if I'd been an accountant, she wouldn't have given me a backwards glance. I know this. I'm not a damn Armani model; I'm a hockey player. I've got a busted nose, scars, tattoos—I'm not what women would call pretty. Stand Matthew McConoughey next to me and people would think I'm a bum.

"Get out of my car," Julia says with a wobble in her voice. "You know, I *thought* we had something special."

"What gave you that idea?"

"I *drove* you to volunteer."

"I'm sorry, here is some gas money." I pull out a twenty and hand it over. "I appreciate the ride. Thank you."

"I'm not a *whore*!"

"I didn't say that!" I throw my hand up in exasperation as she tosses the money back at me, then lands a punch to my shoulder. It feels moderately like a blind bumblebee has crashed into my arm. "I'm sorry, I'm just not interested right now."

"Are you emotionally unavailable?" She sniffs.

"Yes," I say, seeing a loophole and grasping onto it for dear life. "I just got out of a horrible relationship, and my—uh... heart is still healing."

"Oh, you poor thing." Julia sandwiches me between her set of balloons and squeezes hard. "Call me once you're feeling better, okay, honey?"

"Sure thing."

This time, she pockets the gas money and gives me a finger wave as she buckles herself into the driver's seat. Before she pulls away from the curb, she takes one last look out the window. "So, should I call you tonight?"

"I don't think so," I tell her, thinking that suddenly, it all feels exhausting. Julia, the bunnies, the stupid pranks—all of it. "Maybe a different time."

"Okay, honey. Feel better." Satiated with the response, she whips away from the curb nearly crunching my toes in the process.

I hoof it to the entrance of the upscale condo building. I have a nice place in Uptown, a two bedroom penthouse above the city. It's more of a crash pad than a home, since I spend so much of my time traveling. It's close enough to the nightlife to give me a place to rest up while in town, and it's not far from the airport or the rink.

The whole thing works for me. I'm not looking for a permanent place to set up a Christmas tree for the rest of my life; setting down roots is not my idea of a good time now, if ever. I've seen what setting down roots can do to a person when they don't actually want it, and it's not pretty. I know this because the result is *me*—team trouble-maker.

I open the fridge, pop the top off a Corona, and settle into the couch. It's barely afternoon, but it's been an exhausting morning. I'm ready for a nap, a burger, and bed.

Alone.

Chapter 8

Annie

"Nope, not ugly enough." I look in the mirror at the fabric draped over my body. I officially look like some odd combination of a first grade art project and an ancient Egyptian goddess. The suit is probably intended to be cool and edgy, maybe a bit on the upscale fashion side, but it's not nearly horrible enough for my intentions.

"Sweetie, I really love that metal collar on you." Gran pokes her head underneath the stall. She has no shame. I suppose when a person reaches a certain age, the amount of embarrassment they have left in stock begins to vanish. In Gran's case, however, it's evaporated. All of it. "The padding at the back gives you nice definition in your rear end."

"I'm not looking for definition. I'm looking for a parka."

"I thought you wanted a bathing suit."

"I do. A bathing suit parka," I correct. "Something so ugly you can't help but cringe when you see it."

"Pop that door open for me. I'd crawl underneath the stall, but my knees don't work like they used to, and I don't feel like getting stuck again."

"Again?"

"Gertrude trapped her head in one of them new lingerie sets, and I tried to rescue her last week after church. Turns out, security had to rescue us both and call the ambulance while they were at it because Gertrude's hip was on the fritz. But we *were* the talk of the town at bridge club."

"I'll bet," I mumble under my breath, sliding the lock open and letting Gran sneak through the door. "Do me a favor and don't go crawling underneath dressing room doors. That sort of thing can get you kicked out of the mall, and you know mother hates picking you up from security."

"I raised your mother good," Gran says. "Ellie's way more of a tightwad than me. Now, spin around, dear. Let me size you up."

I give her a twirl, Gran's eyes scanning me over from top to bottom.

It's just me and Gran shopping today. Mostly because my mother swore a long time ago that she'd never accompany either of us to Target again. All because of a single incident with marshmallows and a bottle of bubbles. Let's just say the fire department was called.

That's why she's getting her nails done next door while Gran and I are on the hunt for a swimsuit that'll turn Cohen James *off* me for life. I may not be interested in him, and he might be bound and determined not to get involved with me, but I might as well not take any chances.

"Let me get this straight." Gran raises a blood-red fingernail to her lips. "You said this suit is for Cohen James?"

"Sort of. It's like a... let's call it a Cohen James repellent suit."

"I thought he was a hottie."

"Gran, you've got him by fifty years. At least."

"My body might be wrinkled, but my eyes can see just fine, honey."

"I'm trying to prove a point to him."

"Sorry, but I'm missing the point."

"He thinks he can get any girl he wants," I explain, thumbing through the rack of clothes we hauled into the room with us. "But I'm out to prove that he can't."

"Sit down, baby," Gran says. "Let me explain something to you."

I sit, mostly because my grandmother doesn't give me a choice—she yanks me into the seat and stands over me. All she needs is a ruler to smack against my knuckles to complete the picture.

"You want to show a man what he's missing?" She paces back and forth in front of me. "You're going about it all wrong. The way you're doing it, you're *hiding* everything he's missing."

"But—"

"Nope," Gran interrupts. "I take that back. You're burying it halfway to China. Honey, you shouldn't care so much. If you're not interested, just tell him so."

"Oh, I think I made that clear," I tell Gran. "But this is a safeguard. There's no sense tempting the man if it's not going to go anywhere. I *know* what I want, and it's not him. He's not my type, so I might as well ward off the trouble. I can't afford a distraction, not now."

"You're a better woman than I am," Gran says. "Have it your way. But in the meantime, check this out—what do you think?"

Gran slithers out of a dress she'd been trying on and stands before me in... *what the heck* is that? I blink several times, my eyes burning from all that I shouldn't have seen. "*Why* Gran?"

"It's one of them European suits!" Gran turns around, a thong so far up her cheeks it's mostly vanished. "Don't I look edgy?"

"First of all, you *have* to buy that now because... you can't possibly put them back. I can't even *see* it anymore." I shield my eyes with a hand. "Second of all, no. Just... *no*."

"So these won't work for my synchronized swimming team uniform?"

I shake my head. "Not unless you feel like asking mom to bail you out of jail for indecent exposure."

"That's just fine, I suppose," Gran says. "Dolores wants something with a skirt, anyway. Says she has to cover her baby fat."

"I think Dolores has a great point."

"Well, I think it's silly. A woman can't have baby fat after the age of sixty," Gran says. "That's just regular fat."

"Gran!"

"What? It's true. I have fat and skinny days just like anyone else." Gran swivels toward the door, twists the knob open, and halts abruptly before stepping through. "Oh, that reminds me! I signed you up for our synchronized swimming class."

I'm looking in the mirror already, wondering if I could somehow sew a burlap sack together to make an ugly wetsuit. Gran's comment registers with a *thud* in the back of my skull. "You did what?"

"Signed you up for synchronized swim team."

I whirl around to face her, my mouth hanging open. "Why would you ever do that? It's a horrible idea. First, I can't swim. Second, I'm not retired. Third, I'm not graceful."

"Dolores isn't retired. Well, she says she's not, but I think she's a liar. That woman doesn't *work*." Gran shrugs. "Why not join us? We're all old farts and we need one more woman. We're looking for a man, too, but those are harder to come by. Any recommendations?"

A fleeting thought crosses my brain—Cohen James—and I can hardly hold back a smile. The image of him and all his tattoos and tough-as-nails attitude floating around with a bunch of old ladies makes me nearly giddy with glee.

Unfortunately, my sail deflates the second I realize that would mean we'd just have to spend more time together if he agreed to help. Nix on that idea.

"Nope," I say. "Can't think of anyone."

"Well keep your ears peeled because we could really use that masculine touch," Gran says, disappearing from the stall. Now you hold tight dear, and I'll make you the ugliest spinster you've ever seen."

Chapter 9

Annie

"Please drop me off at home," I say. "It'd be easier for everyone."

My mother glances into the backseat of the car at me. Gran is sitting next to her up front, busy playing with her new Target earrings.

"It's not my fault you scheduled dinner with your father tonight." My mother sniffs, her nose in the air as it always is with any talk of my dad. "I'll drop you off and he can give you a ride back."

"He won't care if I'm twenty minutes late. I don't want to make him go out of his way to bring me back."

"Would it kill him to take a second out of his busy, busy, busy work day to drop his daughter off at home? I don't think so."

"Mom—"

"I'm serious, Annie."

My car is at my apartment, which is the first problem. All because my mother insisted on picking me up this morning to deliver my bathing suit. Never in a million years had I thought that swimming lessons would turn into an all day extravaganza—I'd planned to be back at my apartment hours ago.

My mom's nail appointment had run late, then we'd grabbed lunch, and now there's not enough time for me to stop by my apartment before heading to my dad's place. According to my mom, she's now got dinner plans with Claude, so she doesn't have time to bring me all the way to my college housing before she's meeting him.

Apparently, I'm just one huge inconvenience.

I'd considered rescheduling after the day I'd had, but that's also not a great option. My father is a busy man, and we usually schedule our dinner dates weeks in advance around his work schedule.

My mother does have a point—I *never* ask my dad for anything. I don't expect anything, either. Hopefully, he won't mind giving me a ride home later as a one-time deal.

"Tell your father *hello*," my mother says, the familiar stiffness creeping into her voice. "If he can't *possibly* find a way to bring you to your apartment tonight, have *him* call me, and I'll come get you."

"Thanks, mom."

"Don't forget this." My grandmother shoves a Target bag into my hands. "Your suit. It's so freaking horrible that Cohen James won't know what to do with himself."

"Mother, watch your language," Ellie says with a frown.

I shut the door on my mother and grandmother as they argue about whether or not the word 'freaking' should be allowed when I'm in the car. I wave, jog up the front steps, and curl the collar of my coat against the chilling wind. It's almost March but we're in a horrible cold spell—there was a storm last weekend that left enough snow to go sledding.

"Dad!" I pound on the door again. I have my gloves in my bag, but I was too lazy to put them on—I hadn't expected to stand in the cold for so long. "Open up, dad. It's me!"

My phone rings, and I look down. Oddly enough, it's my father's name popping up on the screen.

"Hey, kid, sorry I'm running late at the office," he says in a rush once I've fumbled to answer it. "I completely forgot Maria changed the code to the garage door. Do you mind letting yourself in? It's 4-2-1-1. I'll be home in twenty minutes."

He forgot all about dinner. I exhale a breath that forms a cloud in the crisp night air. "Did mom just call you?"

There's a pause that follows from his end. "She said she's waiting in the driveway until you get inside. *Please* don't leave, cupcake, I want to see you—I really do. It's just this last proposal I'm about to send off, it's almost finished..."

I debate running back to my mom's car. She'd be more than happy to bring me home because *that* would make my dad look bad. She'd gloat silently the entire trip and hold my dad's lackluster parenting skills over his head. They don't have the healthiest of relationships. From what I can tell, mom was still very much in love when they separated. Dad was, too, he just wasn't around to show it.

The thought of my mother and father arguing is exhausting, and I don't want to fuel their feud. So instead of slinking back to the car, I give my mom and Gran a cheery wave and let myself in through the garage.

I'm not a complete martyr, though, let's be honest. My dad has a nice place. A really nice place, and my apartment on campus has been experiencing faulty internet and cable. I'm sort of looking forward to a half hour of peace and quiet with the remote all to myself.

No roommates, no mom or grandmother preaching at me, no Claude walking around without a shirt on, his mouth half-open in a state of perma-confusion. A piece of quiet sanctuary sounds like heaven.

I plop the Target bag on the counter. Inside, there's not one swimsuit, but two. Gran made me buy the second one. It's black, sleek, and beautiful. I'm a bit curvy, so those tiny little triangles never sit right on me. This one, however, fits like a glove.

I'm saving it to wear aboard the cruise. Who knows? Maybe I'll meet the man of my dreams there. It'll be summer break, just after I've graduated college. I don't want a horrible swimsuit on when I meet the man I might eventually marry.

Tottering into the living room, tired from the cold, exhausted from swimming, dead on my feet after shopping with Gran, I settle onto my dad's luxurious couch. It's cushy, and I sink into it as I wrap myself in a blanket. Next up, I flick on some horrible reality show and snuggle down for the wait.

My eyes are closed before the credits roll.

Chapter 10

Annie

When I wake, it's dark.

"Dad?" It feels like I'm home alone, but I call out again just in case. "Dad, are you home?"

No answer. I turn the TV down and call a few more times in case he's wrapped up in his work. I listen for the shower. The garage door opening. *Nothing.*

Sliding the plush blanket around my shoulders, I cinch it tight and tiptoe through the house. It's too big for my dad by himself, and the modern feel is a little too fake. I don't know why he bought this place when he was trying to *downsize*.

But that's not my problem. I head into the kitchen and make one last sweep, but my dad's not hunched over the laptop he keeps at the small, built-in desk. My dad works everywhere, even the kitchen.

Tonight, however, it's just me.

I sink into the desk chair as a flash of annoyance ripples through my body. I'm not *hurt*. No, this has happened far too many times for me to feel upset. I'm focused instead on the *minor* inconvenience of being stuck here without a car. I have to get back to school, home-work, real life—and who knows how long my dad'll be stuck at the office?

I pop a Nespresso capsule into his shiny new machine and press the button, watching as it whirs to life. Once my cup is ready, I plop back into the chair and check my phone—no messages.

I debate texting him, but decide against it. If he doesn't care enough to see me, I'm certainly not going to force him—not at this point in my life. I'm a full grown adult. I don't *need* him for anything; I never have. I've made it a point to pay for my own college, even though he's offered. I don't want to owe him a thing.

But I will borrow his internet to stall as I debate my car situation. Flicking on the computer, I debate getting started on some homework. I *could* just work here all night until my dad gets home, but that's just depressing. I don't feel like working alone on Saturday night because my dad forgot me at home.

Instead, I find myself typing a familiar name into the browser: **Cohen James.**

The results list is quite lengthy. Even more so when I click onto the *Image* tab. There he is, those green eyes glinting off the screen as he's captured in various stages of post-game smiles, candid shots of him on the ice, and a few photos of him out to eat or sharing a drink with friends.

I scroll further. There are a few photos of him with a girl on his arm, but I find myself oddly pleased that it's never the same one twice. Nowhere in the search results is a snapshot of the woman who picked him up from the YMCA today.

A sinking feeling follows. It's just as I suspected—he has a different woman waiting for him every night of the week. I glance toward the Target bag on the counter, thankful for my newest suit. It makes me look like a dinosaur. No way will I let him make me a member of his revolving harem.

I flip back to the results listing and find an article near the bottom of the first page that announces ***Stars Starting Forward Leaves***

Little to the Imagination. My finger presses down on the link, even though I know it's clickbait.

Inside, I don't find naked pictures of Cohen James like the article's title insinuates. Sure, there's one blurry image from a cell phone, but it's impossible to even tell whether or not it's really Cohen.

I've almost hit *back* to return to the homepage when a line at the bottom catches my attention. More specifically, a pair of words. *Indecent exposure*.

Apparently my swim instructor had been hazed by some of the older members of the Stars team. Cohen's a new trade this year, fresh from the LA Lightening, and apparently the captains thought it'd be funny to introduce Cohen to MN with a bang.

Unfortunately, he'd been caught standing outside his teammates' home, serenading the captain with no clothes on. Some poor older woman walking her dog had been scared stiff, called the cops, and Cohen had been slapped with an indecent exposure fine, and another tick against him in the troublemaking column.

It's funny, sort of, the image of Cohen singing at the top of his lungs without pants. For some reason, I can picture it clearly. I can also picture him *not* snitching on his teammates.

As the article suggests, it was all Cohen's fault. I hardly doubt that's true, but he didn't correct anyone, and I give him some grudging points for that. Even more than a jerk, I can't stand a tattletale jerk.

This is where my research must end. Before I feel any more sympathy for the guy. Standing, I rinse my coffee cup, dry it, replace it in the cupboard, and then wipe the browser history clear.

Then, I fork out my phone and make a call to Sarah, my best friend and roommate.

"Hey, how'd it go today?" she asks when she picks up. "I thought you'd be home sooner—oh, are you at dinner with your dad, already?"

"What are the chances you'll let me buy you a bottle of wine tonight?"

"What do you need?"

"My car."

She sighs. "He didn't show?"

I nod, realize she can't see me, and murmur an affirmative answer. "I don't want to call my mom and get him in trouble. It's probably best if I just find my own way home."

"I'm sorry, Annie."

"Hey, don't be—you know how this goes. If you're too busy to come get me though, I'll suck it up and phone her—I know she's just waiting for the call."

"You said wine?"

"I'll splurge and buy you the eight dollar bottle."

"I'm a poor college student. How about *two* of the four dollar bottles?"

"I like that math," I agree. "Two bottles it is."

"Give me fifteen minutes."

Ten minutes into my wait, I text my dad and tell him I have to get going, but thanks for the coffee. He doesn't respond right away. In fact, it's not until I'm with Sarah and chowing on a Chipotle burrito—apparently swimming makes me ravenous—that he texts me to apologize.

I turn my phone off, and instead focus on showing off my Target score.

"What do you think?" I hold the horrid suit up for Sarah to see. "Do you think this will get Cohen's attention?"

Sarah wrinkles her nose, her fingers reaching out for the coarse fabric that, in all seriousness, feels like dragon scales. "*Why* are you doing this again? He seems funny. I liked that article about him serenading his team captain."

"Because," I say cheerily. "I want to drive him crazy."

"Crazy? Then you should *really* go with the black one. It looks great with your boobs." She looks at her own, smaller ones. "I could never wear it, that's for sure."

"Oh, not sexually crazy," I tell her. "Just regular crazy."

"Well, then you've nailed it." She picks at the fabric, unconvinced. "It's horrible."

Chapter 11

Annie

One week later, and I'm right back to where this whole mess started: swim lessons.

At least I drove myself today, so Gran's not marching around in her *Go! Annie!* socks. I'm waiting outside the pool five minutes before class when my phone rings. My mom's picture flashes on the screen, and I can't help but roll my eyes.

"Are you at the Y?" she asks when I answer. "I'm not being nosy, I'm just wondering."

"You *are* being nosy, mom."

"Well, are you there? I paid good money for these lessons. I don't want you to die at my wedding."

"I'm not going to die at your wedding!"

"Well, good. That means you showed up to class?"

"*Yes*!" I hang up the phone with gusto after adding a firm goodbye to my mother.

Glancing in the mirror, it's obvious that I won't have any trouble with Cohen James this morning—not in this hideous thing. The sensation is oddly freeing. There are enough strings hanging off the brown suit to make me look like a cousin to the wooly mammoth.

Before heading out to join my class, I pull one last, brand-new purchase from the bag. A robe made to look like a superman cape, all blue and fuzzy. I don't know why I got it—as a joke, I suppose—for Cohen. After the article I'd read about him serenading the team captain without pants, I thought he could've used it.

But now that I'm standing here in front of the mirror, it feels too personal. I don't even know the man. Instead of feeling goofy and cute, I feel like a creep for buying a gag gift based off an article on the internet. That's like having an inside joke with myself.

I shove the robe back into my locker and slam it shut before I change my mind and embarrass myself further. Before I can chicken out, I force myself to take one step after another out of the locker room and into the pool area.

He's there, waiting. Not for me, specifically, although that knowledge doesn't make this any easier. It was a horrible idea wearing this outfit. A horrible idea to come back to class. A horrible idea to buy the robe as a joke. All of it—horrible.

Cohen's eyes land on me, running over my body in the span of a nanosecond. It sets my skin to tingling and my mind swirling with curiosity. Wondering what he's thinking right this very second.

Maybe it's not too late to pay him off for a certificate to pass the class. I ponder this while waiting for him to speak. After all, what does he care if I show up to class every week? It's not his problem if I fall off a plank at my mother's wedding and drown. I mean, *really*, after three margaritas is it really going to matter whether I know how to breaststroke? I think I'm shark bait at that point anyway.

"You know I can't possibly stick up for that bathing suit, don't you?" Cohen's eyes are dancing green. We're the only two people in here save for an elderly couple sliding into the hot tub. "That thing is tremendously ugly. Where did you find it?"

"I think it flatters my figure."

My fingers trail over some of the coarse streamers hanging off the side. *Where is Leigh?* I can't handle being in a room alone with him.

The pressure's too much. I don't even like the man, and I feel like I'm going to melt into a puddle under the intensity of his stare.

Then, that intense gaze lowers to my lips, and my face heats up all over. Suddenly, I can't think of anything to say, so I start humming the first song that pops into my head. *Night at the Roxbury.*

He recognizes it, and his eyes roll to the ceiling. "You stalked me?"

"No."

"*Really.*"

"I read the news. I'm a well-informed citizen."

"I didn't know well-informed citizens cared a lick about the hazing rituals of a hockey team."

"So it was hazing?"

"It's none of your business," he says, his face now close enough for me to smell the spearmint on his breath. Fresh, sharp, just like his eyes. "In fact—"

He stops speaking abruptly, and I glance up. Leigh's entered the room, and she's holding the door open for Jason.

"Can I speak to you in my office?" Cohen glances at my swimsuit—if it can be called that—and clears his throat. "Please and thank you, Miss Plymouth."

Leigh raises her eyebrows at me, her expression neutral. I follow Cohen out of the room and offer her an eyeroll and a shoulder shrug, enough for her to break into a grin.

"You kids have fun," she murmurs as I pass by.

A few minutes later, he closes the door to the lifeguard office. It's early Saturday morning, another snow softened day, the temperatures dipping just below freezing.

Cohen has his shirt off, swim trunks covering his legs, and it's distracting. I wish I'd brought the robe with me so I could put it over his chest.

"What do you want from me, Annie?"

I'm startled by the question. "What?"

"What are you doing in my class?" Cohen's face is unreadable, and I can't tell if he's upset, or just mildly annoyed at my presence. "You hate being here. You don't want to get in the water, and clearly I'm your least favorite person in the world."

"You're not my least favorite person in the world."

"Is that right?" He crosses his arms and leans against the desk. "Sure feels like I am."

"You're not my least favorite person in the world, but after last week, you're close."

"Who wins that award?"

"Billy Prescott. Pantsed me during gym class freshmen year of high school. Mortifying. Hitler takes a close second."

He runs a hand through his hair, his muscles straining as he perches on the edge of the desk. "Contrary to popular belief, I'm not as big of a jerk as you might think."

"You stole my noodle."

"I brought you in here to apologize for last week." He folds his hands before his body, looks down at his feet before raising his eyes to mine. "I shouldn't have taken your floatation device away without warning. I'm sorry. I hadn't realized you'd react like that."

"I told you that I'm terrified of water!"

"Look, I said I'm sorry!" He straightens from the desk, his hands widening as he speaks. "I'm apologizing because I can recognize when I've made a mistake. I thought you were a *little* nervous of the water. Not *deathly* afraid! Either way, it doesn't matter. I shouldn't have pushed you so hard the first day of class."

I swallow, uncomfortable with the way his gaze has softened, his eyes roving my face, looking for signs of a crack in my exterior.

"What happened, Annie?"

"Nothing," I say. "It's no big deal. Stupid. Can we just get back to class?"

"You never answered why you're here in the first place."

"My mom's getting married on July 7th."

"Congratulations to her."

"On a *boat*," I continue. "As you might've guessed by now, I don't have this whole swimming thing down yet, and she's nervous I'll die."

"Couldn't you just stay on the boat and not jump into the ocean?"

"Well, yeah. Try to get my mother to see things that way, though."

He laughs, the crinkle around his eyes a pleasant change from the hardness that's been there before. "If she's anything like you, I'll bet she's stubborn."

I cross my arms back, but he's too close, and I brush against his bare chest as I do so. It's hard, smooth, just like I'd imagined. "Maybe."

"July 7th..." He taps his fingers against the clipboard he'd carried into the office. "Your mom's getting married on your birthday?"

I reach over and pull the clipboard away so I can see what it says. Sure enough, my birthday is listed there, information I'm sure my mother supplied when she signed me up. "Yep. Special day. On the subject—are you open to bribes that allow me to bypass this class?"

"Bribes? What sort of bribes?"

"I'm a college student. I can give you my used textbooks, twenty bucks, and meals for a week from the cafeteria. In exchange for a certificate that says I passed, of course."

"You have something else I want."

"I do?"

He reaches a hand out and places it on my chin, tilting my face toward his until I'm pinned by his gaze again. I stand there, transfixed, as he runs his tongue over his lips. "Yes."

"So is that a *no* to the textbooks and twenty dollar deal?"

"I want a date with you."

"A date?" I'm floored. "You're kidding. I thought you were trying to clean up your act."

"I am." He pauses. "Annie, I'm trying to do the right thing here."

"How is this doing the right thing?" I shake my head at him. "I'm not interested, and I'm not sleeping with the teacher to get an A, sorry."

"First of all, I never asked you to sleep with me. Your mind went there all on its own. Secondly, that's not what this is about."

"What *is* it about? I thought you had rules and were trying to be professional? This is how you... you *professional*?"

"Professional is not a verb, but I like your creativity." He grins, which irks me even more. "Believe it or not, this is me trying to do things the right way."

My cheeks turn red, and I can't believe I'm having this conversation. Dressed like a wooly mammoth, no less. "I'd love to hear how you justify that one."

"That's easy. How do I justify wanting a date with you?" Cohen sets his clipboard down and leans against the desk. "A gorgeous woman shows up to the first day of class. I mean, it's impossible to miss her."

It takes me a minute to realize he's talking about me. When it finally clicks, I turn over a few noises that never quite make their way into words.

"Then, I get to know her a little and find out that she's also really funny. She makes me laugh, she's obviously smart, witty, all of those great things, and on top of it she's stunning—even in a burlap sack."

"It's not burlap," I say, fingering my suit. "It's—"

"Whatever the hell it is, the suit is offensive, and yet I still can't stop thinking about you. I've tried, Annie, believe me. Every day this week I've tried to make sure you're *not* the first thing I think about when I wake up, or the last person I think about before bed."

"And how'd that work for you?"

His grin grows brighter. "Not fucking great. Otherwise I wouldn't be throwing professionalism out the window and taking a chance asking you out."

"But—"

"You can say *no,* and I won't treat you differently in class. This was never a bribe, Annie, this is all about me spotting an incredible woman and wanting a chance with her."

"Me? No, I'm very, very average."

He snorts with laughter. "Right."

Somehow, it's endearing the way he looks at me next, and I find myself getting all shy on him. "I don't think it's a good idea. I'd still prefer a get-out-of-class free card. Are you sure I can't interest you in a calculus book?"

He raises his hands. "Sweetheart, I didn't even use a calculus book when I took the class. Sorry, no deal. I just want to get to know you."

I bite my lip. "Can you hold that thought? Because I have one more bribe for you."

I spin past Cohen, leaving him to watch as I barrel out of the room. I retrieve the robe from my locker and return in a few seconds.

He takes one look at the fabric in my hands. "What is that?"

"For you," I say, tossing it to him. "For the next time you get the idea to waltz around the neighborhood naked."

"You're kidding."

"No. Actually, put it on right now because I can't make a deal with you while you're naked."

"I'm not naked, I'm—"

"—half-naked, and that's just as bad," I say. "Put it on."

My words are cut off mid-sentence as he takes two steps toward me and slides his hand behind my head. His lips hover above mine for a second, just a split second, leaving me the window of escape. The opportunity to back out from the kiss.

I don't move.

"Do you want me to kiss you?" He waits, his eyes searching mine. "You can say no, and I'll leave you alone."

My eyes are closed, which is a mystery to me, since I don't remember shutting them. Tingles are shooting everywhere, and I can't seem to make myself push him away.

The moment his lips meet mine, two things happen. Simultaneously, I'm melted from the inside out by the best kiss I've ever had in my life, and horrified that it's happened at all. I'd told myself not to fall for Cohen's charms, and... *crap!*

I completely forgot about the girl in his car.

My hand comes up and strikes him across the cheek with a loud slap. "You have a girlfriend, asshole!"

"What? Annie, no I don't!" He reels backwards as I stomp out of the room. "What are you talking about?"

His words follow me, and I wonder if I made a huge mistake. What if that was his sister in the car, or his brother's wife? What if I assumed wrong? I'm flushed from head to toe, staring wildly around the hall as I head toward the showers.

Then I remember that I should get to class still because my mother will know if I skip it. She's psychic like that. Plus, Gran will be coming for her synchronized swimming class, and *she'll* tattle if I'm not here.

So instead, I head to the sauna to cool down for a second, which is ironic because I'm sweating bullets. Someone cranked this heat up *high*. I wait for a minute, two, three before I'm fairly certain he's not coming after me.

Sooner or later, though, I must return to class.

Before I move, the door is pushed open and a rush of cold air washes over my body. It's a welcome relief from all the hot air, and I raise my head to greet the newcomer.

I pause, my hand halfway to my mouth in surprise.

"Cohen?"

Chapter 12

Cohen

I can't figure out if I'm angry or annoyed or curious.

Rubbing my jaw, I wait in the office a little dumbstruck. What have I ever said to give her the impression that I have a girlfriend? I'm the last person in the NHL that anyone would imagine had a girlfriend.

Her slap was hard, but it didn't hurt. My skin stings, but what annoys me even more is I can smell the lingering scent of her lotion, or soap, or whatever it is that's driving me insane. So, instead of standing around and waiting for her to apologize, I storm back to class.

After all, she has to come to me. At least, she does if she wants to pass the class in time for her mom's wedding.

"Where's Annie?" Leigh asks the second I reach her and Jason. "Wasn't she with you?"

"Bathroom," I mutter, wondering what it is about girls and their ability to sense when things have gone belly up.

"Is she okay?" Leigh presses. "Should I go check on her?"

"I think *she's* fine." I rub my jaw again, wincing when I brush over an area where she clipped me with her nail. "Let's get started. Grab a kickboard and take a lap down and back."

"I recommend you go after her," Leigh says, brushing past me on her way to grab the floaty. "Annie's a nice girl."

Before I can respond, she flops into the pool, a sorry excuse for a cannonball. I have to admire her grit. The way she's spiraling and kicking and floundering down the lane makes me exhausted, but she doesn't give up. As far as I can tell, she's floating on nothing but a prayer and a rickety old kickboard.

I offer some constructive feedback to her and Jason as they complete their first lap. I instruct them to practice the changes with another lap, and then tell the lifeguard I'll be right back. He nods and turns an eye on my class as I leave the pool area.

The first place I check for her is the office, but she's not there. Next, I debate asking a woman with a few small kids if she'll check the ladies' room for me, but I don't get the chance because the youngest child starts screaming bloody murder.

I'm about to give up, wondering if maybe she went all the way home, when I turn around and see her. I stop, and so does my breathing, at the sight of her through the clear sauna door. I almost barge right in, my adrenaline taking control, when something makes me pause. Something in the way she's sitting, head in her hands, shoulders slumped.

I feel bad. I should be apologizing about going in for the kiss. There's no excuse for me to pull that sort of a stunt. Even so, I do have one big problem.

I'm not at all sorry that she kissed me back.

Chapter 13

Annie

"Cohen, what are you doing here?" I ask for a second time. "What about class?"

"I'm *not* sorry I kissed you, Annie. I can't pretend that I don't like you."

I blink, processing. He just blurted these facts aloud, and I'm not sure if he intended to say any of it at all.

"Okay," I say cautiously.

"I don't have a girlfriend, either."

"So the girl in the car, that was... a friend?"

He shrugs. "Yes, though I think she had the wrong idea. I'm not—wasn't—interested, and I told her so. Nothing happened between us."

I straighten. "Then I owe you an apology for slapping you. I'm not normally a violent person."

Moving through the heat, he gestures for me to scootch over so he can share my towel. The temperature increases to approximately one million degrees, and it has nothing to do with the sauna. One of his hands comes to rest on my lower back and, try as I might, I can't bring myself to flinch.

"This is what I mean," he says gently. "You don't pull away when I touch you."

"That sounds creepy."

I reach behind my body, pull his hand off my back with two fingers, and deposit it onto his lap. The rest of my body is sizzling, and frankly it's a traitor. My mind tells me it'd be bad news to get involved, but my body seems to like the idea.

He folds his hands over his knees. "So, are you coming back to class?"

"Have you reconsidered the deal?"

"You mean, your bribe?"

"Whatever."

"Sorry, no can do, pretty lady. I'm *professionaling*."

"That's not a verb," I snarl, staring out the door. With a last ditch attempt, I give him the side-eye. "Are you sure about that bribe?"

"The bribe's a no. Have you considered my proposal?"

"I'm sorry, but I'm just not interested in a date." I stand and yank my towel off the bench. It's wedged under his rear end, so I yank harder. "I'll do the stupid front crawl and treading water thing if it kills me."

He stands too, his long, lean muscles shining in the humidity. A new sheen from the moisture coats his skin, and I watch as teensy little droplets slide down the rivulets of his stomach.

"I've gotta teach the breaststroke. Care to join?"

"Breaststroke. Funny."

"I'm not laughing."

"You're looking at my boobs."

"Nope." He shakes his head, eyes landing on my oddly shaped suit. "It's impossible to see anything through that."

"I wore it specially for you."

"I'm flattered." He reaches out, toys with one of the weird, random string-things hanging from the outside. It's almost like Native American tribal wear, but less interesting. "Next time, feel free to drop the shield. I promise I'll keep my hands to myself."

"I'm not sure if you understand how to do that."

"Tell me one thing, Annie." He leans over, his breath dancing across my collarbone. "Would you slap me if I kissed you right now?"

I rub my lips together, my entire body *zinging* with the prospect. It wasn't that the first kiss had been horrible. In fact, I quite liked the feel of his lips against mine, but I'm not ready to admit that to him. Instead, I stick a hand on my hip. "Do you *really* want to risk it?"

"Okay then," he says, leading me toward the pool with a lingering smile. "Just don't forget that two can play at this game, Miss Plymouth."

Chapter 14

Annie

The rest of the lesson passes with surprisingly few incidents. Cohen doesn't try to steal my noodle or kiss me, and I refrain from slapping him. It's almost like we've reached an odd level of truce, and I find the end of the class arriving too soon.

I didn't even hate the water as much today as I normally do. I made it down and back once, all by myself. I might have strapped myself into a life vest and held onto a secondary floatation device, but it was progress.

"See you all next week," Cohen says, ushering us out of the pool as the oversized clock on the wall shows it's time to go. "Nice work today, everyone."

I bid Leigh goodbye and head toward the showers. Cohen catches me, matches my stride.

"You never answered my question," he says, his gaze quite passive. "I was hoping to get a response."

"I thought I was clear. I don't want to go on a date with you."

"I meant your suit." He picks up the streamers between two fingers. "What is this thing?"

"No comment."

"Annie," he says, changing his tune. "You did good today. Really."

"Because you didn't steal my noodle."

76

"At this rate, you won't need to let me take you on a date to pass."

He's grinning, so I smile back. Before I can think up a halfway intelligent response, he's gone—disappeared into the men's room. I wait, surprised for a long second, until I realize he's not coming back.

Heading into the women's locker room, I rinse, lather, shampoo, and realize it's all for naught just as I'm finishing up. I've forgotten that Gran signed me up for the synchronized swim team—the retired version—and today's my first day.

Seeing as I've already showered, the thought of climbing *back* into a wet burlap sack holds absolutely zero appeal for me. Luckily, I have a second option; I fish the black two piece I picked up at Target out of my locker.

Once it's on, I glance at my body in the mirror. It's not half bad, I think, which is about as good as it's going to get. Bonus points if Cohen catches a glimpse while he's got his hands tied up teaching baby class.

Because whatever Cohen's opinion on the matter, we're off limits to each other. Completely and utterly off limits.

Chapter 15

Cohen

Now she changes into some hot little number.

Now that she's over there doing stretches and cartwheels and who knows what else with the old lady squad, she's decided not to wear the strangest swimsuit on earth.

What the hell are they doing, anyway? I squint, trying to make out some sort of routine, or dance, or... *something.* I'd overheard Annie telling Leigh that her grandmother had signed her up for synchronized swimming lessons.

One problem. There is nothing synchronized about these ladies. One of them has her hands in the air, another one's floating on her back, and a third is sitting on the edge of the pool.

Meanwhile, Annie, sexy as hell in her new black bikini, is patiently helping one of the women twirl around like a ballerina. In the water.

"Cohen!" One of the mother's in my infant class calls me, her voice sharp. "I dropped Thomas into the water. Is he okay?"

I look at the baby—I'm not *great* with babies. This little man is somewhere between three months and three years old. When my PR lady got me the class, I went through some training before teaching, and they *said* I wouldn't be doing the holding of babies. Just singing songs and splashing around.

Which is why I'm completely unprepared when Mrs. Erickson thrusts her kid at me. He's somewhere between the size of a watermelon and a yardstick. He doesn't talk yet, just gurgles and smiles and farts.

"Oh, hello there," I say, wrapping my arms around Thomas. "You're a tough kid, aren't you?"

Thomas blinks water out of his eyes, looking a little confused.

"It's okay," I tell him. "I'm confused about what we're supposed to do with you, too."

I hold him out at arm's length, my fingers getting a little sweaty. He's heavier than he looks, and I don't want to drop him. *What comes next?* It's like all the training I took before teaching just flies out of my head and is replaced by blankness.

Am I supposed to cuddle him? Plop him in the water? I know I'm not supposed to dunk him underneath, but the rest seems to be fair game. *What's the song about the wheels and the bus?*

Thomas kicks his feet and squeals, and I take that as a good sign. I lower him ever so slowly until his feet hit the water, and he begins to splash. The smile on his face splits even wider, and then this bubbly little laugh comes from his throat that makes me laugh right along with him.

"I think he likes it," I say, surprised to feel a tiny sense of accomplishment. "Well, look at that, you punk."

Mrs. Erickson is smiling now too. "He won't splash for anybody except me!"

"Way to go, buddy."

"So that means he's okay?"

"Kids are tough," I tell her, handing Thomas back. "A little water in the eyes won't hurt anyone."

I do my rounds with the class, realizing sometime later that thirty minutes have passed in a whirl. I haven't even checked out Annie *once*. Before ending the class, I take Thomas for another spin around the pool, surprised to find myself wanting to earn another laugh.

That's when I catch Annie's eye. She's watching me with this look of amusement mixed with curiosity on her face in the middle of her routine. I shrug when our eyes meet, and she snaps to attention, making an effort to ignore me.

I take no small amount of pleasure in the fact that the back of Annie's neck is bright red. Music pumps from her side of the pool, some old song from *Grease*. She's clearly distracted, wildly off the beat. Even her Gran is keeping pace with the song.

Her class runs fifteen minutes longer than mine, so I take the opportunity to say goodbye to my miniature students before hitting the showers. I'm clean, and dressed by the time Annie's class is done, so I dawdle in the front lobby for ten extra minutes.

I help myself to the godawful coffee, chat with the receptionist—whose voice is as thrilling as a paper towel—and listen as she recounts the medical mishaps of her seven cats. I'm debating putting myself out of my misery when, out of the corner of my eye, I see the woman I've been waiting for.

Annie's deep in conversation with her grandmother as the pair climbs the stairs, and it's Grannie Plymouth who sees me first.

"Hey, Mr. Teacher," she calls. "You were looking good out there."

"Thank you, Mrs..."

"Call me Lucy."

Annie swivels her head to face her grandmother. "Your name is not Lucy."

"Nah, you're right." The older woman sticks her hand out. "My name is Margaret. But don't you think I'm more of a Lucy? Or, why don't you just call me Gran?"

I glance between the two, a smile frozen on my face.

"Her friends call her Maggie," Annie clarifies, her cheeks filling with a new shade of pink. "Feel free to do the same."

"Maggie." I extend a hand. "Pleasure to meet you. Caught a glimpse of your synchronized swimming moves and, let me tell you, they are *something* else."

Gran shakes my hand, the blush on her face matching that of her granddaughter's. "Well, thank you, my friend. I pride myself on my flexibility. Did you see me doing the splits out there?"

"Alrighty, then." Annie gently guides her grandmother through the front doors. "Keep this up, Gran, and we'll put you in that home you've been eyeing."

"Oh, relax." Gran pats Annie's arm. "Aren't I charming, Mr. Teacher?"

"Call me Cohen."

"Cohen, aren't I charming?"

"Sure are, Maggie."

"Great," she says. "You have a good day now, Cohen. It was fun watching you with them babies. You've got a knack for teaching the little tykes."

Her comment is surprisingly sweet, but I don't tell her so. Instead, I do the next worst thing and turn to Annie. "Hey, I was wondering if I could talk to you for a second."

"What?" Annie looks up, eyes wild. "Fine, sure, whatever. You can say it right here."

I give a look at her grandmother, but it's not enough to deter me. I haven't sat around listening to the receptionist talk about her cats for fun, and I'm not giving up this easily.

"Okay, then," I say, lowering my voice so the *entire* bridge club upstairs can't here. "Is there any chance I can get your phone number?"

"No."

"You can have mine," Gran says, fluttering her eyelashes. "But it's a landline, so don't try to text. I've tried texting from the landline before, and things get a little wonky."

"I'll bet," I say, holding a straight face. "What about it, Annie?"

"I said I'm not interested in dating."

"This isn't about a date."

"What's it about?"

"Since when is it against the law for a handsome man to ask a beautiful women for her number?" Gran turns to Annie and gives her a poke to the chest. "Tell him yes, kiddo. You can always tell him no to a date over the phone."

Annie's jaw sets in a firm line, and I'm sure she's going to tell her grandmother off first, and then round on me.

But she's full of surprises. "Don't you already have it?"

"Have what?" I ask.

"My number." She shifts her purse higher on her shoulder. "I'm pretty sure it's on the roster, along with my address."

"You don't mind if I call you sometime?"

I watch Annie's face flash through a rainbow of emotions. From the outside, it looks like she wants to say yes, but is stopped by something resembling pride. I should know, I have plenty of it, along with the stubbornness to back it up.

"Whatever," she says. "See you next week."

She leaves with her grandmother, and I pull my backpack closer. Inside, I've got my wet swimsuit there, wrapped in a plastic bag, along with the gift from Annie. That Superman robe is the most thoughtful gift I've received in the last five years.

Annie might not know it, but that's the reason I can't find it in me to give up on her yet. Even if it'd been in jest, there was meaning behind it. A certain thoughtfulness. She'd done her research, and she'd been thinking about me.

In fact, I have one idea left. It's a gamble, and it's risky, but Annie's already proven that it'll take extraordinary measures to get her to trust me. To let me take her out to dinner. To wiggle my way into her life.

I'll have to wait until the right moment to follow up on my plan. For now, I'll be patient and wait. The only thing that I can guarantee for certain is this: chasing after Annie Plymouth will either be the stupidest stunt I've ever pulled, or just maybe, it'll be the very best thing.

Chapter 16

Annie

"Am I horrible?" I ask Leigh after our third class. "Do you think I'm a terrible person?"

"What are you talking about? Of course not." She tilts the nozzle of the shower higher and cranks the water warmer. We're both rinsing off in our suits after our latest almost-drowning session at the YM-CA. "What'd you do this time?"

"Did you see how he acted toward me?"

"Who?"

"*Cohen!*"

Leigh blinks in my direction. "I thought you said he asked you on a date last week, and you said *no*."

"Well, that's true, but..." I trail off, hoping Leigh will pick up the slack.

"But what?" Leigh looks over at me. "I know what you want me to say, honey, but I'm not going to say it."

"Was I terrible to him today?"

"No! You're allowed to tell him you're not interested in a date. But then you shouldn't be surprised when he backs off." Leigh reaches for the shampoo and squirts some into her hand. She begins washing her hair as she gives me the side eye. "I know what's happening here. You're not very sly."

"What's happening?"

"You're playing hard to get, and Cohen's respecting your wishes. It's frustrating you."

"I said no to the date. I didn't say that he couldn't ever talk to me again."

"He talked to you just fine today. Just like he talked to me and Jason. Like a professional."

"Stupid professionalism."

"Hon, if you're interested, why don't you give him a sign?" Leigh extends the shampoo bottle over to me, and I press some into my hand and mutter a thank you. "Believe it or not, it's a good sign he backed off. If he had started pursuing you continuously after you told him *no*, well, that's called stalking."

"Fair enough."

"Hey, I get it, Annie. Every woman wants to feel pursued. Wants to feel like even if she pushes her man away, he'll fight for her."

"Maybe."

"The thing is, he's not *your man*. Not yet, at least. The rules are different. You're going to have to relax and throw him a bone."

"I thought I did."

"When?!" Leigh snorts with laughter as she rinses her hair. "You glared at him all class and threatened him with a painful death if he took your noodle away."

"I didn't mean it to be rude."

"Even if you don't want to date him, it might not kill you to lighten up a little." Leigh turns the handle and shuts the water off. "Yes, he stole your noodle on the first day of class, but he apologized. He asked you out on a date—so what? Is it *really* so bad he finds you attractive and smart?"

A tiny layer of unease settles over me. "I guess not."

"He took a risk asking you out, and you shut him down. He's not going to read your mind, honey. In my experience, men don't even read a To-Do list if their name is stamped across the top."

"Great. Now I feel like the jerk."

"Neither of you are jerks! You're just all young and in lust."

I wash my hair more furiously. "I'm not *lusting* after him."

"What are you doing?"

"I just want..." I sigh. "I don't know what I want."

"Ding, ding, ding. Figure out what you do want before you play games with him. Decide if you want to be professional or... more than that."

"What's your advice?"

"Just relax! Have some fun. I don't mean that in a reckless way, I just mean if you like talking to him, don't be afraid to say *hello*. If he asks you for coffee and you want to go, then go."

"But what about professionalism and all of that?"

"It's *swimming lessons*. Most people sign up for them *voluntarily*."

"Not me."

She rolls her eyes. "If you both decide to spend some time together, no one is going to care."

"There's a chance you might be right."

"*Of course* I'm right." Leigh grabs her towel and wraps it around her body. She eyes me, and my swimsuit, before speaking. "And don't be afraid to look like a woman. I don't know *what* that thing is, but if Cohen notices you in it, he'll be knocked unconscious when he sees the real you."

"Thanks, Leigh. See you next week?"

"Yes. And if you bring that suit again, I'm bringing a torch."

Chapter 17

Cohen

For the first time ever, I wonder if she doesn't hate me.

Last week, Annie iced me out like I'd been infected by the plague. Every time I looked over at her, I'd caught her glaring back. I'd leaned over at one point to help adjust her noodle, and she'd just about taken my eye out with her elbow.

I'd gotten the picture and backed off. Probably better for both of us, anyway. I'm supposed to be professional, and if Annie ignores me completely, it makes it a helluva lot easier on my end.

This week, however, it's as if a light switch has flipped. I'm standing on the pool deck when she arrives for class a few minutes early and offers up a bright and cheery smile. She even addresses me by name. I'm so stunned I can't think of a response.

"You okay?" she asks. "Did I startle you?"

"Annie! No, sorry. I was, uh...nice suit." I cringe internally as she glances down and surveys the black bikini that's replaced the weird burlap sack. "I just mean—"

"Thanks." She smiles, almost shyly, and moves toward the pool. "Maybe this week you can help me try to tread water without the noodle?"

"I won't pull your noodle away from you, I promise. I apologized, and I meant it—"

"I'm serious! Actually, if we have a few minutes now, maybe you can help me out."

I stand there dumbly. My brain considers speaking, but it never makes its way to my mouth. Almost cautiously, I step forward as she tests the water with a toe.

I'm getting mixed signals here. Her tone is light and unassuming, but I can't help the shock of having her talk to me in a pleasant sort of way.

"Unless you're busy?"

Her question brings me back to reality. "Not at all! Of course I'll help. Why don't you slide in, and I'll grab the noodle."

She dips her toe again into the shallow end, testing the water for a second time. Daintily she eases in up to her hips, then to her chest, as a shiver wracks her body and her lips tremble.

Part of me wants to jump in there next to her and hold her against me. For body heat, of course, and because I'm a nice guy.

Not because she looks smoking hot in that bikini and finally doesn't want to kill me.

"Did you have a nice week?" I ask, careful to keep my tone even as we move along the edge of the pool. I walk along the ledge while she holds the wall for balance. "Do anything fun?"

"Not too much. School, exams, all of that crap."

"What are you studying?"

"I'm an econ major. Pre-law."

"You're going to be a lawyer?"

"Why do you sound so surprised?"

I extend the noodle to her as we reach the halfway point in the pool. A few more steps, and she won't be able to touch. "I'm not surprised. If anything, your argumentative nature makes a lot more sense, now."

For a brief flash, she looks offended. Then she laughs, snatches the noodle, and takes a few more steps until she's floating. "My mom said I was born to be a lawyer."

"Your mom must be a smart woman."

"Yeah, she's great. Except for this whole forcing me into swim lessons, thing," she says, then jerks to a stop. "I'm sorry, I didn't mean... it's not *so* bad."

"I'm sorry, did you just say it's not *so* bad?"

She grins broadly. "Mediocre bad."

"I'll take that as a compliment."

Another laugh from her as she agrees. "You should. I don't use my insults lightly."

"So do you—"

"*Cohen!*"

"What?" I glance down, heart pounding at the panic in her screech, but nothing seems amiss. "What's wrong?"

"I can't touch." Sure enough, her toes have just passed the point where the water is taller than her, and she's floating using the noodle. She offers a half sheepish, half terrified grin. "I take it back. I don't think I can do this. I'm going to die."

"Hold on, don't move. You're not going to die."

"I *can't* move. If I could swim, I wouldn't be here."

By the time she's done arguing, I've slid fully into the water and have a hand on her wrist. I offer what I hope is a comforting smile. "Come on, we'll go down together."

"But... you got into the water just for *that*? All wet? Freezing cold? Voluntarily?"

"It's my job."

"It's not your job! You stand on your ledge. This is—"

"This *isn't* law school. Stop arguing. Do you trust me?"

She hesitates for a second. "Well, I—"

"I'm not going anywhere, Annie. I'm right here. Trust me. Just this once."

Reaching out her other hand, she takes mine in hers. Gently, I guide her to the deep end, the noodle still under her arms as I kick my legs to keep my head above water.

"How's that?" I ask. "Feeling okay?"

"Terrified."

"Other than terrified, how are you?"

"I'm..." she hesitates, glances at our clasped hands, and then below her to where the bottom of the pool shines beneath the bright blue water. "I'm okay."

"Of course you are! I promised you would be okay, didn't I?"

She nods. "What next?"

"Do you trust me?"

The hesitation is shorter this time as she bobs her head yes.

"Good. I'm going to remove the noodle slowly, but I will not let go of you."

"But—"

"We'll go slow."

"Okay." She breathes out, her eyes panicking with every inch of the noodle disappearing from under her arms. "I'm scared."

"Don't be. I'm right here."

Before she can resist, the floatation device is on the side of the pool, and the only thing Annie is touching is me. In some odd, primal sort of way, I like this—I like her hands on me, the way she looks into my eyes as if I'm the only thing keeping her alive. It's everything I can do not to brush the damp strands of hair away from her face.

"I'm doing it," she says, a whisper of excitement in her voice as her feet flutter below the surface. "We're alive."

I can't help but laugh. Her voice is full of nothing but excitement. "*You're* doing it. Look! I'm barely holding onto you."

As I begin to remove my fingers from her grip, she holds on tighter. "No. Don't you dare let go, Cohen."

"I'm not going anywhere." I reaffirm my grip on her hands as her legs flail wild underneath us. "You're doing this all by yourself."

"I'm holding onto you."

"Just barely. You're keeping yourself afloat."

"Omigosh. I'm doing it."

We stay here for several extended seconds, and I dread the moment the other students in class will arrive. They'll shatter this moment, this first truce we've had together, and I'm not ready for that to happen.

I need more of this, of her, of this wonderfully vulnerable side to Annie Plymouth. I've backed down from the chase somewhat, but I haven't abandoned my plan. If anything, with each passing minute I spend next to Annie I'm more determined than ever to get to know her. The more I see of her, the more I'm convinced she'll be worth it.

"*Cohen*!" She shrieks my name as she dips slightly below the surface of the pool, her mouth garbling with water as she yells for me again.

I'm there in a second, my arms wrapped around her torso and my legs moving double speed to keep us both afloat. She's warm, soft in my arms as I bring us together to the side of the pool and rest her arms against the ledge.

"You okay?" Without thinking, I reach out and brush those wet strands of hair off her cheek as her eyes widen and fix on my face. "Sorry," I mutter. "I just—"

"Did I see you treading water without a noodle?" Leigh breaks any private moment as she reaches the side of the pool, sits down, and swings her legs into the water. "You looked awesome out there."

I'm not stupid, and I don't miss the raised eyebrow or the cheeky grin Leigh gives her friend as she waits for a response. I mutter something about toweling off and pull myself out of the pool after depositing Annie with her noodle safely at the edge. At the same time, Jason steps onto the deck.

The girls whisper behind me, and I do my best to ignore their murmurs, pretending instead to fill out the attendance sheet on my clipboard. Really, I'm watching Annie out of the corner of my eye as she recounts her latest near-brush with death, and how fabulous it felt to be swimming almost on her own.

It's then that I decide tonight is the night. With swimming lessons today and hockey practice this afternoon, I won't have time to corral Annie before this evening to get another conversation going. The last thing I want to do is scare her off or push her away, just as she's opening up.

But even worse would be letting her slip through my grasp without knowing how I feel. I don't know that Annie wants anything to do with me, and I don't *know* that we have anything between us except physical chemistry. All I know is that I need to find out.

Chapter 18

Annie

I'm in my room when the noise begins.

It's a howl, sort of, or a screech. Like a cow in labor or a pigeon on its deathbed. I plug my headphones tighter to my ears, crank up the movie soundtracks, and return to studying.

I'm at my grandmother's house tonight—on a Saturday night—studying because of this stupid exam. Sarah wanted to have friends over to our apartment, and I didn't want to spoil her weekend just because I'm feeling anti-social and grouchy. So, I vacated the premises while her friends piled into our apartment.

This anti-social and grouchy mood has nothing to do with the fact that I spent all day thinking about why in the world I didn't stick around after class and ask Cohen James out for a cup of coffee. I could've had plans tonight if I'd *wanted* to, but I hadn't gotten up the guts. Hence the reason I'm studying at my grandmother's house on Saturday evening.

My mother also took advantage of the situation by requesting I join her for a day of shopping tomorrow. She wants to find me the perfect dress to wear as her maid of honor.

I'm not thrilled about the dress, but she sweetened the pot and offered to buy brunch and lattes from the fancy place on Grand. What can I say? Unlike Cohen James, I'm easy to bribe.

I'm trying to read through my notes again, pushing away all thoughts of Cohen James, but that noise outside just won't quit. I'm not sure what's worse—the dying pigeon, or the incessant thoughts about Cohen's naked torso. They're both equally annoying and equally persistent.

Finally, I throw off my headphones and make my way over toward the window. It's my childhood bedroom, and most of the decorations—the boy band posters, the collage of high school photos, the earring display and nail polish jars—remain largely intact.

Cranking the window open, my heart begins to race as I realize that the sound is neither a pigeon dying nor a cow giving birth—it's distinctly human. I can't make out the exact words, but it's definitely a *voice*.

My palms get slick with sweat as my brain starts to ponder the worst case scenarios. *Is someone getting mugged*? Do I call the police? Run outside with my dinky pink can of pepper spray? I could yell downstairs to Gran, but I don't expect she'd be able to do much to help.

Leaning out the window, I begin to breathe easier. I catch sight of a man's figure standing on the street below, and it looks like he's talking on one of those Bluetooth earpieces. It's still *odd* that he's standing outside in this weather, but at least nobody is in mortal danger.

I'm about to turn back to studying and crank up the volume when my back shoots ramrod straight, and a flash of recognition streaks through my mind. *The robe*. I recognize the robe.

"Oh, *no*," I breathe, flinging the window open even wider. I lean close to the screen and, sure enough, as the blast of icy cold air steals my breath, another jolt of recognition hits me hard.

Cohen James. I don't know what the hell he thinks he's doing standing outside in a robe, but suddenly, I'm wondering if he's trying to *sing*. He might have the body of a Greek god, but he's got the voice of a rooster with laryngitis.

Tapping my toe against the floor, I wearily scan the neighborhood and impatiently wait for him to wrap up the verse. He does so with an extra flourish of his hands, and a bow halfway to the ground.

"Cohen *James*!" I shout through the arctic blast. "What do you think you're doing?"

"I'm serenading you."

"I thought someone was getting mugged!"

"You don't like it?"

"There's nothing to like; it's not *music*."

He fingers the edges of the robe, pulling it tighter around his body. "I thought you might appreciate seeing your gift in use."

"It's freezing. Go home, Cohen."

"All of this for nothing?"

"What did you expect?" I ask, lowering my voice as our neighbor's light clicks on. We live in a fairly normal, pint-sized community just outside of the Twin Cities that likes to gab. I don't want to bring attention to myself or my family. "You can't just show up here in the middle of the night."

"It's nine p.m. on a Saturday."

I hesitate, glance at the clock on the wall. It's technically eight thirty, but I've been studying since the sun went down and it feels like three in the morning to me.

"I'll leave if you reconsider my offer of a date," he says into the silence. "It's just dinner, Annie."

I pause, which is unexpected, even to myself. By the time I snap back to attention, someone else has joined the conversation, and it's too late to keep this private.

"Well, lookie here!" Gran opens the front door downstairs. I can picture her easily, standing there in her own fluffy robe and bubblegum pink bunny slippers. "That's a nice robe you've got there. Wait a second... don't I know you?"

Cohen rubs a hand over his forehead looking shockingly unembarrassed. "You do. We met earlier at the YMCA. I was trying to win over your granddaughter, but I think I've struck out."

"That's a bummer. She's a tough cookie to please."

"So I'm beginning to see."

"Anyway, don't freeze your buns off! Come on inside. I'll fix you a warm drink."

"Gran, no!" I call down. "Cohen was just heading home."

"Where are your manners?" Gran yells up the stairs. "He seems like a perfectly nice man, and he's practically freezing his buns off out there. Come on in here, Cohen. It's nice to see you again."

Before I can resist further, Gran has shepherded Cohen into the house and, judging by the clatters coming from below, she's begun a quest to warm him up.

Sighing, I look in the mirror. It's not pretty. I've got my hair whipped into a studying ponytail, and I have absolutely no makeup on my face. I've borrowed clothes from my high school self, and let's face it—Annie Plymouth wasn't any sort of fashionista, even in her prime. It's snowmen flannel pants and a tank top for me.

Long story short, I'm in no state to be going downstairs to greet company.

If I stay here, however, Gran will have a tongue lashing for me. She might be kooky, but she insists on good manners. Why? I have no idea.

Since there are no great options, I decide to suck it up and face the music—or rather, the horrible screeching. Cohen's already seen me in a fugly swimsuit and no makeup, so there's no need to get fancy. I shrug into a big sweatshirt that won't show a single curve and make my way downstairs.

I'm still not convinced that I should get tangled up with Cohen James in any way, shape, or form. There might be enough chemistry between us to light this place on fire, but sooner or later, the flames will be doused and I'll be the one left hurting. Best if I stay sensible—it's worked for me so far, and there's no reason I should stop now.

Gran's got two cups of hot chocolate sitting on the kitchen table by the time I arrive. Being in my gran's kitchen has a calming effect on me; I've always liked the way it's set up.

There's a small, cozy table centered in the breakfast nook. Old, yet well-kept, wallpaper lines the walls, yellow and bright, and it brings me right back to the mornings I spent here as a kid.

"Enjoy," Gran says, pushing a bag of marshmallows toward me. "I've gotta get some cucumbers on my eyes and a head start on my beauty sleep, so I'll just be upstairs trying my darndest to turn back time. And wrinkles."

"But—" I start to argue, but find myself speaking to Gran's retreating figure before I can form a sentence. I turn my glare on Cohen, who is watching me with a grin on his face. "What are you looking at?"

He lifts the hot chocolate to his lips, takes a sip, and closes his eyes. "This is delicious."

"Gran has a special recipe," I say, swirling the spoon in mine. "She's never told me what it is exactly, but I swear it's magic."

"I'd agree."

"I used to come inside after sledding with my friends when I was little, and we'd leave our boots in the entryway," I begin, unable to stop the story from tumbling out once I've started. "My mom would get so upset by the puddles we'd leave there, but Gran never cared. She even threw a snowball in the house once."

"How am I not surprised?"

I laugh. "I know, right? Anyway, she always had these hot chocolates waiting for us, so every time I have one, I remember..." I trail off, realizing I'm babbling. "Sorry, boring."

"You grew up in this house?" Instead of looking bored, Cohen glances around the room, his eyes landing on a few of the old trinkets that line the walls. A picture of my Gran and Gramps on their wedding day sits in the place of honor behind the table. A few photos of me, sometimes surrounded by friends, sometimes with Gran, sometimes alone, are scattered around, too.

"Yeah," I say, following his line of sight to the photos. "I've always loved this room."

"I can see why." He points to a few photos with me in them. "Your parents aren't in any of these photos?"

"My mom was usually the one taking the picture."

"And your dad?"

"They're divorced."

Cohen nods, and thankfully, he doesn't press any further. I'm not in the mood to discuss any of that with him. In turn, he doesn't offer any pity, no sympathy, just an understanding expression, and it's nice. Almost as if he understands.

"He worked a lot when I was young," I say, taking another sip of hot chocolate. Something about the silence made me feel the need to speak. "I think that's probably one of the reasons why my parents didn't work out. My mom and I moved in with Gran and Gramps after they split up."

"This wedding in July—is it your mom who's getting remarried?"

"Yeah, to a guy named Claude. He seems to make her happy."

Cohen gives a tight smile. "That's what counts."

As it turns out, Cohen's a good listener. I realize I've been talking this whole time, and I've hardly asked a word about himself. "You just moved here from California, didn't you?"

"Well, moved back. I'm from here, originally. Took a few years to play for the Lightning, but something called me home."

"Did you miss this place when you left?"

"Let's just say that I didn't have a lot holding me here."

"And now that you're back?"

Cohen ignores the question, peers into his cup. An adorable little frown appears at the sight of one lone marshmallow there. "I could drink this for days."

"Are you sad to be home?"

I should stop prying, but I can't help myself. I'll never admit it to him, but not five minutes before he'd serenaded me outside the window, I'd had an article pulled up with his face on it. *Research.*

"I'm indifferent. Except for the damn weather. My blood's thin, and I feel the cold."

"I'll bet."

"I do love skating on the lakes though. First time I've done that in a few years."

My worst nightmare. I cringe outwardly at the thought of ice skating, but I recover quickly and pepper him with more questions so I don't have to think about it. "You never came back to visit?"

"I did, but like I said, I hadn't left much when I went away."

"Your parents are—"

"Just me and my dad," he says.

"Oh, that's fun!" I'm trying to be peppy, but he doesn't seem to be interested. "Just two guys hanging out?"

"Sure," he says shortly, without an explanation. "A real joy. So, have you been reading more about me? How'd you know I just moved back?"

My face burns. He already knows I don't follow hockey. If I did, I'd have recognized him on the first day of class. So I ignore the question and fire back with my own. "Why are you always doing stupid stuff?"

"Stupid stuff?"

"It's like you're looking for trouble." I shrug my shoulders, well aware that I'm playing with fire. "In the last year alone, you've been involved in a bar fight, serenaded your teammate naked, mouthed off to the press, and fired your agent."

"The agent was a crook, the reporter an asshole, the bar fight a necessity, and the serenading..." He pauses and graces me with a light-hearted smile. "That was just for fun."

"How can a bar fight ever be a necessity?"

"If you'd seen someone steal your best friend's fiancée's purse right out from under her nose, what would you do?"

I look down at my own arms. "Call the police?"

He grins. "Yeah, well, I forgot the number. And they wouldn't have been faster than my fist."

"Ah, I see." I sit back in the chair, crossing my arms and layering on the sarcasm. "So it's all a giant misunderstanding? You're not a troublemaker at all—really, you're just one giant teddy bear out to save the world?"

"Well..." He gestures toward his attire. "I do have a Superman robe."

It doesn't take a genius to figure out he's dodging the question. I should just let it go. I've already decided that getting involved with him is *just* not an option. Not at this point in my life.

But there's something bothering me about him, as if there's more to him than meets the eye. I get the feeling he's a tough nut to crack. Not that I'm thinking about nuts.

"What do you want me to tell you?" Cohen's face flashes with a whisper of frustration. "I don't have a good answer for you, Annie."

"It's not that hard of a question," I say. "I'm just trying to understand."

He shrugs. "Do you want some sob story? Does it make it easier for you to understand me if I tell you that my dad has always preferred to drink beer instead of watching my hockey games? He's never seen me play in person. Does it make it better to know my mom walked away from us when I was a baby?"

"Cohen, I didn't mean—"

"Sometimes a person doesn't fit into a neat little box, Annie." He stands up, carrying his hot chocolate cup to the sink. "I'm sorry it's not black and white for you."

"I'm not trying to upset you. *You're* the one who showed up here in the middle of the night. You're the one who's trying so hard to get us together. I'm just trying to understand *why*."

"I'm beginning to wonder the same thing." Turning to face me, he gives a shake of his head. "Maybe it *is* a mistake. I've never in my life worked so hard to try and get a girl to dinner. Especially one I'm supposed to be *professional* with."

"That still doesn't answer my question."

"It just feels worth it to me."

"Worth it?"

"You're different. There is so much more to you than any woman I've ever met. Of course you're beautiful. But I also really enjoy talking to you. Being around you. Hearing what you think about things. What am I supposed to do, sit back and let someone else ask you out first?"

"Oh."

"Look, I'm sorry. I should be heading home so you can get back to... whatever you were doing."

The robe is open now, and I realize he's got jeans and a sweater on underneath. More practical than I expected.

I grudgingly gesture toward his body. "The robe is a nice touch."

Cohen's already turned to leave, but he stops in the doorway. "Humor me, Annie. Why do you dislike me so much?"

"I don't dislike you, I'm just... I'm not at a place where I want to date." My hands circle the hot chocolate mug for strength. "I have a lot on my plate—I'm graduating, my mom's getting remarried, I'm going to law school in the fall. I don't need any distractions."

"And that's all you imagine I would be?"

"It's not *you*, Cohen. I'd turn down anyone right now."

"Really?" Skepticism is written on his face. "*Anyone?*"

My hesitation is a second too long.

"I see." He nods. "Girls like you don't mix with guys like me. I understand."

"No, Cohen, I just have to focus on studying and working and... I don't have time to goof off."

"Have a nice night, Annie. See you next week."

"That came out wrong!" I call after him. "I didn't mean you're... a joke or something."

"It's fine." He pauses at the door and gives a tight smile that doesn't reach his eyes. "I'm the one who showed up here unannounced. You don't have to apologize for anything."

"Please don't be mad."

"I'm not mad in the slightest."

"Upset?"

"Goodnight, Annie."

He's gone, out the door and into a sleek car parked at the curb. When he gets into it and pulls away, there's a strange tightness in my chest, and a sinking feeling in my gut. I might not want to date the man, but I didn't want to hurt him, either.

"Well, that went well, huh?" Gran asks, coming up from behind me. She reaches for my shoulder and gives a squeeze. She's stronger than she looks. "Come upstairs, honey. I'd like to tell you a story."

Chapter 19

Annie

Gran has us both in green aloe masks with cucumbers over our eyeballs in a few minutes. She's brought up a pot of tea, a couple of teacups, and a small jar of honey arranged on a cute silver tray.

"Comfortable?" she asks as I squirm into position.

"Not really. My skin feels like it's splitting off my face, and the cucumbers are frozen solid, and—"

"Beauty is pain, darling."

"I thought we were *past* the days of getting all dolled up for men."

"Whatever made you think this was about men?" Gran turns toward me, both of us peeking out from under the cucumbers. "This isn't about men at all. This is about pampering yourself."

I lay back and close my eyes. I'm annoyed, and it's not fair to take things out on Gran—she's just trying to help. I'm not happy with how things ended with Cohen.

"What happened downstairs?" Gran asks. "It seemed like you two were getting along so well."

"Don't pretend you weren't eavesdropping."

"I heard the ending, and that was enough awkward for me."

"I didn't say anything wrong!"

"Okay then, dear. Whatever you say."

I fall silent, replaying the conversation in my head. "Was I a jerk?"

"You tell me."

I sit up and pop the cucumbers off my eyelids. "I didn't try to hurt him."

"I know that, dear."

"He really shouldn't care what I think. We barely know each other."

"He hasn't tried to kiss you?" Gran readjusts a cucumber so that it rests on her forehead. "Seems like there's chemistry."

"How'd you guess about the kiss?"

"I'm old. I know these things." Gently, she removes the other cucumber from her eye and sits up straighter. She preens, glancing at a set of shiny red toes before stretching her arms and letting out a long, loud yawn. "It's clear the two of you like each other, so why don't you let him take you out on a date?"

"I don't like him." I mean to say this firmly, but it comes out a little stuttery. "I *can't* like him."

"Whyever not?"

"Because..." I trail off, my cheeks burning at the way my conversation with Cohen ended. "I have my reasons."

"Because women like you don't date guys like him?" Gran raises an eyebrow at me. "I can guarantee that's the way he heard it."

"I tried to clarify! That's *not* what I meant."

"Men are stubborn, among other things. He heard it one way, so it'll be hard to convince him otherwise."

"Well, he's not my type, anyway. I'd prefer someone more like Gramps." I lapse into silence. It feels like yesterday he was here, reading beside me, the two of us sharing my Gran's perfect hot chocolate by the fireplace. "Grandpa was smart and gentle, mostly. Kind. Really funny when he felt like it."

"He was, wasn't he?" Gran's smile is paper thin on her lips. Her eyes, however, hold a burst of starlight in them. "He was something else."

"He wasn't like Cohen."

"What's Cohen like?"

"Cohen is..." I try to think of something to prove my point, but I can't.

The first picture that pops into my mind is the one from this morning during swimming lessons. He'd taken one of the babies in his class and splashed around the pool, singing songs and making silly faces.

It was odd seeing Cohen like that, in a different element. Gentle, despite his playful grin and colorful arms littered with tattoos.

I feel my face flush. Gran's watching as all of these thoughts flash across my face, and I force myself to stop thinking about him.

"I see," Gran says. "No need to say more."

"He's... he doesn't have a stable job. He travels a lot for hockey, so he'll be gone all the time. One day he won't be able to play any-more—what then? And he does dumb things!"

"Like serenading you on the street in a Superman robe?"

"Yes!"

"He has a horrible voice," Gran says. "Truly awful."

"Terrible."

"Is that everything?" Gran asks with a raised eyebrow. "Can I talk now?"

"Oh, um. Okay."

"Your grandfather wasn't always responsible."

"Are we talking about the same guy? Gramps had everything or-ganized down to his sock drawer. He wouldn't ever stay out after nine p.m. on a work night. He paid the bills, went to work every day, came home every evening."

"Yes, later in life. Once we had kids—your mother and her sib-lings—to think about."

"My mother always told me that I shouldn't expect a man to change. If he doesn't treat me with respect before we're married, then it's only going to get worse after."

"I agree one hundred percent." Gran gives a nod. "Good advice from your mother."

"Sorry, then I don't understand your point."

"What's Cohen done to you? You don't trust him?"

"He yanked my noodle out from underneath me on the first day of class."

"Did he pull your pigtails, too?"

"It's not that simple! You know I'm terrified of water."

"He *believed* in you. If he didn't care, he wouldn't do anything at all—so what if he pushed you a little?"

"I hated it!"

"He made a mistake underestimating your fear of water. Did he apologize?"

"Well, yes—"

"Has he done it again?"

"No, but—"

"I'm not telling you whether you should let Cohen take you out on a date or not—that's up to you, honey. What I am trying to tell you is that sometimes, men act out in certain ways, and it's not a reflection of who they really are on the inside."

"Are you trying to set me up with Cohen?"

"The day I met my husband was his first day out of jail."

"What?" I gape at my grandmother. "Gramps?"

"Well, yes. I was only married once, of course."

"But... he would never do anything to get put in jail."

"I was a waitress at the diner near my parent's house when we met. I remember the day like it was yesterday," she says, sounding quite dreamy indeed. She ignores my expression of complete and utter shock. "Your grandfather waltzed into that diner with three bucks in his pocket. He didn't have enough money to buy breakfast, so he bought a piping hot cup of coffee."

"Jail?"

"I'm getting there! First, we got to talking. That's how I learned that he'd gotten in with the wrong crowd of friends."

"How have I not heard this story?"

"Let me finish!" Gran shushes. "He was hanging out with a couple of guys from high school. The others wanted to steal a twelve pack of beer from the local gas station. Your grandfather had no interest in breaking the law, so he stayed in the car."

"Sounds more like grandpa to me."

"But the idiots your grandfather had been hanging out with made a mistake. The cops came, caught them, and somehow, the blame landed on your grandfather. He was just eighteen, and the cops made him spend the night in jail as a lesson against shoplifting."

"That is *so* unfair! Grandpa would never do anything like that."

"This isn't a lesson in the justice system, it's a lesson in getting to know a person," Gran says, playing with the stack of cucumbers on the tray next to her. "When your grandfather came to the diner, all I knew was that the man sitting there was as poor as dirt and fresh out of jail."

"I can see how it was a little misleading."

"It might have been, but when he asked if I'd sit down with him, I had to make a decision. Take a chance, or play things safe?"

"I'm guessing you took a chance?"

"I was working! I told him if he held onto his shorts, I'd join him for lunch."

I cover my mouth with a hand and suppress a laugh. "Your first date was lunch, then?"

"It started there, but we talked straight through dinner, drinks, and a midnight coffee. A week later we were dating, six months later engaged." She pauses to wipe her face with the back of her hand. "I never stopped loving him. I still do, honey. Some days, I find myself wishing he'd walk right through the door of that diner again so we could start over and do it all again."

My eyes sting. I blink quickly, then struggle to swallow until I trust myself to speak. When the lump in my throat is nearly gone, I reach over and squeeze Gran's hand. "I'm sorry."

"There's nothing to be sorry about. I spent over sixty years with a man I loved more than I ever thought possible. I'm not sure how many people can say that." She clears her throat, leans over, and pops the pedicure toe separator onto the floor. "But I didn't pull you up here to talk about me, believe it or not. I brought you in here to tell you my story, in case it means something to you."

"What do you want me to say? I hardly know Cohen."

"Your grandfather was a stranger the day he walked into the diner. If I'd told him that nice, hard-working girls like me didn't date jailbirds like him, I would've never found my other half. If I hadn't taken that chance, maybe you wouldn't be here today."

"How'd you know it was the right thing to do?"

"I didn't know if it was right or wrong, but I did it anyway. All I knew was that there were little butterflies in my stomach when we started talking. They lasted—well, forever. I still have them when I think about the times we shared together."

"That is so sweet."

"Just because a person is spontaneous doesn't make them irresponsible, and just because they make you heat up inside and feel like the world is flipping over every time you see them, it doesn't mean they can't be gentle. Kind. Honest."

"I suppose."

"Your Gramps taught me how to have fun, how to lighten up and enjoy the little things. I used to be uptight, you know. More uptight than him. We changed together."

"Really?" I can't picture my sparkling, tube-sock-wearing, thong-displaying grandmother being anything but vibrant. "I don't believe it."

"Your grandfather didn't try to change me. The point of getting married, of sticking with one person for your whole life, is to learn these things *together*. To grow and change as a unit, not as an individual."

"What if it's too late for us to even have a chance? I think I pissed him off."

"I don't think you pissed him off, I think you hurt his feelings. He just didn't want you to know that."

"Oh, great. Even better."

Gran grins. "Is he dead?"

"Uh, no?"

"Then it's not too late!"

"I won't see him for another week."

"Well, then either you wait for a week, or you chase him down. We're past the days of having to get dolled up for men." Gran rolls her sleeves up and flexes her shiny new nails. "Get dolled up for yourself and go after what you want."

Chapter 20

Annie

"You can't possibly think this looks good, mom." I'm hiding in the dressing room with a gown even uglier than my bathing suit hanging from my shoulders. I don't know what it is with my mother and ruffles, but there are so many. A sea, and I'm drowning in them. "Tell me you were kidding when you sent this in the room with me."

"Are you dressed?" she asks. "I'm coming in, Annie."

Without allowing me any time to respond, my mother barges into the dressing room of the wedding shop, followed closely by my grandmother.

"Oh, you look adorable! What is all this moaning about?" Gran asks, patting me down from head to bum. She focuses on the bum. "Look, I've got the matching version of your dress on—we can be twins. I think you inherited your rear end from me."

"I look like a bumblebee."

"You do not," Gran says. You look like *Beauty and the Beast*."

"Yeah... the *Beast*, maybe."

"It's not so bad," my mom says, but even she doesn't sound convinced. "Maybe if we take it in a little bit..."

"Just go for something simple!" I look in the mirror, wincing at the brilliant shade of yellow. It's not the yellow itself that's offensive, it's the vibrancy of it. And the amount of it. The shade an eye-water-ing color of sunflower. "What happened to the black one I showed you?"

"I will not be having my maid of honor wear black at my wedding. I refuse."

"How about that dark purple one?"

"The one that *looks* black from a distance?" My mother gives me the side eye. "No. This is a happy time, and I want everyone to know it. Would you prefer orange?"

"Probably not the best idea," I say. "It wouldn't go well with the theme."

"The theme? The theme is bright and happy!" My mother's staring at me with a look of puzzlement. "How does orange not go with that?"

"The dress will clash with Claude."

My mother still doesn't look convinced, so I pull out my phone and find a recent photo on my mother's Facebook page of her and Claude. She's worse than most high schoolers. Her profile picture is an image of her macking on Claude's cheek.

"Here." I zoom to show a close-up of her fiancé's nose. Then I place the phone beside the newest dress in my mother's hands. The women of my family compare Claude's face to the orange loofah that is supposed to be a dress. "Well?"

"Ellie, your daughter has a point," Gran murmurs. "They're the perfect match."

My mom's face is getting paler by the second, so I put the phone away. "I'll change," I offer. "Whatever you want mom. It's your day, really. If you want the yellow, I'll wear yellow. If you want orange, I'll wear orange."

Turning, my mother stomps off toward the lobby, out through the front door, and finally stops, pacing back and forth. She pulls a cigarette from her purse. She tried out smoking after the divorce, but it didn't last long. However, she'll still whip out a cig when she needs time to think.

"I'm going to go after her," Gran says, eyeing my dress. "Don't you worry, I'll talk her into the perfect dress."

"I shouldn't have said that, huh?"

"We couldn't have done orange. I'm just glad you said it before I did. Now she's mad at you, and I get to console her."

"Gee whiz, that's great of you."

"Before I go out there..." Gran gives me a searching stare. "I want to know if you've thought any more about our conversation."

I shift my weight from one bare foot to the next. "Conversation?"

"Don't tell me you forgot last night already."

"I didn't."

"So?"

I shrug. "I already hurt his feelings. It's probably too late. Apparently I'm getting very good at upsetting the people around me."

"Don't be foolish."

"I'm being realistic."

"You want to get married someday, don't you?"

"Well, yes," I admit. "That was always the goal."

"Well, marriage ain't gonna work if you give up on it every time you're in a pissy mood and have a little tiff with your husband."

"I wasn't in a pissy mood."

"Fine. Then let him go."

Gran twirls in a flurry of fabric, and begins stomping toward my mother, who's coughing out front. She sometimes pretends to smoke when she's stressed. Usually, she just holds the cigarette and flicks it every now and again until it's gone.

"Hang on a second," I call after Gran. "What am I supposed to do if I want to see him again?"

"You could wait a week for swimming lessons," she says. "*Or*... you can take this old thing I found in the paper this morning."

She shoves the slip into my hand and whisks herself away to console my mother. Peeling the crumpled sheet back, I find Gran has ripped out the Stars' upcoming schedule from the paper. One game in particular is highlighted, and the date is for *tonight*.

Oddly enough, I already knew this. Although I may hate admitting I'm wrong, I know when I owe an apology.

I text Sarah to see if she's available tonight. Dishing out an apology might be easier to stomach if I have my best friend next to me, reminding me why I'm there in the first place. Unfortunately, she's busy.

On a whim, I find Leigh's number from when she plugged it in my phone after our last class. I ask if she's available and interested and, to my surprise, she agrees to join on one condition—that she can bring her oldest son.

I reply that it's a deal, and give her the time and place to meet. Then, surrounded by piles of chiffon and the smell of someone steaming a wedding dress hot in the air, I scroll through my phone until I find a website to purchase tickets.

I click purchase, my heart fluttering with nerves, and then shimmy out of the yellow dress. Scurrying into my street clothes, I decide that today is the day of apologies. First, I have to apologize to my mother and find a dress that'll make her happy.

Then, tonight, I'll hunt Cohen down and apologize all over again.

I can only hope it's not too late.

Chapter 21

Annie

I'm pretty much an idiot when it comes to sports. I can't swim, I am uncoordinated with my hands, and playing soccer with my feet has never made sense to me. The whole *working out* thing doesn't make all that much sense—I prefer to *not* sweat, if at all possible.

Sometimes, I do yoga and Pilates when the mood strikes, which isn't often, or I'll go for a walk with Sarah if we both need coffee and have the money to splurge for a latte. Those are rare days. Occasionally, we'll walk to get ice cream if they're offering free samples.

Because I'm *horrible* at all things athletic, I had to Google photos of the latest Stars' home game—not, as one might think, to look at Cohen. Instead, I needed to study the crowd and find out what girls *wear* to a hockey game. Jeans? Dresses? Face paint?

After extensive research, I've settled on jeans, mittens, a cute sweater, and my winter jacket. It's reasonably comfortable and reasonably cute, and I suppose that's the best I can do if I'll be freezing my butt off in an ice rink.

I leave my car in a downtown St. Paul parking ramp and get plenty frozen while waiting for Leigh and her son to show up. They arrive ten minutes later, and they're adorable. I watch as they approach our meeting area, but they don't see me yet. They're too wrapped up in their own world.

Her son must be twelve or thirteen, almost to that age where hugging and touching is really, really uncool, but it's clear the way this kid looks at his mom that they're close. He leans into her, speaks quietly, and then she laughs at whatever he's said.

"Hey, guys!" I chirp, hugging Leigh before extending a hand to her kid. "You must be Leigh's oldest son."

"Dominic," he fills in. He's got dark hair, just like hers, and eyes that hold the same twinkle as his mother's. There's a level of calmness about him that's different than what I would've guessed for a boy his age. "Thank you so much for the tickets, Miss Plymouth."

"Annie," I say with a wave of my hand. "Glad you guys could come. Shall we head inside? I hear they sell popcorn, and I'm hungry."

Dominic nods, but Leigh shoots me a knowing *look*. "You owe me a story."

"Later," I promise. "First, popcorn."

We make our way inside and take our seats as the players are warming up on the ice. I don't see Cohen yet, but it's difficult to make out individual faces with all the gear the men are wearing. I realize I don't even know his jersey number.

"Nine," Leigh says, watching me as I scan the ice. "He's not out yet."

I feel my cheeks burn a little and hunker down in my jacket. Leigh pulls a few bucks out of her pocket and asks her son to grab us some snacks from the stand just above us. As he leaves, her eyes follow her son, but her attention is directed toward me.

"Spill the beans," she says. "You've got about eight minutes until he's back here. I won't have you corrupting the mind of my baby. Talk fast. Why are we here?"

"There's nothing to corrupt! I promise."

"Well, you didn't feel the need to come here because of your love for the game," she says. "So what happened?"

It's just the nudge I need to spill the beans. All of the beans. She's surprisingly easy to talk to, which is a good thing, but it also inspires me to babble and carry on about every little detail until thankfully, she interrupts.

"Look, I get it," Leigh says finally. "You said something you didn't mean. Apologize. No big deal."

"You all make it sound so easy."

"Well, I *am* divorced, so I don't know if you should be taking advice from me. Then again, I like to think I learned something from the whole ordeal."

"I'm so sorry."

"Oh, it's fine. I don't mind talking about it anymore. It was hard at first, but... I've had time to digest."

"Can I ask what happened? You can tell me to bug out if I'm being too nosy."

"I still don't really know. One day, my husband told me he wasn't in love with me anymore. Simple as that. Clinical, as if he'd fallen out of love with me some time ago and had merely gone through the motions for awhile. Weeks? Years? I don't know, and he wouldn't tell me."

I clear my throat and reach for Leigh's hand. She lets me take it, hold it, her fingers small and cool against my own. "I'm so sorry."

"I don't know what I did. I thought everything was going fine. We have three beautiful kids, and... now they barely see their dad. I just don't understand it." She pauses, shrugs. "He was always so stable in every sense of the word—an eye doctor, no less. He had a great job, came home every day in time to eat dinner. He was the most predictable guy I'd ever met. And then one day, he just *wasn't*."

"I'm really sorry."

"Really, it's fine. I manage. It's not the end of the world; I have my kids."

I put my arm around her shoulder. "You do more than manage. You're brilliant, and you're great with your kids. As a friend, you're the best. I promise. Dominic is growing up to be a great guy, all because of you."

"You're sweet. I just wish he had his dad around."

"I didn't have my dad around," I say, and then offer a short bark of laughter. "Although, I'm not sure if that's any consolation. I'm a bit of an oddball."

"I like oddballs."

"It's going to be okay," I tell her, as Dominic returns with his hands full. "I promise."

"Mom, I got you Peppermint Patties," he says, handing over the change. "Your favorite."

Leigh pulls him in and kisses him on the cheek. "You are the best. What'd you get for yourself?"

"Popcorn to share with Annie."

I wink at Leigh over his head. "It'll be just fine."

The announcer interrupts us then, and I find my eyes drawn to the ice as a bodiless voice calls the players one by one. Sometime during my conversation with Leigh, most of the team has made their way onto the ice. I squint, looking for number nine.

Next to me, Dominic goes wild. One second later, the announcer's calling Cohen's name, number, and position. He skates forward and takes his place center rink. *Found him.*

Cohen's focused on the game, as he should be—and not once does he look into the stands. My heart's beating too fast at the sight of him. I can't help but wonder if he'd glance up and look around if I'd told him I'd be here.

To distract myself, I turn to Dominic. He's chomping popcorn, eyes glowing like flashlights as he watches the rink.

"So, Dom," I say, once the anthem has played and the game has begun. "Can you help me understand the game? I have no idea about the rules."

"Sure. Have you heard of the penalty box?"

"Let's start with the very basics," I say. "For example, what do you call the little black thing everyone's whacking around?"

Chapter 22

Annie

By the time the end of the third period rolls around—they are not called halves, as Dominic clarified—the poor kid has gone hoarse. As I requested, he's detailed every second of the game: rules, player names, the score, strategy, penalties—everything.

"Do you play?" I ask him as the clock ticks down.

The game is tied, and his eyes are fixed on the rink. "Yeah."

"I bet you're pretty good."

"Nah," he says. "I'm okay. Not like these guys."

"Someday you will be," his mom says. She speaks over his head to me. "He's very good. Just shy to admit it."

"*Moomm*," Dominic whines. "Watch the game. There's only a minute left."

I had never known one minute could be so thrilling. I watch, cheering when Dominic cheers and holding my breath when he does, too.

"Don't watch me," he scolds. "Watch the ice. Your boyfriend is going to score, I know it."

"He's not my boyfriend—"

I'm interrupted by the roar of the crowd. Everyone's on their feet, cheering like maniacs. The few stragglers from the opposing team's cheering section remain seated, heads in hands, frustration and disappointment scrawled across their faces.

"Told you." Dominic turns to look at me, grinning openly. "Tell your boyfriend good job from us. That was *awesome*."

"He's not my boyfriend," I say, but again, the sound is drowned out by the crowd. I stand along with the rest of them, clapping and cheering, wondering why I'm arguing with a twelve-year-old.

"Do you think you can get me his autograph?" Dominic looks up at me. "My mom hasn't gotten up the guts to ask for it, yet."

"I do too have the guts!" Leigh gives him a look of mock anger. "I told you I'd ask if you got straight A's this semester. I have yet to see your report card, mister."

His shoulders slump. "But history is *so* hard."

"If it's okay with your mom," I tell him. "I'll see what I can do."

"We'll see," Leigh agrees. "If Annie gets you the autograph, you owe her all A's."

"I *promise*," he says, eyes glowing. "I *seriously* promise."

"It's past our bedtime," Leigh says. "Are you okay here, Annie? Can we walk you to your car?"

I give a weak gesture toward the ice. "I think I'm going to stick around for a bit. I have an autograph to hunt down."

Dominic squeals with excitement. Leigh hugs him to her and nods, giving me a conspiratorial smile over his head. "You've got your phone, right? Text me if you need anything. We're not far away."

"Thank you." I give both of them a hug. "Thanks for the Hockey 101, Dom."

Dominic offers me a fist bump. "Anytime."

"I want details on *everything*," Leigh calls over her shoulder. "Good luck!"

I sit back down in the bleachers while I let the crowd clear out. Most of the folks on this side of the rink are laughing and jolly, swigging the last of their beers as they reminisce over the recent game highlights.

It's a festive crowd, but I find it hard to get swept up into the feeling. My stomach churns with nerves, and I fumble with my phone, pretending to scroll through Facebook even though my eyes can't focus on a thing.

Cohen still doesn't know I'm here. When he plays, apparently he focuses on the game— and only the game. He didn't once look into the crowd. I should know, seeing as I stared at him like a lion watching an antelope for all three periods.

I couldn't take my eyes off him; the way he moved on the ice was impressive. Smooth, clever even, and with confidence. And *of course* he scored the winning goal. He'll be a hot commodity at the bar tonight, I'm sure, celebrating with teammates and fans.

Maybe I should go home for tonight, I think, pulling myself to my feet as the janitors start cleaning the floors, sweeping up stray popcorn kernels, gum, and other miscellaneous treasures from the crowd. It'd be easier to call him, or talk to him after lessons on Saturday.

I shove my hands in my pockets, letting the crowd push me toward the entrance. I pass the food stands, the girls in mini skirts, the parents with stars in their eyes... and somewhere among the latter, a sudden thought hits me.

If what Cohen said was true, neither of his parents would be here. His mom is long gone, and his dad is uninterested in his son's career. Cohen wouldn't have had any family around to see him score the winning goal.

The thought sent a jolt of discomfort toward my stomach. I *know* how that feels—how disappointing it is to realize that, after volleyball practice, my dad had forgotten to pick me up. Or, how it feels to prepare for a piano recital for months, only to find out that my dad had shown up so late he'd missed my entire song.

For me, however, my mom had been there. Always. Clapping and cheering and rooting for me, no matter what. It's this memory that makes up my mind. I'm staying tonight, and I'm finding Cohen. I'm going to apologize, congratulate him, and then let the powers that be do their thing.

I find myself shuffled toward a back entrance where there's nothing but vending machines and stray spectators putzing on their phones. Everybody wanting in on the action waits closer to the main doors, but it's a zoo over there, and I'll never find Cohen.

I figure I have a few minutes, since none of the players have arrived yet, so I push the nearest exit door open to get a breath of fresh air. It's cool out here, but it's also calming. I need a moment of peace and quiet to gather myself. My heart is pounding, and the crisp air is a jolt to the system.

I'm about to close the door when I catch a glimpse of movement out of the corner of my eye. There, a little ways off, is a selection of cars that must belong to the players. Several men in suits are hopping into cars, and there's a bus nearby filling with the opposing team's players.

Maybe Cohen's snuck out a back entrance. I can't take the chance of him leaving before I get to say my piece, so I take a look around, step further outside, and let the door close behind me.

To my surprise, nobody tells me that I don't belong back here. It's pretty clear I'm not affiliated with the team, but either nobody notices, or nobody cares.

I scan the crowd, looking for the only man I came here to see. Cohen's car isn't in the lot—at least, not the one he'd driven to my house last night, so I scan again. This time, I see *him*.

There's just one problem that, stupidly, I hadn't even considered before showing up tonight.

Cohen's not alone.

He's standing next to a bright red car, almost girlish in nature, near the passenger's side entrance. The woman from the driver's side leans over and manually unlocks the door. Cohen pokes his head inside, laughing as he sees her.

The woman's arm, now resting out the driver's side window, is long, thin, clothed in a beautiful jacket, and I can tell just from the way she moves that she's got a level of confidence I'll never have. She tips one of the valets, and then turns to look back across the console, saying something that makes Cohen laugh even louder.

I'm frozen. Literally, and figuratively.

It's not that I hadn't anticipated some female attention on Cohen tonight, it's just that this *particular* female seems very...friendly. From their laid-back interaction, I'd guess they know one another well.

I shouldn't be here. I shouldn't have come. I back away as I hear my name called, and I don't stop when he calls a second time.

"Annie?" Cohen's voice carries across the low chatter of players finding their vehicles. "What are you doing here?"

"Oh, hey." I somehow manage to raise a hand and give a wave. I have no clue why I'm acting nonchalant, since there's nothing nonchalant about this situation. "Came to say hi."

Cohen leans down, murmurs something through the open car window, and then makes his way toward me. That dark hair of his is still a little damp, and as he approaches, I catch a scent of something delicious which makes me think he must have showered post-game.

"What are you doing here?" He stops a foot away from me and repeats the question. He's close enough to keep my heart pumping, but too far for me to touch. "I didn't know you'd be here."

"I didn't know I was going to come," I say. "Not until today, actually. Leigh came too, with her son."

"Ah."

"It was my idea." I'm babbling. Probably because his eyes are almost luminescent they're so green, and they're distracting, holding my gaze as if we're the only two people around. "I wanted to see you play."

"Why?"

"Oh, um." Again, I hadn't prepared for Cohen to actually speak to me. I'd mostly practiced a speech in my head to tell him exactly what I wanted to say. Oddly enough, it hadn't dawned on me that he'd talk *back*. "Well, I felt bad."

"About what?"

"Last night." Finally, I'm in the zone. I've practiced this part. I even rehearsed in the shower. "Look, Cohen... last night I was surprised when you showed up. I'd been studying all night, and my brain was fried. Then Gran invited you inside, and I said some stuff that I didn't mean. I'm sorry."

"Those are a lot of excuses." He offers a wry smile. "Don't worry, apology accepted, but I'm not upset. You didn't have to come here tonight. It's my fault for pushing you so hard to go on a date with me. Why don't we just forget I ever asked?"

"No, Cohen, that's not what I meant."

"What *did* you mean?"

My mind goes blank. I haven't rehearsed this part. Mostly, I just wanted to apologize and get the heck out of here, but now I'm stuck. He's given me every opportunity to tell him how I feel, and I can't string a sentence together.

A lot of thoughts flood my brain, I just can't seem to make any sense of them. I think about Leigh and her husband—the perfect, doting father—who one day up and left out of the blue. No explanations.

I remember Gran who, on the other hand, married the wild card. Decades later, she had a beautiful relationship to show for it; not only had Gran and Gramps maintained their relationship, but they'd let it grow, flourish, and bloom until the day he died.

I take a deep breath, swallow my stubbornness, and speak from my heart.

Chapter 23

Cohen

I can't shake the frustration streaking through my bones. I scored the winning goal and somehow, I'm still pissed, even now as I take my skates off in the locker room. I should be social, but I'm not feeling like talking to anyone.

"Good game," Coach tells me. "But I don't know what bug crawled up your ass and died tonight. Go out the back door and don't talk to the media, hear me? I don't know what shit you'd say tonight."

I grunt, and he leaves me alone. It's as close to a truce as we'll get. After my trade from the LA Lightening, we're still getting used to one another. It hasn't been easy.

The guys here are good guys for the most part, but my reputation precedes me. As it turns out, Hollywood provides plenty of opportunities to get into trouble, and I'm pretty sure I found them all.

I shower, dress, and head through the backdoor. The team's going out to celebrate at a line of bars nearby, and I'll join them later. I've got a friend in town, and we're going to grab a drink first and catch up.

"Hey," I say, grinning once I see Chelsea. She's in a flashy red Miata, a cute car that fits her. Completely impractical for the Minnesota winters, but she won't care. She's not about *practicality*. "Great to see you, Chels."

She unlocks the doors and rolls down the window. "I hear you scored, sorry I missed it. Flight landed not that long ago."

"Yeah right—you just didn't want to come watch the game."

"Yeah, actually you are right. I landed hours ago, and I would've preferred to sit around *bored* rather than come watch you play." She rolls her eyes. "Are you hopping in or what?"

Chelsea and I *almost* slept together once—nearly a decade ago, now. We'd never made it all the way, though, because once we'd started making out, we'd mutually decided there wasn't a connection. We'd ended up popping some popcorn, watching a movie, and heading home early from the date.

At this point, we're like siblings. She's even gone and gotten herself engaged. In fact, she met her husband-to-be at a party in my LA condo when she was visiting. Now, they're both living out there and about to get married. She's back for a family visit this weekend with her fiancé, and the three of us are grabbing drinks before I meet my teammates later.

I'm about to throw my stuff in the trunk and slide into the passenger's seat, but something gives me pause. I'm not even sure what it is until I look up and find a set of eyes staring back at me.

"Annie?"

I squint. It's her—but I can't figure out what she's doing here. Last night, she was pretty clear about her feelings toward me when she sent me home. I'm not usually one to throw myself pity parties, but all at once, I realize why I've been pissed all day.

She's frigging confusing, and I'm on edge not knowing what's going through that brain of hers. Does she like me? Hate me? Just when I've started to swallow the bitter pill of rejection from yesterday, she shows up out of the blue at my game. No wonder today's been a roller coaster.

To make things worse, she's standing a good ten feet away, hands in front of her body, these huge puppy dog eyes that have me wanting to wrap her in my arms. For a second, I can't even remember why things are weird between us. I throw my bags in the trunk, still processing.

"Are you going to go *talk* to her, or are you planning to stand there all night with your thumb up your ass?" Chelsea calls from inside the car. "I'll wait here—I've *gotta* see this."

"Shut it, please."

"It's been a long time since you've been speechless over a chick, my friend."

"She's not a chick."

"Then move."

I walk toward Annie, though it's not a logical decision. My feet drag me toward her before I can think about what I'm doing. Then I'm there, standing before her, and we're making some inane conversation about why she's here tonight.

Finally, I can't stand it any longer. I need some answers. "Honestly, why did you come here tonight, Annie?"

She inhales a rattling breath, and finally, she begins to speak in a clear voice. "I didn't mean what I said last night, and I'm here to apologize."

"Accepted." I don't mean to be short, but if she really has no interest in me, I should leave things alone. I don't want to make things *worse* by having her think I can't move on from rejection. "Anything else?"

"Do you still want to take me on a date?"

Her question surprises me, and I blink a few times first. "Yeah, Annie. I didn't change my mind overnight."

"If you're free this week..." She stops talking mid-sentence, a sudden realization dawning on her face. "*Ohmigosh*, I'm so sorry. I didn't realize that you're here with someone."

I glance back at Chelsea. "That's just a friend—I promise. She's in town for the weekend, and I'm meeting her and her fiancé for drinks before I meet the team to celebrate."

"Celebrate?" A smile blooms on her face as she realizes what I mean. "That's right! Nice goal."

"I didn't know you enjoyed hockey."

"I don't." She grins, a laugh bubbling up and spilling over like sunshine. "But Leigh's kid does, and he explained everything to me."

"So you came just for me?" I take a step closer, my hands itching to touch her, hold her close, show her the words I can't seem to say.

"No."

"No?"

"I came for the popcorn."

I close the gap, pull her to me. My hands find the sides of her face, her cheeks chilled from the night air. She's wearing the hood of her coat pulled up, her chestnut hair spiraling beside her face as my hands twirl through it.

Her lips reach for mine, and that's the only permission I need. Her hood slides from her head as our lips connect, a ring of fire lining the place where we've made contact. It's soft at first, exploratory, and then her lips part and she emits the tiniest of moans.

I press against her, more needy than I'd ever expected, and she melts into my arms. Annie might've fought off a first date harder than any girl I've ever met in my life, but the payoff is worth it ten times over—even if this is the only kiss I'll ever get from her. I'd do it all over again—the volunteering, the serenading, the talking to Gran—because this is the most intensity I've ever experienced from a kiss.

By now, we're in full-on make out mode, and my hands are slipping down her back, sliding over the curves I've forced myself to stay away from over the last couple weeks.

She's even softer than I imagined, and she fits snugly into my hands. If only she wasn't wearing a stupid sweater and jeans, and if only we weren't in the stupid tundra of the north where we'll freeze at the first sight of exposed skin, I would have stripped her bare and touched every inch of her. If, of course, we weren't in public.

"Wow," she breathes, breaking the kiss before I open my eyes. "Did you like that?"

I wasn't ready to be done. "Like it?" My voice escapes in a husky tone that I barely recognize as my own. "Babe, I'm ready to call a cab and take you home."

Immediately, I wonder if I've gone too far, but her cheeks merely flush pink, tickled by the winter breeze, and she gives a shy sort of laugh.

"I'm not ready for that," she says. "But I might be interested in accepting that date."

"A date sounds nice. How about I pick you up tomorrow at noon?"

"Noon?"

"I was going to take you out to dinner, but I'm not sure I can wait that long."

"I have class until one."

"Skip it."

"One hour!" She rests a hand on my chest and walks her fingers up to my chin. "You can wait an extra hour, can't you?"

I groan, clasping her wrist in my hand. "I've been waiting weeks for this. I can't wait an extra hour."

"Try."

"Fine."

"Who knows?" She gives a flirty shrug of her shoulder, and I wonder where this side of Annie has been all along. "Maybe it'll be worth it."

"Tomorrow can't come soon enough."

Her eyes widen as she realizes what she's said. "I didn't mean... I'm not *sleeping* with you tomorrow, Cohen. It's our first date—it's innocent."

"How innocent?" My pants are suddenly too tight, and it's difficult not to feel disappointed. I hadn't expected to sleep with her right away, but damn if she hadn't gotten all kinds of thoughts circling through my mind.

"Kissing only," she says. "That's as far as I go on a first date."

"Master of the tease."

"I just want to get to know you," she says, her eyes clouding. "I don't... I don't want—"

"I'm sorry, Annie. I'm just teasing. We go at your pace. I've worked hard enough to get you on a date, I'm not going to ruin it by trying to move things along too fast."

"That's really sweet."

"Careful, I'm not known to be sweet. If that gets out, it'll ruin my reputation."

She's smiling, and I can't help but grin back. I scored the winning goal in a nail biter of a game, and somehow, it's not the highlight of my night. I have a date tomorrow with Annie. She's already shot down the idea of us hooking up, and somehow, I'm still in the best mood ever. I hardly know who I am anymore.

"I guess I'll see you tomorrow then," she says. "Do I need to plan anything?"

"I'll take care of it all," I tell her, already wracking my brain for things Annie might like. I'll bet Chelsea will have some insights, and that thought reminds me the Miata's still waiting. "Well, I'm heading down to the Lion's Tavern next, and we usually end up at the Lucky Pig by midnight, if you care to join."

"Oh, well..." She hesitates, and her eyes flick ever so briefly toward the car behind me. "No, that's okay. I have class in the morning."

"If you change your mind, you know where to find me." I lean in to kiss her forehead. "Can I walk you to your car?"

She gestures behind me. "I'm right there. Don't keep your friend waiting."

With a kiss on my cheek, she's gone.

I walk back to the car, barely noticing the stares from several of my teammates.

"Watch your head," Chelsea says when I reach the car door. "You're floating so damn high you'll clock your noggin on the way in here."

"Floating?"

"Who's the girl, and why didn't you invite her out with us?"

"I did. Said she has an early morning."

"What did you say to her about coming out tonight?" Chelsea pins me against the window with her eyes. "What did you say *exactly*?"

"Uh, I told her that I was meeting with a friend and that she could join us if she wanted."

"You idiot."

"What?"

"Idiot," she says, pulling away from the curb and shaking her head. "Every girl knows that means you don't want her to come. You have to tell her that you want her there *specifically*."

"I thought I did."

"No, what you said means: *hey, if you feel like third-wheeling, I guess you can hang around with us.*"

"Those aren't the words I said."

"Those are the words she heard."

I swivel around in the car, but she's already gone. "What should I do?"

"We have to meet Rich at the bar, so that's where we're headed. Call her if you want her to come—I'd love to meet her."

It takes a few minutes for me to nut up and dial Annie's number. By the time I do, we've parked and are walking through the front door. The bar is close by the rink, and Annie can't be more than five minutes away.

I push through the main entryway, hold the second set of doors open for Chelsea, and hit dial. It rings as I make my way toward my usual seat. During the season, I'm a regular around here. It's close to the rink, and the combination of good food, cheap drinks, and friendly faces make it a pleasant place to de-stress after a loss or celebrate after a win.

When I glance toward my chair, however, I'm in for a surprise.

There, in my seat, sits a familiar face.

Annie.

Chapter 24

Annie

I tried convincing myself to head home.

I *want* to see Cohen tonight. That kiss in the parking lot has broken something open inside me—a dam that's been holding in all of the reasons why I shouldn't let him in, all of the reasons he was wrong for me.

Then, he'd gone and turned all those reasons inside out, and the only thing I can think of is seeing him again. As I get further and further from the arena, I can't help but think about tonight. Gran's words run through my head. If she hadn't said yes so many years ago, things would be oh-so-different for all of us.

That's the final straw. I whip the car around, make my way toward the Lion's Tavern, and park. It looks like I've beat Cohen here, so I order a drink and find the first open seat at the bar when my phone rings.

My heart stutters, skips a beat—it's him.

I click *answer*, but not before I hear his voice speaking aloud, and it's *not* filtering through the speaker.

"Well, look who it is," he says, smiling when my gaze rises to meet his. "I'm glad you showed up, sweetheart."

I gurgle a response, one that's interrupted as he swoops in and plants a kiss on my lips that would've knocked my socks off had they not already been knocked off once tonight.

"Hi," I say, once we pause for breath. "I don't have to stay long if you want some time with your friends. I just needed one more kiss."

"Well, we can fix that." His other hand slides up to meet his first, and together they frame my face in his warm palms. Then he pulls me in, and presses a gentle kiss to my mouth. It's slow, sensual, and it heats me up from the inside. "How about that?"

"Better." I smack my lips. "But feel free to keep practicing."

"I can't believe you came here. I thought for sure you'd gone home."

"Maybe it's all a dream," I say with a grin. "Because it feels pretty surreal to me. I *never* do things like this."

"I can think of a solution to that." Cohen traces one hand down my cheek, his fingertips leaving a trail of sparks behind. "What if you come home with me tonight? That way, once the sun rises and we're still together, you don't have to wonder if you've imagined it all."

I rest my fingers on his chest, and I now understand why women everywhere have swooned over professional athletes since sports were invented. It's not that Cohen is beautiful —he's not in the traditional sense—but seeing him play tonight was eye opening.

All the adrenaline, the testosterone, the raw athleticism in his blood—there's something inherently male about it, and the aura swirls around him now, and I sink further into his embrace.

"Sorry," I say, feeling a very real sense of sadness that I can't accept his offer. "I have class tomorrow. Plus, we haven't had our first date yet."

He frowns. "I want to argue with you, but I didn't expect to win this battle, so I'll let you have it."

"I'm going to see you tomorrow."

"I know." He sighs, and blinks long and hard. "I'll try my damndest to be patient."

"I'm here now," I say, a hint of light-hearted in my voice. "In case you want to make the most of it."

"Honey, I don't want you to ever wonder if this was a dream," he says, leaning toward me and smelling of spice and need and desire. "So let's make this something to remember."

"Oh..." I can't form a full response as his lips inch toward mine, tantalizing. I surrender to him, body, mind, heart because it's *more* than a kiss. It's almost as if he's marking me, taking me as his own in front of all these people.

The hand he's rested on the bar smooths over my back, sliding lower, lower, until the tips of his fingers reach the top of my waistband. He reaches the danger zone as his fingers dip inside, toying with the thin band of lace.

"Holy smokes, Cohen James," a female voice says. "I thought you already played one game tonight. Round two for tonsil hockey?"

Cohen pulls back, but he keeps one arm snug around me. "Great timing, Chels."

The brunette—probably the one who'd driven Cohen to the bar—sticks her hand unashamedly between us for a shake. I meet her fingers, looking up to find pretty brown eyes brimming with energy.

"I'm Chelsea," she says. "Just so we make sure nothing's weird, I want you to know that Cohen and I go way back. Childhood friends. We tried the kissing thing once when we were sixteen, and it went horribly wrong. Zero chemistry. Ever since then we've been friends. Siblings, really."

"I'm Annie," I say, digesting her words while struggling for a response. "I'm... uh, well, I'm Cohen's..."

He watches me, amusement in his eyes as I struggle to find the right word. "I'm listening," he says. "What *are* we?"

"I met Cohen at the YMCA," I say, turning to Chelsea. "He's my instructor."

"Oh, how romantic," Chelsea says without batting an eye. "Anyway, just wanted to say hello while we're waiting for my fiancé to show up—he'll be here any second."

"Congratulations! When are you getting married?"

"We haven't set a date yet." She flaunts a hand in my direction, bling shining from her finger. "This just happened last weekend. We did a trip to Seattle, then went exploring the wine country. Isn't it gorgeous?"

"Beautiful," I say. "So sparkly."

"Yes," she sighs dramatically, "I love it, too. Then again, I picked it out. Enough about us old boring engaged folks. How long have you been dating?"

"Oh, uh, we just met," I say. "We're not dating."

"Well, we *will* be," Cohen clarifies. "She finally agreed to go out on a date with me tomorrow, and I'm determined not to screw it up."

"Yay!" Chelsea pinches Cohen's cheeks and gives him a cheesy smile. "You've found a winner, Annie. If I didn't see him as a brother, I'd have taken him myself."

An unfamiliar male voice clears his throat. "We talked about this," the newcomer says, throwing an arm around Chelsea. "You can't run off with the best man."

Cohen turns to the newcomer. "How are you, Rich?"

Rich—tall, handsome in a shiny sort of way—clasps Cohen to his chest. Where Cohen is rugged, a bit battered even, Rich has the sleek polish of a Wall Street banker. Rubbing a hand over his fiancée's back, he's quiet in his affection toward her. If she's all bright and festive, he's more of a dull, metallic color that shines underneath her light. They complement one another.

"Have you ever been to New York? We're debating a wedding there next fall." Chelsea says, gesturing toward the waiter for a refill on her vodka soda. "Extra lemon, please."

"No, always wanted to, though," I say.

"This'll be the perfect opportunity, won't it Rich?" Chelsea slides her hand over his shoulder and gives a squeeze. "Cohen, you'd better hang onto this one long enough to bring her. We only allow for plus ones that we both like, and Annie fits the bill. Right, Rich?"

"Absolutely," he says.

"Rich is a man of few words," Chelsea says. "That's why he can put up with me. I talk enough for four people."

"We'll have to see," I hedge. "My mom's getting married this summer, so I'm getting booked up with weddings."

"Around here?" Chelsea asks.

"No, it's down in the Caribbean." My eyes give a shifty glance toward Cohen. "On a boat."

Chelsea puts a manicured fingernail to her lips. She points it between the two of us, her jeweled fingers glittering under the dim lighting. "That's how the two of you met? Swimming stuff? I knew Cohen was doing that volunteer thing."

"I really hate water," I admit. "And I promised my mom that I'd learn to swim by my next birthday."

"Lucky for me," Cohen says.

"Freaking adorable." Chelsea grins. "We'll keep you guys posted on the bachelor and bachelorette party. If you're coming to the wedding, you might as well attend the pre-party. I promise it'll be a blast."

I wait for Cohen to take the lead which, thankfully he does by pestering Rich with questions about the impending bachelor festivities. I excuse myself to use the restroom and slide away before I'm forced into any more talk about happily ever afters.

When I return, Chelsea and Rich are in a conversation about flowers, and Cohen is staring with a somewhat wanton expression into his beer. I want to stay longer, but I *do* have class in the morning. I thank them for the invitation and say my goodbyes.

"Let me walk you out," Cohen says, despite my protests. Slipping a hand behind my back, he leaves me with no real choice in the matter. "Wait here," he tells the others. "I'll just be a minute."

The temperature has dropped even lower, and I hide underneath all my layers of clothing. Cohen reaches over, his hands bare, and tugs the fur lined hood of my jacket up and over my head.

"Stay warm," he says with a wink. "Can't have you getting sick before our date tomorrow."

"I'll be there," I promise.

When we stop next to my car, he continues one step further to engulf me in a warm embrace. His breath is hot against the top of my head as he leans closer and plants a kiss just below my hairline.

"Do you want me to drive you home?" he whispers. "I won't ask to stay over, I promise."

"No, stay with your friends. Chelsea's great, and Rich too. Plus, you have to celebrate. You're the hero tonight, after all."

"Just say the word, and I'll hop in your car and leave it all behind. My place, your place—your choice."

I let my hands find their way around his back, slipping underneath the thick winter coat. My fingers rest against his shirt as I lean into him, the sheer size of him offering a wall of safety against the wind. I'm not looking forward to letting go.

"Thank you. Drive safe, okay?"

"Thank you for what?"

His face cracks into a smile. "For giving me a chance."

I nod, since I can't think of a way to respond that won't have me asking him to come home with me. Instead, I beep my car unlocked and step backward. I slide into the driver's seat and halfway *wish* my car won't start. Then I'd have no choice but to stay with him longer.

Unfortunately, I've had *reason* and *logic* engrained in my brain for too long, and they win out this time. "I'll see you tomorrow," I say through my cracked window. "Sweet dreams, Cohen."

Chapter 25

Annie

"Good morning, sunshine!" The words rain down on me, harsh pellets in the early darkness just before dawn. "Rise and shine, darling."

My eyes crack open, screaming with reluctance, as I pair the screeching voice with the face of my grandmother. She's dressed in a suit that looks like her Sunday best, except it's pink and velvet. I believe she thinks it's trendy.

"Gran, what are you doing here?" I pull the covers up to my chest. "How did you get inside my apartment?!"

"It wasn't my fault." Sarah pokes her head into the bedroom behind Gran, obviously anticipating my questions. "She bribed me. You know I can't resist her homemade cinnamon rolls."

"There are homemade cinnamon rolls?" I tilt my head to the side, considering this new piece of information. "Why do I feel like this is a trick? Don't eat the rolls, Sarah, she wants something from us."

"Nope," Gran corrects. "Just from you, darling."

I sigh and collapse back against the pillows. "It couldn't wait until the sun rose?"

"I need you to come eat breakfast." Gran reaches for my covers and pulls them back. "With your new teammates."

"What *team*?"

"The synchronized swim team—The Dolphins—has a planning meeting today, and as an active member of the team, you need to be there."

"You named yourself The Dolphins?"

"Because we're beautiful and graceful."

"I can't come. Not today."

"Unless you have a smoking hot date waiting for you outside, you're coming with me." Gran puts a hand on her hip and watches my face. "Holy guacamole, Annie. You've got a hot date!"

Sarah barrels into the room behind Gran. "Is this true?!"

I groan and pull a pillow over my face.

"Who is he?"

"Is this the swim stud?"

"Where are you going?"

"What are you doing?"

"Pictures? Can I come?"

I wave them away and try to inch the blankets higher, but seeing as they're both sitting firmly on my comforter, it's impossible.

"Cohen James," I say. "You both know him. Of him, at least."

"Good thing it's barely six a.m." Gran raises her eyebrows. "Surely you have time for a quick breakfast before your date."

"No, I need *beauty* sleep."

"We're buying," Gran says. "Really nice latte. From your favorite place down the road."

"Brewberries?"

"The one and only."

I inhale, letting the breath sizzle out in a frustrated rush. Breakfast from Brewberries is a tough offer to turn down. Especially since the damage of *waking up early* had already been done.

"Fine," I agree. "But I have to be back in time for class. No exceptions. You've got an hour."

"Deal," Gran says. "Sarah, you're welcome to come with us, but you'll be sworn to secrecy. Either that, or you have to join the swim team."

"I'll stay here," she chirps, and it's suspiciously cheery. "Cinnamon rolls."

"Something with the museums?" Miranda Shaun says. "I'm on the board for the Natural History Museum, maybe we could work out some sort of deal with them."

"Nope," Gran says. "Too boring."

"Car wash?" Lottie Bolt asks. "After all, we have those really sexy swimsuits that go up your hiney. I think we could make a nice chunk of change with a car wash."

"Now you're talking." Gran grins. "I like Lottie's idea. What do you think, Annie? You've seen the suits I found."

"Oh, um... I don't think that's the best option. And those are *not* the suits we're going with; we decided on skirts."

"Really?" Lottie asks. "Why not?"

"Well, it's not *exactly* original," I say. "Pretty much every cheerleading squad and dance troupe in America uses car washes for fundraisers. Also, the suits Gran found would get you kicked off the streets for indecent exposure."

I survey the ten ladies here, all of them having dragged themselves out of bed at the crack of dawn to talk about fundraising for a retired synchronized swim team.

They want to buy matching suits for the competition, and they want to do it the *old-fashioned* way with real, honest-to-goodness fundraising. My mind is boggled. It's not like these ladies can't just *afford* a suit.

"What about selling candy bars or something?" Miranda asks. "It must work. Kids are still coming around with them."

"Nope," Gran says. "We're old. Half of us can't eat candy anymore. As for me, I want to be skinny for the competition."

"I like chocolate," Lottie says. "But not nuts. I'm allergic to nuts."

"What if we didn't do chocolate, but some other treat?" Miranda looks around. "We could bake. Everyone loves baked goods."

"Then we need everyone to bring something, and it's a lot of work," Gran says. "Something easier."

"What if we all cooked together?" I raise a hand and glance at the ladies. "Pancake breakfast! Those can be fun."

"I like this," Gran says. "That's where we all cook and sell tickets for five bucks a pop, right? It's like a social gathering *and* a fundraiser. I bet everyone from church will come."

"Donald loves pancakes," Miranda says. "He'll bring all of his poker friends."

Gran leans over and whispers, "Donald's her husband. He's a grouch, but he's rich. Fancy dentist or something."

"Donald's friends tip *very* well," Miranda says, not disagreeing with the rest of it. "I think this is a great idea. We'll have swimsuits in no time. Anything extra we can donate to charity."

Lottie gives a resounding cheer all by herself. Then, she gestures for the waitress to pour another round of coffee and raises her mug like a mimosa. "All for it, say *aye*!"

An excited chorus of *aye* reaches my ears, and I squint at the enthusiasm.

"My church has a gathering area in the basement they don't use much Saturday mornings," Lottie offers, pulling over a napkin and scribbling the name on it. "So long as there's not a funeral, we should be good to use it there. We can make a donation with the leftover funds."

"Done." I take a napkin from Lottie. "I vote sometime in April. Give the weather some time to warm up, but it's still early enough that we're not running up against the dress rehearsal for the swim competition."

"I'll call and book a date so people know not to die that week," Lottie says. "Even if there is a funeral, maybe we can combine the two and get some mourners in for pancakes."

"Lottie!" Miranda says, her voice hushed. "Have some sensitivity."

"It's not a horrible idea," Gran says. "It might cheer them up. Pancakes always make me happy."

"Gran!" It's my turn to scold. "Okay, I'm glad this is settled. I have to get to class."

Calls of *thank-you* drift up from the table as Gran stands next to me. Together, we wave, call goodbyes to all, and head out the door. Once in the car, I look over at Gran who's smiling happily behind the wheel.

"One question," I tell her as she flicks on a pair of bright purple sunglasses and throws the car into reverse. "Why on earth do you need a fundraiser? Miranda's got a ring on her finger the size of Jupiter. She could afford all of them."

"Yeah, but it's fun. I'm old, honey." Gran rests her hand on my leg and gives a squeeze. "Let a woman have some fun. Who knows? Maybe I'll meet a dashing young man there who'll ask me on a date. Now, enough about me. Are you excited for today?"

"Sure."

"You're guarding yourself."

"Am not."

"Fine, then let's try this again. Are you excited for today?"

"Maybe." I offer her a small smile. "It's too early to tell."

"Take a leap, dear. Let yourself feel excited."

"It's too soon! When did you *leap* with Gramps?"

"Oh, goodness gracious. We leapt so many times we lived life on a trampoline, darling. There's not *one* instance, but many. You have to trust over, and over, and over again."

"I don't even *know* him."

"But you have to start somewhere."

"What if he lets me down?"

Gran slows the car to a stop. We're outside of my apartment complex already, and without realizing it, I'd worked myself into a tizzy. My breath comes in short waves, and my hand is grasping the handle tight.

Gran's fingers close around mine, the car warm and toasty now that the heater's blasting. She moves our intertwined fingers into her lap and hesitates a long moment before answering. "Just because some people in your life have let you down time and time again, it doesn't mean that you shouldn't try to trust another man."

"This isn't about my dad," I say, and it comes out sharper than I'd intended. "Mom was always there for me. So was Gramps. I had a man I could depend on with him."

"Okay, then," Gran says. "I'm done preaching. Just *try* to remember that any relationship worth having will make you nervous. There are a million and one ways everything can go wrong."

"Gee, that's uplifting."

"Which is why it's a miracle when things go right. When you find that right one, there's nothing better. Let yourself open up—you might be surprised to find what you need."

"I *know* what I need in a man, Gran."

"Yeah." She speaks so softly it's barely a whisper. "I thought so, too. I was wrong."

"But—"

"Let's just say I'm sure as hell glad that I wasn't right." Gran's fingers tighten as she brings my hand up to kiss the back of it. "Have fun, honey. If nothing else happens, you get a free meal out of it. That's what I told myself, too."

As I scurry across campus a few minutes later, backpack hunched over my shoulders and thick mittens added to my outfit, I can't help but wonder if Gran's right.

What if I'm wrong about everything?

What if Cohen *isn't* wrong for me?

Chapter 26

Annie

He's late.

I've been waiting here for ten minutes, and I'm starting to turn into a popsicle. I'd texted Cohen the address to my apartment late last night and agreed to meet him out front since the campus layout can be confusing.

Huge mistake—now, I'm stuck waiting out front while my body temperature steadily drops to zero. Gritting my teeth, I pop a thumb out of my glove and scroll through my phone's touch screen. No messages, no phone calls, no texts. Minutes are ticking away, and I'm about ready to call it quits.

I'm not surprised—not even a little bit.

I know men like this. My father, for one. I've been in this situation so many times the rejection doesn't even sting anymore. That's not the part that bothers me—it's better that way, actually. The part that bothers me is the fact that I'm disappointed.

I start back into my apartment and catch a glimpse of myself in a nearby window. My cheeks are pink, thanks to the biting wind, and my eyes are all squinty. On my lashes, however, there's an extra swipe of mascara. An extra dot of eyeshadow. An extra *puff* of foundation. To think I actually put on makeup for this gets my blood boiling.

I'd be fooling myself if I said I wasn't disappointed. Truth is, I *hate* that I'm disappointed. I hate feeling helpless, and I hate the fact that there's a tear sparkling down my cheek about to freeze into a tiny pinprick of ice.

"Annie, wait!"

Thankfully, it's cold enough that my red cheeks and shiny eyes can be blamed on the lack of temperature. I turn around to face Cohen and force a smile.

"Where were you going?" His breath appears in a visible rush. "I told you I'd show up. I am so sorry I'm late. I got stuck behind an old woman at the grocery store paying her thirty dollar bill in coins, and... God, you're *freezing.* I am so sorry."

"It's okay, really." My somewhat frosty smile thaws at his bumbling apology as Gran's reminder to take a leap hits me hard. "I'm Minnesotan. We're built for this."

Dimples appear as he grins, relief written in his eyes. "Hop in the car. I've got the heat cranked up, and I'll make this up to you, I promise."

"Where are we going?"

"You'll see."

Twenty minutes later, we park in a quiet field that's situated atop a high hill just outside of the Cities. Our tire tracks are the first ones down this road, wheels crunching with effort as we cross loose gravel meshed with fresh snow. Fat flakes drift in lazy circles around us, spiraling in the wind until they rest on top of the ground.

"I used to come here as a teen." Cohen climbs out of the car, opens my door, and helps me out. "Right when I first learned to drive."

"How'd you find the place?"

"Friends."

"Girlfriend?"

His lips quirk up in a half-smile. "I plead the fifth."

"It's fine. You're not my first boyfriend."

"We're doing titles now, are we?" Cohen leans against the car, his eyes glinting as if he knows a secret that I don't. "I'm not opposed to being your boyfriend, if you're asking."

"You know what I *meant*!" My face flames red despite the dropping temperatures. "We're not a *thing* yet, this is a first date. We've barely kissed."

"Oh, honey, that's where you're wrong." He winks, and it sends butterflies soaring in my stomach. "We *definitely* kissed."

The memory of last night has me flushing warm despite the goose bumps on my skin, and I make a disgruntled noise deep in my throat. Meanwhile, Cohen clicks the trunk open and exposes two sleds—bright green and bright pink—immaculate in their newness.

"I had these laying around the house," he says, "and I figured it'd be a sin to waste the perfect snowfall. What do you say?"

"I say bullshit."

"Sorry?"

"These weren't laying around," I say, resting a hand on one of them. "These are beautiful, brand new sleds. Did you just buy these at the grocery store?"

"Am I that obvious?" He smiles, and I can't help but laugh. "I thought you seemed like the sledding sort of girl."

I yank the pink sled out of the trunk. "You guessed right... but now you're in trouble. I happen to be the reigning champ of sled races."

"That sounds like a challenge."

"It's more like a fact, actually."

"You're on, sweetheart."

Before I can turn away, however, he hooks a finger into the front of my jacket. I spin in a circle and crash against his chest with a *thud*. Snowflakes reflect in his gaze, spinning, swirling in circles, our breath fusing into one cloud of smoke.

The warmth from earlier is still there, and now with this close-ness, there's a twist in my gut that has me wanting more. I lean into him as his arms wrap around me, hold me tight, so perfectly tight, the beat of his heart matching mine.

When he brings a hand to my face, strokes a stray hair from my cheek, my lips reach for his, desperate for a touch, a kiss, a caress. Anything. As if all of this waiting has me pent up and needing him more than ever.

His lips brush against mine, and it sends me circling toward the heavens, the feel of him against me so right, so sweet, so—

"Ready, set..." He pulls back, grasps the free sled from the car, and gives me a quick flash of a smile before setting off in a sprint toward the hill. "*Go!*"

For a moment, I'm stunned. I stand there, aching for more of his kisses, frustrated beyond belief at the sudden absence of his body against mine, until I realize his sneaky little game.

"Hey!" I call after him. "Not fair!"

Though it feels like minutes, it's only a matter of seconds before my body catches up to my mind, and I take off after him.

I dive onto my sled just behind him as I reach the top of the hill. "You play dirty, Cohen James!"

He gives me a cheeky grin, slowing his pace to wait. Even so, he's got athletic grace on his side, while I have awkwardness on mine, and it's no competition as we take off down the hill.

"So," he says, lazing in a heap in the snow at the bottom of the hill. His sled has curved off to one side, so I make my way over to him. "What's my prize?"

"Prize? You didn't win fair and square."

"Come here, we'll call it a tie."

"Eat my dust."

I stomp toward the top of the hill, and it's not until I'm halfway up that I realize he's following me. We're a few feet from the top when he makes his move, hooking an arm around my waist and pulling me down with him onto the sled, directly onto his lap.

The sled loses all traction and takes off down the hill, the two of us a tangle of limbs as Cohen struggles to situate his arms around me. The wind whips across my face, snow pelting us from every direction until finally, I succumb to the warmth that is Cohen, and sink into his embrace.

By the time our sled skids to a stop, we're both giggling like schoolkids, and I find myself disappointed the ride has come to an end. I sigh, not yet ready to stand up, which works out fine because he doesn't seem keen on moving, either. If anything, he leans closer, his breath fresh as spearmint and spicy against my cheek.

"Can I kiss you, Annie Plymouth?"

I swallow, wishing I could see him. We're wedged tightly into the sled, however, so I'm stuck. When I give the slightest of nods in response, his mouth lands gently on my neck, a tender, soft spot just below my ear.

Shivers rock my body at the surprisingly sensitive touch, and I only lean further into him as he slides his mittens off and eases his hands under my jacket. It takes a few seconds of fumbling through layers of clothing before he inches his hands toward the edge of my shirt, skin finally brushing skin.

I need to have my arms free to hold him, too, so I swivel around and attempt an awkward sort of straddle. My gangly limbs wreck my best attempts at being suave, however, and I accidentally knee him in the gut.

He lets out a *whoosh* of air at the impact, but with minor difficulty, he guides us out of the sled and into a tangle of more awkward limbs in the snow.

Once we're finally situated somewhat comfortably—Cohen on his back while I'm perched on his lap—he grins, looping his bare hands through my gloved fingers. "Better?"

I lean forward, one leg on either side of his body, and press a kiss to his lips. "Perfect."

"You feel fantastic just like this," he says, a smirk playing at his lips. "But I promise that one day, I'm going to get you on a date that doesn't require a parka."

I laugh a little, wiggling my hips against him, my lips lingering just above his. "You can try."

Before I can say anything more, his mouth closes on mine. It's hot, swift, and all-consuming. His hands reach up and find my bottom, grasping tight as he pulls me against him. He groans as my hips press against him, a slow grind as he deepens the kiss.

"I want you *so* badly," he says, breaking the kiss for just long enough to run a tender line down my cheek. "You don't understand."

"Oh, I think I do."

It's my turn to shut him up with a kiss. Ironically, it's safer this way—if I let him use his words, he'll sweet-talk me right out of my pants. That wouldn't be good—at least not out here, in the snowy tundra. A lady can't let her best parts get all frostbitten.

I don't know what we're doing here, I'll be honest. I never expected to fall in love with Cohen James—but then again, I'm not sure this is love. I'm not sure it's friendship. I'm not sure if it's something in between, even, or if it's pure lust. I just don't know.

Cohen's hands come up through my hair, his fingers sliding through the loose curls as my hat hits the ground. I don't feel the chill in the air, or the brush of melting snow. I feel only Cohen, his desire for me, pressed against me.

It's a good thing we're not in a bedroom right now because there's a chance I'd be in danger of losing my self-control. As much as I want Cohen, I'm not quite ready to give myself to him—not fully, not yet.

There's still a wall inside me that's keeping him out despite these last few weeks of a burgeoning friendship. I don't know why, I don't know how to break it—I just know that it's there. We're still so new at this: new at talking, new at kissing, new at being together.

"Where'd you go?" he asks, running a thumb softly over my chin, lightly breaking the kiss. "Annie?"

"What are you talking about?" I blink down at him, shaken out of my smoochy haze. "I'm right here."

"No, you *were* right here." He gives a smile, but it's tinged with confusion. Almost sadness. "Did I do something wrong?"

It's now that I realize he didn't stop kissing me—*I* backed off from him. "Oh, no. I'm fine. Sorry, it's nothing."

"Why do you run away every time I kiss you?"

I find those green gems locked on me, asking for the truth, and I shake my head. "I don't know."

"Sure you do."

"No, I don't. I like kissing you," I tell him. "I just—"

"You're trying to keep us in some odd sort of friend-zone, and I don't like it. I want you. *All* of you. I'm not talking about sex, I'm talking about you trusting me."

"I am not trying to *friend-zone* you. I don't kiss my friends like that."

"I *know*, and I will be patient. Because you're worth it." Cohen shifts. When I try to move off his lap, he curls his arms around me, hands landing on my lower back. "But I'm done pulling your pigtails, Annie. Playing games and flirting and pretending I don't like you."

"Pulling my pigtails?"

"All of that surface stuff. The jokes, the banter, the fun stuff. I want to have fun with you, but it's okay to open up around me and have a real conversation. You are so incredible, so smart and funny and yes, so beautiful. I want to know each part of you."

He presses his lips to my forehead, and the gesture melts a place deep inside of me. The words are gone, and I can't form a response that seems good enough for the moment.

He brushes a stray snowflake from my jacket. "Please give us a chance."

"I want to," I confess. "But I'm scared."

"Of what?"

"Of whatever happens next. After."

"After what?"

"After this, us..." I hesitate, my fingers shaking as I hold onto his arms. "That's what all men say at first. *I love you, I want you, you're beautiful.* Then one day, you're just gone."

"You're not talking about me, Annie. I'm not going to do that to you, or to us."

"What makes you so sure this will work? How can you say *us* already?"

"I'm not sure at all, but I am willing to try."

"I *am* trying—"

Though we're mid-argument, he leans in and takes the words away with a press of his lips. It's soft this time, and gentle. When he pauses, his eyes land intently on mine. "How can I prove to you that I'm serious about us?"

I exhale a breath. "Look, I'm sorry. I'm a little on edge today because when you showed up a few minutes late, I felt stupid."

His eyes go wide. "*I'm* the one who showed up late. How could you possibly be the one feeling stupid?"

"Because I was *excited* for you to show up. I hate getting my hopes up. If you hadn't showed, I would've been disappointed. I don't like being disappointed by others. Waiting outside, shivering...I got really upset even though it was irrational."

"It's not irrational. It's—"

"It made me realize something." I bite my lip, shivering against a fresh breeze. "I'm starting to like you, or care about you, or something. And it's terrifying."

"Give me a way that I can earn your trust. I don't care what it is—*anything*. I want to prove that I won't let you down."

"It's not that simple."

"I need to start somewhere," he says. "Anywhere. We'll go slow. Then one day, with any luck, you'll *allow* yourself to feel excited again. And when that day comes, I promise you I'll show up."

"You said anything?"

"*Anything*."

"Well, there is one thing I've been meaning to ask you."

"Name it."

"My grandmother's looking for one male to help out with the synchronized swim team. We don't have many options, and I'm guessing you can see where I'm going with this..."

"You want me to join a ladies swim team?"

"Not *join* it, but maybe just show up for the competition. We can't find anyone else strong enough to do the twirl."

"You're kidding me."

"You said *anything*."

"Fuck me," he says. "Where do I sign?"

"Really?" I grin as he pulls me to my feet, an expression of disbelief on his face. "You'd do that for me?"

"I said anything."

"I admire your dedication, Mr. James."

He holds my hand and, together, we march toward the top of the hill. We're wet, the wind is cold, but I'm feeling buoyant inside, even giddy. Our kisses, this talk, his promises—maybe Cohen James isn't the playboy the media makes him out to be.

"One catch," he says, turning to face me, a look of utter seriousness on his face. "I am *not* wearing a Speedo."

Chapter 27

Annie

The man knows how to win over a girl's heart, I'll give him that.

He'd shown up packing a bottle of wine and a warm thermos of hot chocolate, and that was enough to make me swoon. Add on a plate of cheese and crackers, and it's the perfect picnic. Mr. James earned bonus points when he pulled out the bag of marshmallows as an accompaniment to watch darkness fall over a nearby lake.

"It's been *two hours*?" I look at the clock on the dashboard of his car. "*How?*"

We've been alternating between sitting in the car with the heat cranked up and bundling up against the cold outside. There's a scenic little overlook near the sledding hill, and we decided to stop and watch the sunset with the goodies in his grocery bags. Then the temperature dropped, and we retreated to the heated car.

"Time flies, doesn't it?"

"It does," I agree, swaying toward him with a quick grin. "Too fast."

That's probably the wine talking, or maybe the sugar high from the marshmallows. There's a bit of a warm, fuzzy sensation happening in my stomach, and as I lean across the center console, I catch a whiff of Cohen's cologne. It's delicious.

I want to kiss him, even though I've been avoiding it these last couple hours. We've been getting to know each other, and it's been fun—comfortable. Too comfortable, maybe. His hand closes the gap between us, guiding my head to rest against his jacket. I nuzzle in, enjoying the quiet peacefulness in this moment.

"Are you happy to be back in Minnesota?" I ask, punctuating the question with a kiss to his chin. "Or do you miss Los Angeles?"

"The sunshine, sure, but there are plenty of nice things about being here, too."

"Like what?"

"Like this." He tilts his head so that his mouth meets mine. The kiss is a delicacy, a tiny treat that promises so much more. "God, I love the taste of you."

"What do I taste like?"

"I'm not sure, actually." He pauses a moment. "Let me check."

Dipping his head, he goes in for another round, this time more urgent, pressing. My body arches in the passenger seat as trickles of warmth skitter across my skin.

When I finally break the kiss, his eyes linger on my lips as I whisper to him, "Any conclusions?"

"No, there's no way to explain it, except that you taste..." He pauses, runs his tongue over his lips. "Familiar. When I kiss you, it's like I've kissed you a million times before."

I wrinkle my nose. "So... I'm *boring*?"

"Did that kiss feel boring to you?"

"Well—"

"Be honest."

"No." I sigh. "I loved it. I sort of want to do some more kissing."

Cohen laughs, and the sound is a jolt of bright in the fading light. "Lucky thing I can accommodate that request. Can you swing your leg over?"

I maneuver the best that I can, but we're shoved into an incredibly uncomfortable position as I've sort of half-straddled him, and my groin is on fire—*not* in a good way. "Yeah, this isn't working."

He winces. "Dare I ask where the shift stick ended up?"

"You're horrible, and you're ruining the kissing mood."

"I can think of some place better to do this."

"Where?"

"My place."

"Cohen..." My voice changes, cracks with nerves, even as I try to keep it strong. "I'm not ready for that."

"That's fine, there's no pressure. I was just offering to warm you up with a shower and cook you dinner."

"You? Cooking *me* dinner?"

"Does ordering a pizza count?"

"I like pizza."

"Does that mean you'll come home with me?"

I slide off his lap, giving the shift stick a glare for ruining a potentially fabulous make out session. "I don't know."

"Come on, Annie. A chance. It's just dinner."

"Fine. But no hanky panky."

"Hanky panky?" His eyebrow crooks up in amusement. "Okay, then. We'll only go as far as you want."

"I mostly just want to use your shower. My dorm room never has enough hot water."

"I see how it is. You're using me for my facilities."

"And your lips." I bring my mouth a centimeter from his. "And, for the record, I know what you mean."

"About?"

"You taste familiar, too."

He groans, the sound causing a whirl of pleasure through me. I've never made a man moan with need, and I like it. It's empowering, in a way, to know that someone as experienced, as worldly as Cohen James might want someone like me. Even if only for a little while.

"Cohen," I say, this whole train of thought dredging up the dreaded questions that I've been trying not to ask. "What are we doing here?"

"I think we're about to make out."

I roll my eyes, but he's looking so adorable with those big, puppy-dog green eyes that I can't bring myself to have a serious conversation with him. Instead, I let my lips pull me toward him, magnetized by that elusive sense of familiarity.

He smells like rain, or like freshly cut grass—the first snow of the year. Like something I'd always known existed, even before we'd met. It was like coming home.

When we connect, the need is stronger for both of us. His fingers curl through my hair, teasing out the hairband I'd used to toss my locks in a bun. He pulls the strands tight against my scalp in a way that has me letting out a moan that's completely involuntary.

"You are perfect. You know that, don't you?"

"Shut up, Cohen. Kiss me."

One of his hands runs all the way down my hair until it reaches the base of my neck. He stills, looking me in the eyes, the moment frozen. "I'm *getting* to that."

The gentle kisses start on my forehead. Soft touches at first, and then more on my cheek. He continues the trail down past my chin to my neck, and when he brushes my skin it sends an involuntary shiver down my whole body.

"Cold?" He reaches past me to adjust the heat.

I rest a hand on his and shake my head. "Not at all."

The green in his eyes darkens, turning into that wild jungle I've seen on precious few occasions. "Well, damn."

He resumes the trail of kisses after unzipping my jacket, pressing one to either side of my collarbone, and all the way down my chest.

His hands are grazing up my body until they come to rest on the sides of my breasts, and his thumbs slide over to toy with my nipples through my shirt. I feel them harden at his touch.

"Interesting," he says.

"Yeah?"

"I'd like to get my hands on you," he murmurs. "And then my mouth."

I suck in a breath. "What did you say about using your shower?"

Chapter 28

Cohen

Apparently wine works. Or hot chocolate. Maybe it was the damn marshmallows.

I don't care, I'm just glad it made her happy.

I have no idea what sort of romantic gestures women expect on a winter picnic—I don't do "romance" as a general rule. I wouldn't say I consider myself relationship material.

But Annie Plymouth makes me want to change that.

I want Annie to be mine. I don't deserve her and, frankly, I can't think of a man who does. She's like a poster child for the perfect woman, all gorgeous on the outside and smart as hell on the inside.

I haven't figured out what she's doing spending time with me. She's not after my money, not after the fame... and she's *definitely* not after sex. Quite honestly, I can't figure out what the hell she wants.

All I know is that she's in my shower right now, and I'm sitting on my couch trying to wish away a boner that doesn't want to quit. For a girl who says she doesn't want sex, she sure as hell kisses like she does.

The things that woman can do with her tongue make my mind go blank.

Literally, it's empty inside my head.

You can't find a single thought in there with a magnifying glass, except how much I want to take her to bed, to relish her with my hands, my mouth, my everything. She deserves to feel good, to let loose, to be worshipped. And when she figures that out, I want to be the one she comes to for help.

Maybe it's the wine, I think again. When we were sitting in the car, she held my hand as the sun went down like she'd never let go. Her laugh danced like starlight, and her whispered stories about the years gone past were music to my ears.

We'd talked and touched for hours, and it'd been comfortable. Until she'd kissed me, and then she'd let loose a fury like a starved woman, desperate for more. If only she'd let me give her everything.

The shower clicks off, and I sit back in the couch. My palms are sweaty. *Freaking sweaty*. I haven't been this nervous since Varsity tryouts in high school.

For the first time ever, I sense parts of her defenses beginning to crumble around me, and whatever happens, I don't want to screw that progress up tonight. She's got these guards built up around her, tall as the Great Wall of China, and I have a feeling I know who put them there.

The only person she didn't talk about in that car was her dad, and I know he's still a part of her life—she's mentioned him briefly before. Whatever he's done to get her all skittish around men, a part of me hates him for it. Now, I have to disassemble her walls brick by brick. Inch by inch. Day by day.

I can be patient, that's not the problem. I know it'll be worth it. Today, for the most fleeting of moments, I caught a glimpse of what she's hiding inside that fortress.

And let me tell you—there's nothing more beautiful in this entire world.

"Hey, you." Annie's shyness is back as she peeks her head around the wall. She raises a hand to cover her mouth, a cute little giggle bubbling up in her throat. "Sorry to interrupt. You doing okay?"

I'm startled, even though I expected her. She's caught me daydreaming about her, and the end result is embarrassing. With a look at my pants, I run a hand over my face and shake my head. "Ignore me."

"Any chance you have lotion? My face is so dry."

"Let me check." I stand, willing my excitement to go away so I can finally be comfortable again, but it's impossible. My boner is persistent, I'll give it that. "Have a nice shower?"

"It was perfect. So hot."

I raise an eyebrow at her. Does this woman know what she does to me? Every word out of her mouth sends my mind spiraling to places she's *explicitly* said she doesn't want to go. "Hot. That's how you choose to describe it?" I say, brushing past her. "*After* telling me we're not allowed to have sex tonight? You are a tease, Plymouth."

"Like... the *temperature*!" Her face colors red. "And I *liked* it. Lotion?"

"Here." I hold up a bottle of goop from underneath my sink. The maid stocks it—I don't have a use for lotion normally, but tonight, I don't mind. When Annie reaches for it, I hold it out of her reach. "You can use it on one condition."

"What's that?"

"Let me help you."

"Cohen..."

"Just your back. You can't reach it anyway!"

"But—"

"I'm an excellent masseuse. Very professional."

"Somehow, I doubt that."

"Let me prove it to you." I feel her resolve cracking as I waggle the bottle back and forth. "Unless the thought of a backrub is really so horrible; I suppose I could trade it in for a kiss."

"A naked kiss?"

"Well, I wasn't going to ask, but I'll take it."

The pink tinges her cheeks again, and there's a new glimmer in her eyes. The brown and green intermix, sparkling with mischief. I'm glad it's been hours since we opened the bottle of wine—there's no way she's still under its influence.

This is Annie. The real Annie, and the bricks are tumbling down.

"Where?"

I cough, wondering if she'll recoil if I suggest the bed. "Uh, I suppose the couch?"

"The bed is fine," she says, and leads the way out of the bathroom. "But I mean it—no sex."

"No sex," I murmur, wondering how the hell that's going to be possible with a naked Annie wrapped between my sheets. "Fantastic."

Chapter 29

Cohen

"Oh, God, your hands are amazing!"

Annie's moans have me so turned on I can't even perch on her back to massage her shoulders. I have to sit off to the side, or we'd both be uncomfortable. She doesn't need a hockey stick poking her in the back while I'm trying to rub knots out of her shoulders—that would be distracting.

Just like the sounds she's whimpering into her pillow.

"You're going to have to stop that," I say, a little cross. "Otherwise, I'm going to spin you around and kiss you until you change your mind."

"Change my mind about sex?"

"*Yep*," I grit through clenched teeth. "It's not on my mind at all."

"Right." She peeks at me with a sideways glance from the pillow. "Yeah, I can see that."

I never knew a woman's back could be so damn sexy. I'd lent Annie a robe, and she had thrown it over a set of lingerie, leaving only a thin layer of cloth between us. It was more intensely erotic than anything I'd ever known.

To make matters worse, she'd climbed onto my bed—a huge king with a thick white comforter— and face-planted there with gusto.

Then, she'd morphed into Moaning Myrtle which did crazy things to my imagination.

Around three minutes into the massage, she'd ditched the robe. Five minutes in, she'd wordlessly unhooked her bra. I'm praying the panties come off next, but I'm not getting my hopes up. I've almost died from excitement twice already.

She's relaxed now, I can see it in the way she's breathing. Soft puffs of air against my pillow, her hair damp from the shower. She smells fresh, clean, and as my fingers knead into her tense muscles, that familiar scent washes over me again.

"Why are you so tense?" I ask, working on a knot just above her right shoulder. I let one hand stray, dragging my fingers down past her ribs to the curve of her lower back. I groan as my thumb brushes the lace lining of her panties. "Something on your mind?"

"*You*," she says. "Your hands are inching a little low there, buddy."

Reluctantly, I make my fingers obey my brain and inch them back to her shoulders. "Swimming lessons stressing you out?"

"Yes, that's why I'm here in your bed. Bribing you for a passing grade."

"You know I don't accept bribes, Miss Plymouth."

"Bullshit. You put the offer on the table."

"And you counter-offered with... *textbooks*?"

"I'm poor!"

"You won't be forever. Lawyers make good money—that's the goal, isn't it?"

"That's the goal," she repeats. "But it's a long road ahead of me, so we'll see if it pans out."

"Of course it will."

"What?"

"I said *of course* it will."

She rolls onto her side then, not fully, but just enough so I get a massive peek of side-boob. I'm a goner.

By the time I manage to drag my eyes away from the tender curve there, she's speaking to me. Again, and again, and I'm oblivious. Because side-boob.

"Hey, earth to Cohen!" She snaps her fingers and waves. "I'm talking to you."

"They're nice."

"What are nice?"

"Your... breasts?" I feel like the word boobs doesn't suit Annie. I also feel like an idiot saying breasts. The word *tits* is out of the question for her, so really, I'm screwed any way I look at it.

"You can see my boobs?!"

Noted, I think. *Boobs* it is.

"A little." I let one of my fingers trickle down the side of her body and brush against the softness of her chest. "Just a taster."

"That's like, one inch of it!" She opens her mouth wide in shock. "What happens if I show you the real thing?! You can't even concentrate with a peek of it showing."

"Good question. We should try it and see."

"You may continue the massage." She flops back down on the bed and tucks herself away. "Please and thank you."

I don't mind continuing. I'd love to continue the massage. Anything to keep my hands on her bare skin.

"What did you mean about becoming a lawyer?" she asks again.

"Lawyer?" I'm still thinking about her boobs. But now I'm thinking she'd make for one hot lawyer. I can picture it now, her dressed in a pencil skirt, sky-high heels, and... *shit*. She's talking again, and I missed half of it.

"It would be much better for my focus if we just had sex," I say. "I'm having a hard time concentrating on the law knowing you're undressed. In my bed. While I'm right here."

"I'm not undressed," she says, "I'm wearing underwear."

"I can fix that... *so* fast. I'm like lightning."

"I'm sure," she says dryly. "But you didn't answer my question."

"What question?"

She expels a sigh of frustration. "How are you so sure I can become a lawyer?"

"Uh, well... doubt never even crossed my mind."

"But it's hard, and I might not get into law school, and even if I do, I have to pay for it and study for classes and work while in school, and—"

"You're exhausting me." I brush a hand over the nape of her neck, and she sinks deeper into the pillow. "You can do it, Annie. I know that for a fact. You have more willpower than anyone on this earth."

"How do you know?"

"Because you are lying in bed here and resisting all my charms. Goddammit, Annie, you don't kiss like a woman who is waiting for marriage. If you can restrain your normal human urges like that, you can pass your damn boards."

She freezes, and then laughs. "I think that might be a compliment?"

"Sure, if you want it to be. I was just stating facts."

"Could you ever see yourself dating a lawyer?"

"I don't spend time thinking about that sort of thing. I know what I like when I see it. Then, I go after it. I happen to have a penchant for incredibly beautiful, very smart women, and they're rarer than you'd think."

"You are really trying to get me to bed with you, aren't you?"

"I already *got* you to bed."

"I'm sorry, Cohen," she says, speaking softly. "I don't think I should have come here. It's mean, doing this. I should go."

"No, no, you were up front. The massage was all my idea. I wanted to do it, and you deserve the pampering." A long pause follows and, though it hurts my heart, my stomach, every inch of my body, I re-fasten her bra. "What do you say I order pizza?"

"You're not upset?"

"I'm the opposite of upset. I'm begging you to stay for dinner."

"Well, then..." she rolls over, and I barely glance at her chest. "Give me a kiss, and then you can order."

Chapter 30

Cohen

The pizza arrives after I've showered. I pay for it and haul it onto the couch. Annie's already got Netflix queued up on one show or another—I don't give a damn which show it is, so long as I can sit next to her—and a grin waiting on her face.

"I like your pajamas."

I look down at my long, hockey-stick covered flannel pants. They were a gag gift from a teammate but they're freaking amazing. So soft. It feels like little clouds of bliss are cupping my legs, so I wear them even though they're ridiculous.

"Seriously," she says again. "I really like them."

Her voice is soft, and she's not looking at my pants. She's looking at my chest which I've left bare after the shower. I hadn't really thought about it—I'm in my own house, and I generally prefer to be naked than wear clothes. Hence the no-shirt policy. The fact that Annie seems to like this rule is a major bonus.

"Shall we eat?" I plop the pizza on the table and pour two glasses of wine from a nice bottle I received at Christmas last year. I watch Annie's expression as she takes a gulp, and her eyes light up at the flavor.

Excellent, I think. I have no clue what good wine tastes like, so if she's happy, I'm frigging ecstatic.

"Wait!" Annie reaches out, her hand resting on mine, blocking me from taking a sip. "First, a toast."

"A toast?" My mind is blank again. Mostly because Annie *also* decided to forego a shirt and is wearing my robe. The top opens a little as she twists to face me, and words suddenly don't make much sense. "To your boobs."

"What?" Her forehead crinkles in confusion. "Cohen, you can't say the first thing that comes to your mind. This is serious."

I sigh and drag my eyes away from her body. I stare at the Netflix sign on the television and pray for inspiration. Somehow, somewhere, God is listening to me. He gives me words.

"I would like to make a toast," I say, starting again. "Ready?"

Annie nods and raises her glass to mine. "Oh, I love toasts."

I smile, hold in a laugh, and let the words pour out as they come into my brain. It's some sort of divine magic there are sentences in my head at all. "This is a toast to the bricks."

"The bricks?"

"The wall you have around you, Annie. The shields, the guards that protect you from getting hurt." I look into her eyes, watching as her expression softens when she realizes I'm not toasting another of her body parts. "I think a few of those bricks came down today. This toast is to leaving them off, and to letting me chip a few more away tomorrow. And the next day. And the next."

She swallows, her eyes locked on my face. All of a sudden, her eyes dart away, quick as a squirrel, and she's clearing her throat and looking all uncomfortable.

"Your turn," I tell her.

"How can it be my turn?" She glances up at me. "We haven't completed the toast."

Leaning her glass toward mine, she punctuates the speech with a clink, and then raises it to her lips. She waits for me, holding there, until I follow suit. Together, we take a sip.

I'm surprised when I set my glass down. It *is* good wine. I'll have to thank Boxer next time I'm in Los Angeles—he's an old teammate who stocked up my collection for Christmas.

Annie sets her glass down on the table, too, but I stop her before she can pull her hand away.

"Nope," I say. "Your turn."

"You already made the toast."

"It's a double toast sort of night."

A smile flickers on her face. With achingly slow movements, she lifts her glass and turns to face me. Thankfully, she cinches the robe tight this time, so that when she begins to speak, I'm focused on every word.

"This is a toast to the person patient enough to peek between the bricks of my walls." She stops, her eyes going wide. "No, that is not an innuendo."

I'm grinning because she's nervous, and it's adorable and sweet, and I want to wrap her in my arms. But I think she'll take it the wrong way if I slide my hands underneath that robe in the middle of the toast, so I lock my fingers tighter around my glass.

"I can sometimes be... hard to deal with." Her free hand comes to rest on my fleece clad knee. "You have been really patient, Cohen, and I appreciate it. Thank you."

"You don't have to thank me for that. Plus, it's selfish. I like you, Annie. Any man would be *lucky* to be patient for you."

"Well, thank you. For that, and for your creativity and persistence."

"Is that a reference to my showing up outside your bedroom window?"

"Among other things. You never cease to surprise me."

Gesturing toward the table, she urges me silently to finish the toast, clink her glass, and take another sip. Once we've done so and replaced our glasses on the table, we find ourselves sitting on the couch, mostly naked, hands free.

I'm aching to take her into my arms, to kiss those pink cheeks of hers, warmed by wine, and bring her back to bed. For sex, yes, but something more, too. I want to be next to her, close to her, and ease away those bricks one by one.

I clear my throat instead, determined not to ruin this night. "Pizza?"

"Oh." Her mouth is round, and she shakes her head, flustered. "Yeah, sure."

"Unless you had something else on your mind?!"

"Nope." She picks up a slice in a hurry, shoves a bite into her mouth, and clicks *Play* on Netflix. "Let's watch."

We settle in for the night and, though it's only six p.m. on a weekday, it might just be the best day I've had in quite some time.

Sure, I'm eating dinner at the same time my grandfather does in his retirement home, and yes, I'm wearing fleece pajamas made for a newly toilet-trained child. It's perfect. It's all perfect.

When Annie finishes her pizza and rinses her hands, she returns to the couch and nestles under my arm. We're halfway through the second episode of whatever stupid show is on the television when her breathing evens out, and she sinks into sleep.

I can't resist leaning over, brushing one more kiss on her forehead. I give her another hour or so, but as the clock approaches nine, I decide she's not waking tonight, and I move her into my bedroom.

She shifts, moaning ever-so-slightly as I cradle her body in my arms, and I take epically quiet steps into the room. The mattress is so damn large we could both sleep on it and never worry about touching, but something tells me that Annie might freak out if she wakes up and finds us in bed together.

Especially since I have no shirt on, and all she's wearing is underwear beneath my robe. Thin underwear, I happen to remember. I snuck glimpses of it all night. That robe and its inability to remain cinched tight is friggin awesome.

I ease the covers over her shoulders and watch for a long moment as her chest rises and falls, her hair splayed over my pillow. She looks good there, at home in my bed, on my pillow, in my clothes.

I've never been one for relationships, never felt the urge to dedicate myself to a single woman for more than a few weeks, let alone my lifetime, but I find myself wondering if that could change. It might, if Annie has any interest in the idea.

Pulling an extra blanket from the closet, I drag my ass back to the couch and curl up underneath it. Oddly enough, this might be the first time in my life I've invited a girl over, and then proceeded to put *her* in my bed and *myself* on the couch.

I press *Play* on that stupid show and, three episodes later and five quick checks on Annie, my eyes sag shut, and I ease into sleep.

Chapter 31

Annie

I wake to sunlight streaming through a window.

In a house that is *distinctly* not mine.

It takes a second of frantic thrashing about before the memories from last night come back in a flood, and everything makes sense. I fell asleep in Cohen's arms—that much I know. The memory comes back with a burst of warmth and comfort. The only thing *not* adding up is the empty half of the bed.

I squint at the extra pillow, struggling to remember if Cohen had climbed in with me, but I've got nothing. Blankness. Beyond the sensation of happiness and the mushy feeling of curling into his warmth, the snugness of the couch—the rest of the details are lost to me.

Tiptoeing out of the bedroom, I find him sprawled on the couch in nothing but those fleece pajama pants. If you'd bet me a million dollars that Cohen James owned pants with hockey sticks plastered all over them, I'd have lost a lot of money.

There's the spirit of a kid somewhere in Cohen James, and I like that about him. There's an innocence to the hockey star that even I hadn't expected, a wide-eyed thirst for life lost in so many adults.

I take a moment to appreciate the sight of him. It's not that I haven't seen his bare chest before. Or fleece pants. But the morning glow softens his skin, smoothing the worry, the stress of responsibility away, enhancing features with a sweetness that give me an ache inside.

I imagine slipping onto the couch with him, opening my borrowed robe to let his hands caress my back, my shoulders, my skin as we slip into sleep together. The image sends warmth swirling through my veins.

I remember how he hadn't even climbed into bed with me last night, and because of that gesture, another few bricks melt away from my guarded walls, opening my heart to him, urging me closer and closer.

I want nothing more than to run a thumb over his cheek and trace his smile, but I don't want to wake him. Instead, I let him sleep, sneaking into the kitchen and beginning World War III with the coffee machine. The thing is complex and annoying, and it takes me fifteen minutes to grind out two cups of something resembling coffee.

Now that I have an offering, I figure it's fair to wake him. With a coffee in each hand, I return to the living room and watch him sleep for one moment longer. His eyelashes fan out over his cheekbones, beautiful and thick, and I'm envious for a moment.

Then, I realize that I'm the lucky girl who gets to look at him and his gorgeous lashes. I lean forward, pressing a whisper of a kiss to his forehead. The second his eyes open, another brick from my wall crumbles away.

Clear, green eyes stare back at me, a brightness there. Then a burst of confusion, followed by a flash of pure joy.

"You stayed," he whispers, bringing an arm around my neck to pull me close, dusting a kiss against my cheek. "Good morning, gorgeous."

"Good morning, handsome."

"What time is it?"

I glance at the clock under the television. I have to check again to make sure I'm reading it correctly. "Oh, I'm so sorry! It's only seven—I don't need to leave until nine, but—"

"Hey, it's fine," he says, swinging his feet to the floor and rising to a sitting position. He runs a hand over his face, through his hair, clearing the sleep away. "More time to spend together. Are you rested? You got almost twelve hours of shut-eye, sweetheart."

"I am so sorry that I fell asleep on our first date!"

"Hey..." He slides one hand onto my exposed knee, the touch of his fingers cautious, tender. "You don't have to apologize for anything."

"I stole your bed."

"I let you have it. Look at it this way, you're doing me the favor." At my questioning look, he grins. "I didn't have to argue with you about spending the night. You made the decision all on your own."

"Okay, fine. You got lucky."

"Well..." His fingers inch up the slightest amount. "I can think of one thing to make me an *even* luckier man."

"*Cohen!*"

"Just testing the boundaries. Sorry."

"Keep testing," I tell him with a foxy smile. "Who knows? Someday, it just might work."

"I'll pray for that day."

"And in the meantime?"

"I'm practicing my patience." He swivels to take one look at the coffee, giving me a sideways glance. "That's for me?"

"Yeah, but it'll cost you one kiss."

The next thing I know, he's removing the coffee mugs from my hands and depositing them on the end table. His hands then snake around my back and pull me onto his lap. The robe, wide open by this point, covers the pair of us like a cape. I take inventory of the items between us: my bra, my undies, and his fleece pants.

And let me just say that fleece pajamas don't hide much of anything.

He takes control, situating me right where he wants before lowering his mouth, teasing with the threat of a kiss. All the while, he keeps his eyes locked on mine, desire clouding his gaze.

I can feel him under me, every inch, and it's so incredibly sensual, even though we're barred by clothes. We're not kissing, we're barely even touching, save for his fingers finding a place on my hips to hold me close. I shift my weight unconsciously, and he grips me tighter, a devilish grin appearing on his lips.

"I think you want me, sweetheart," he murmurs, his lips dancing over my neck. He pauses to press a kiss under my ear, at the top of my shoulder, in the center of my chest. "Admit it."

My head falls back, just enough to give him better access to my neck, and he takes advantage of it. A treasure trail of kisses across my chest, goose bumps spiraling over my skin.

"Let me taste you," he says, his voice gruff. "Touch you, at least. God, Annie, I need you so badly."

I lean into him, pressing against his desire, resting my body against his. I'm throbbing with need, but I can't bring myself to act on it. *Not yet.* Lowering my mouth to his, I kiss him with everything I have in me, needing to let him know my confusion, the conflict warring inside of me.

I don't have the words for it, so instead, I show him.

I hold him close, feeling him as I move against him, bringing forth a groan from his lips. He holds me, rocking my hips back, then forward, then back again, until the friction is so intense I'm gasping.

It's more than attraction—it's chemistry. I've never experienced anything like it, this desire burning through my veins, ripping through all sense of logic. I'm drunk on him, on everything he has to offer, but still, it's not enough.

There's that tiny part of me, the voice of reason that reminds me we will *probably* never work out. The two of us—we're different, so very different, and my fears are shouting that the second I let my judgement lapse, the moment I give myself to him fully and completely, I'll be vulnerable. My softness, my soul will be exposed to Cohen James, my heart resting in his hands.

I'm not ready for that, not yet, and the thought brings a sob to my throat. I swallow it, masking it as a moan as I ride against him harder, faster through our clothes, a frenzy between us that acts as a disguise.

"I can't keep kissing you," he says, his hands sinking into the skin of my waist as he stills me on his lap. "I don't trust myself to stop anymore."

I take a breath, calm my nerves, and then I bring my hand to his cheek. The stubble there is rough against my fingers. He closes his eyes in pleasure as I drag my fingers through it, down to his chest. I rest my hand on his heart.

"I trust you," I whisper. "Please kiss me."

If we don't do something, I'm going to explode from passion. Thankfully, he moves first, curling me to him as he shifts, spreading me on the couch before he climbs on top of me. His hands never stop moving, tracing every inch of exposed skin.

We rock together as he crashes his lips, his body against mine. He's bringing me to a dangerous verge, ascending a mountain I'm not sure we can leave without shattering together. His hand carefully caresses my breasts, taking care to move in ways that make me cry out with pleasure.

Then he moves on, letting his fingers brush downward, across my stomach, past my belly until he rests against the outer edge of my panties. He stops, our chests heaving in sync.

I'm breathing heavily, waiting to see what comes next. The air is thick with lust, thick with need, and I know he's waiting on me. But I can't seem to gather the oxygen necessary to respond.

"I'm not going any further unless you ask for it," he says, his voice with a desperate note to it. "I need you to tell me what you want... if you want me. If you want me to touch you, kiss you, take you."

"Cohen, I want you, but... "

He looks into my eyes, his gaze softening. Understanding. "Can I touch you?"

I nod.

He brings a hand lower, brushes against the outside of the silky material. I exhale a moan that has him closing his eyes and biting down on his lip. "You're okay?"

I can't speak, so I nod again. His eyes lock on mine as I arch my hips toward him. His fingers add more pressure, and I withhold a whine of pleasure. My fingernails dig into his shoulders, my thoughts blank, my entire being focused on holding him.

With painstaking patience, Cohen watches my face as he slides one finger past the fabric, hesitating just long enough for me to give him the signal to continue. When I grit out a cue to keep going, he does, a finger dipping inside me for the first time.

He groans first, leaning toward me, begging for a kiss.

I meet him halfway as he gently teases me with his fingers, finding the places that make me writhe with pleasure. My arms wrap around his neck and the magic between us lights my nerves on fire. There's a blind ecstasy to this moment, a blur of everything good I had never known.

"God, Annie, you're incredible," he says. "I want to make you see stars."

"What about you?" I say, more gasp than voice. "If you want—"

"No." He cuts me off sharply. "Today is about you."

If I'd been able to think, maybe I would've responded. I can't do more than bite down, however, as he raises my hips higher, brings the kiss deeper, and carries me toward the edge of all logic.

It's too late to slow down, to bring him with me—I'm frozen in bliss, and it's all I can do to hold onto him as he murmurs my name, warms my neck with his kisses, and sends me spiraling into the stars, just as he promised.

I cry his name as the waves come, carry me through with an intensity that has me crumbling to him, the wash of adrenaline slowly winding to a halt. I repeat his name, pressing my head to his chest and dragging him down so his weight, his beautiful body, is rested against me.

"Cohen..." I whisper again, my hands stroking his hair a few minutes later. "I don't... I don't know what to say."

"You didn't like it?" A flicker of uncertainty crosses his eyes as he tilts his gaze to meet mine. "God, Annie, I haven't asked—are you a virgin?"

"Oh, no! Not at all." I can't summon more energy, so I fall silent, stroke his hair some more, until I can pull together some thoughts from my scrambled brains. There are no words to do this moment justice, so I whisper against his ear. "That was incredible. Thank you."

"No, thank *you*." He draws tiny circles on my chest, his lips curled into a smile. "For trusting me. It *was* incredible."

"I feel bad," I say. "You've done all of this work to get me on a date, all of these sweet gestures, all of this foreplay, and then here you are ready to go, and I keep saying *no*—"

"Stop." He says it matter of factly, as if there's no sense in my arguing. "Whatever you're going to say, stop it. I care about you, Annie, and that means I'll wait. However long you need. Believe me when I say I get more pleasure out of watching your face than you can imagine."

"But I'm worried that when... er—if we sleep together—"

"When," he says with a smile. "I prefer *when*."

I laugh, but my hands are twisting around his neck. I'm anxious, anxious about something I've never before voiced. "What if you're disappointed?" I clear my throat. "I'm not exactly, uh... *great* at sex."

"Where'd you get that idea?" He raises an eyebrow, a ghosted smile on his face. "You rocked my world, and I haven't even been inside of you. I'd say you're *just* fine."

"It's just... I've only been with one other person," I tell him. "My ex. And he told me that I had a lot to learn before I'd be any good at...well, *it*."

"Well, *fuck*. That's a flat-out lie, Annie." Cohen's fingers are shaking, a rage burning in his eyes. "Does he have a name? What an ass. I'd like to find this idiot and see what—"

"No, Cohen, don't. He was probably just being honest with me."

"False." He shifts onto his elbows, holds himself over me, his eyes piercing. "If he were honest, he'd be telling you this: *Annie Plymouth*, you are the most beautiful woman on the face of the planet. But not only are you beautiful, you've got more brains than most men or women can dream of possessing. You're sexy, and the way you move—"

"You don't have to do this, Cohen." I shift under his gaze. It's as if he's staring straight through me and analyzing my soul, and it puts me on edge with what he might find. "It's ok. Forget it."

"The very way you *exist* is elegant. The way you breathe, hold my hand. The way you curl up next to me during a movie and try to pretend you're awake when really, I can see that your eyes are shut."

I'm blinking now, fast, furious blinks, but Cohen doesn't let go of my arms. His eyes are locked on me with an intensity that's almost frightening, and I can't do anything but return his gaze.

"When I saw you sleeping in my bed last night, I wanted you more than I've ever wanted anything in this world. You're perfect. The way you look at me..." He shivers, as if the words are too much to say aloud. "You have more passion in a single touch than anyone I've ever met. Believe me, there is *nothing* wrong with you, Annie. If sparks weren't flying before, it's because he didn't deserve to see them."

He leans in, brushes his lips against mine in a kiss that's as tender as cotton candy clouds—soft, almost non-existent. It sends chills across my body.

"If you'll let me, I plan on making you feel this good day after day, night after night, for as long as you'll have me."

"Oh," I say, and it's more of a reaction than a logical thought. "Well, what a horrible burden to bear."

"Yes, I'm a fucking martyr."

"Let me touch you now. *Please.* Let me show you how good you make me feel."

Something flashes through his eyes, and he seems to consider my offer for a moment. But he shakes his head *no.* Standing, he reaches for my hands and pulls me to my feet, landing us an inch apart, nose to toes.

"Not today, sweetheart. *Someday,* if you'd like, but not now."

My cheeks heat with the thought of *someday*, delicious ideas swirling in my head. "Someday, then."

"Can I take you out tomorrow?"

"On a date?"

"No, on a horse. Yes, of course a date."

"Well, yes," I agree, surprised to feel my heart beating quicker. "I suppose that'd be perfect."

"I won't even try for sex. That's how patient I am."

"No! I told you to keep trying."

"Well, hell, Annie Plymouth." He holds out a hand and twirls me into his chest. "Your wish is my command."

Chapter 32

Annie

A few weeks later, I'm freezing my butt off in the hockey arena as the final whistle blows. Cohen's on the ice, skating toward his teammates when he pauses, glances into the crowd, and locks eyes on me. Even though I've been coming to his games for weeks now, this moment still gives me the thrills.

I cheer as he gives a big, unabashed smile, and salutes in my direction. I wave back like a slightly nutty fan girl. Meanwhile, next to me, Chelsea is making vomiting sounds in her mouth.

"You two are *gross*." Chelsea turns from the seat next to me, her jaw open. "Girl, what'd you do with the real Cohen James?"

"Sorry?"

"I don't get it." She shakes her head in slack-jawed amazement. "He *lost* the last game of the regular season, and he's smiling? That's *not* the Cohen I know. The Cohen I know would sulk, and then go straight to the bar, order a whiskey, and ignore everyone for the rest of the night."

"I guess he's changed?"

"He's acting like a big old butterfly instead of an ugly little caterpillar." Another laugh-snort from her. "Must be some awesome sex."

"Oh, no." I wave a hand, watching as the teams leave the rink to head to the locker room. "We haven't slept together."

As I let that sink in, a stream of curse words all colors of the rainbow punctuate the air. Chelsea's clearly in shock, poor thing. A disgruntled mother strolling past us ushers her child away, hands clamped over his ears and a frown on her face.

"You're kidding me," Chelsea says finally. "You're freaking kidding me. Pulling my leg. Lying."

"No, really. It's true."

I like Chelsea—she's great, really. She's the one who invited me out tonight for the final game of the Stars' season, which is convenient because both Leigh and Sarah have seen more hockey than they ever wanted to see over this past month. And since the actual act of "doing sports" is lost on me, I enjoy the company more than the game.

We wait, somewhat patiently, for Cohen to finish up whatever business that needs attending. Meanwhile, I polish off our popcorn while Chelsea quizzes me in the hallway about 'this no sex thing' that Cohen and I have going. No matter how much I try to explain, she's baffled.

"There you are." Finally, Cohen sidles up to where we're waiting. "What'd I do to have the prettiest girl in the room waiting for me?"

Chelsea rolls her eyes as Cohen plants a chaste kiss on my cheek.

"You two are sickening. I'm going to pick up Rich from the airport and do some swooning of my own. Good*bye*."

"Oh, Chelsea don't go!" I call after her. "When are you leaving?"

"Few days." She gives a shrug. "We didn't find a dress yet, so I need to go one more time with my mom."

Chelsea had flown into town to do some wedding dress shopping with her family, and we'd hung out a few times. As it turns out, it's nice to have a girlfriend who knows Cohen. Sure, I have other girlfriends, but Sarah is shy and develops a strange tick where she loses the ability to speak coherently every time Cohen's in the room.

Then there's my mom, but I haven't exactly told her I'm dating anyone. I just get the feeling she *might* not approve—not now, when I have so much else going on in my life with school, *her* wedding, graduation, and more.

Meanwhile, Gran is more interested in hearing the details about Cohen's washboard abs than anything else. She's big into abs.

"How do you feel about lunch tomorrow?" Chelsea asks me. "Girls only. Sorry, Cohen."

"One o'clock?"

"Great," she gives a smile. "Let's go to that cute place next to the chocolate store we went to after the bread restaurant."

"Yes! I've been wanting to go!"

Chelsea leans in to give me a kiss on the cheek. Almost as an afterthought, she waves at Cohen. "See ya."

"Gee, and to think we used to be friends," Cohen says as Chelsea struts in the other direction. "I'm glad you two get along."

"Oh, we do. We both love those crappy hot dogs that are actually delicious."

Cohen's not listening anymore, instead focusing on his hands, which have taken to winding underneath my puffy outer layer, searching for the warmth of my body. I have on a tank top and a long sleeve underneath my winter jacket, which leaves Cohen with quite a labyrinth to work through in order to reach skin.

"Success," he says, his fingers finally finding gold. "So many damn layers."

I shiver, yelp softly as his fingers connect near my lower stomach. He's dangerously close to a zone that makes me weak at the knees, and I wriggle away because other people are starting to watch us with interest.

"*Cohen*," I hiss. "People are staring."

We might not have *formally* consummated our relationship yet, but we've done plenty of other fun things. There's only one problem

now. Things are going *so well* between us that the mere *thought* of
screwing everything up by sleeping together has me terrified. What if
everything goes wrong once it finally happens?

What we have now is not enough, I know that. It's special. He's
special. We're special, and the closer we get to one another—the
more time we spend together—the more I want him, all of him. This
period of blissful existing as we are won't last forever, but I'm afraid
of what will come next. The next leap, the next jump, the next hurdle.

Meanwhile, Cohen makes no secret about his intentions. Even
now, in public, his hands roam wild and free in a hungry sort of way.
When he reaches my rear end, he gives a possessive squeeze, his arms
around me as he backs me against the nearest wall.

"I don't know what you do to me," he murmurs, that post-game
adrenaline giving his eyes a brighter gleam. He tucks us behind a
vending machine in the now mostly deserted hallway, out of the way
of prying eyes. "I can't keep my hands off you."

"I'm not complaining."

"Chelsea's right," he says. "I've just lost the last game of regular
season, and all I can think about is getting you out of here, back
home. Alone. You don't have plans tonight, do you?"

"With you, I do."

I let my fingers trail down his chest. Those bricks he speaks of, the
wall around my heart—it's started to crumble these past weeks, one
brick after another until a whole section of the wall has completely
disappeared. My defenses are collapsing, and I'm not sure how it happened, just that it has.

"Good," he says, the hoarseness in his voice a mix of post-game
laryngitis and a hint at what's coming later. "But first, I need to kiss
you, or we'll never make it home."

He lifts me with ease, and my legs wrap around his waist. We fall
back against the wall in a tangle of heat as he takes the brunt of the

impact. One of his hands drags through my hair, the other supporting my weight as I wind my arms around his neck.

We have one moment of a whirlwind kiss before it comes to a crashing halt. A sound emerges from the other side of the vending machine—once, twice, finally three times before I recognize it as a male clearing his throat. A male that is definitely not Cohen.

Cohen hears it too, his hands stilling under my jacket as he glances over his shoulder. Based upon the widening of his eyes, he recognizes the figure standing before the vending machine, a dollar frozen in the newcomer's hand.

"Hi, uh, coach," Cohen says, somewhat groggy. "How's it going?"

I freeze, mortified. *Coach.* Coach?! I poke my head around Cohen's to catch a view of a well-dressed man, his hair slightly ruffled with frustration, stalled with a bill halfway inserted into the machine.

"Uh, hello," I echo. "Coach."

"This is Annie," Cohen says.

"I'm Annie," I say.

"Annie," Coach says. "Pleasure to meet you."

"Yep, same to you." I wiggle my hips, hoping Cohen will recognize it as the signal to let me down. I grit my teeth, wriggle harder, but still, Cohen doesn't move. It's like his brain has stopped working.

"I think the lovely lady can stand on her own two feet, Mr. James, don't you?" Coach gives him a half smile. "Though it's generous of you to give her a hand. Or two."

Cohen nods absently along with his coach's words. It takes some time for them to sink into his brain, but when they do he moves in a hurry. He doesn't just set me down, he drops me like a hot potato.

I clatter to my feet, using the wall to stabilize myself for balance. When I gather myself into a somewhat normal standing position, I come face to face with Coach giving Cohen a weird look.

"I didn't mean you had to drop her on her ass, James," he says, before turning to me with a concerned look on his face. "Are you all right?"

"Just dandy!" I straighten my tank top under my jacket, which has somehow gotten all sorts of bunched around my boobs. "I'm great."

"You must be the mystery girlfriend."

"Excuse me?" I glance between them. "Mystery girlfriend?"

"I've been dying to put a face to your name for weeks."

"Cohen's girlfriend?" I murmur. "*Weeks?*"

"Oh, Cohen didn't say anything." Coach reaches out, claps his star forward on the shoulder. "I put two and two together when this guy stopped acting like an idiot on Friday nights and showed up to practice with a smile on his face."

Cohen cinches me tighter, not bothering to disagree. Just being around him, next to him, has my heart racing, my emotions swirling like a pot of chocolate fondue—sweet, warm, perfect.

"You two are either sickening or adorable. I don't know which," Coach says. "Anyway, nice game, James. Don't lose focus now though. Playoffs are coming. Keep him on the straight and narrow, will you?" Coach turns a searching gaze on me.

A wave of nerves rushes through my body. The man's intense and serious and intimidating. He makes the perfect coach, seeing as he can melt a grown man with one of his scorching glares. "Absolutely. I will keep my *boyfriend* on the straight and narrow."

"Good. Then I suppose congratulations are in order. Goodnight, folks." Coach stares at us intently, since neither of us move. "Well?! Do me a favor and take this—whatever the hell is going on here—somewhere private. Don't need the media on you now, do we, James?"

Cohen takes my hand. "Yes, sir."

"Great." Coach finishes inputting the dollar bill into the vending machine and raises his eyebrows. "Glad we understand each other."

"Yes, sir."

Since Cohen has reverted back to his frozen state, I take charge, pulling him down the hallway and out a back entrance. Once we burst into the parking lot, it's as if we're both released from a spell, and the pair of us collapse in a fit of laughter against the wall.

When Cohen finally calms enough to speak coherently, he pulls me to my feet, balancing me against him as he pushes a loose strand of hair away from my face.

"So," he says, watching every one of my features. "Did you mean it?"

"Mean what?"

"You called me your boyfriend."

"Didn't seem like I had much of a choice."

"Then let's make it official," he says, swinging me into his arms. "Will you be my girlfriend, Annie Plymouth?"

Chapter 33

Cohen

I think Annie just agreed to be my girlfriend.

We slip into the car, and I hold her hand as we drive toward my place. I'm still contemplating what just happened. I asked her again after we got outside if she meant it. She said yes.

I'm still feeling a little out of my element, somehow having acquired a girlfriend in the last half hour. I hadn't thought it'd happen so soon—not with how slow Annie's been moving things along.

I can't help but wonder if tonight will be the night. The one we've both been waiting for—the night she'll trust me enough to take things further. Because as much as I *want* her, I *need* her to come to me, to tell me she's ready. But damn if waiting ain't hard.

"Cohen..." Her voice is soft as she looks over to me. "About what just happened—are we dating? Really?"

"Do you want to be?"

She hesitates, then nods. "I wasn't seeing anyone else. Wasn't planning on it, and I don't want to."

"Me neither."

I've been needing her since I laid eyes on her, but I don't tell her this. I already know that there's no one else who can give me this feeling, this crazy desire that's been driving me nuts for months. The only way to quench this need is with her. When she's ready.

"Now that we're official," I begin dryly, "you can ask me to be your plus one to your mom's wedding. I'm a lifeguard, so that should put her mind at ease."

"You're not a lifeguard."

"No, but I have a pretty good handle on mouth to mouth."

She laughs and leans toward me. "I don't know, maybe you need some more practice."

The light turns red at the perfect time. We trade a kiss hot enough to melt ice and, when the light turns green, I've got a woody ready for action. *Fabulous.* I shift, adjusting my boxers.

"Oh," she says, glancing over. "Wow. That was fast."

"Yeah, well..." I shrug. "You've been doing that to me for weeks, honey."

"Maybe I can do a little something to help that tonight."

I *fly* home.

By the time we park and make our way to my unit, we've cooled down a bit. I'm just going to let her take the lead and show me what she wants. If she's doesn't make a move, that's fine by me. But her suggestions sure as hell have me standing at attention.

"Mind if I use your shower?" Annie asks. "It was *freezing* at the rink."

I eye her hair with suspicion. It's still damp from a shower she probably took before my game. "Uh, okay."

She smiles, but doesn't offer any further explanation. Unfortunately, I can sense when her smiles are fake, so I reach out and grab her wrist.

"Annie—" I hold her arm while I lock the front door. "Is everything okay?"

"Yeah, why?"

"No reason."

She makes her way down the hallway toward the shower. I wouldn't mind following her, undressing her along the way and easing into the steam behind her, but I'm getting strong vibes that's not on the agenda tonight.

I kick off my own shoes, hover around the doorway, and practically scare away the teenage kid who rings the doorbell with the Chinese food. I'd almost forgotten I'd ordered it.

I give him an extra ten for a tip to make up for my growl of a hello. "Girl issues, man," I tell him as an explanation. "Just you wait, kid."

He looks at me, his mouth parting as he scans me up and down. "You've got girl problems?"

I shrug. "I think so. I'm not sure."

"There's no hope for me, then."

He's scrawny and has a mountain range of pimples across his forehead. He probably doesn't have it easy in high school.

"What's your name?"

"Brian."

"Brian," I say. "You have some friends from school?"

He nods.

"How do you feel about some playoff tickets to the first home game for the Stars?"

"What sport?"

"Never mind."

"Wait!" Brian holds out a hand. "There's this girl."

"Right."

"I've been wanting to ask her out on a date."

"Give me your email," I tell him, "and tell this girl to mark her calendar. Do yourself a favor and have your mom buy you a new shirt before you go, got it?"

Brian takes in his own shirt, stained with fast food grease, and bobs his head so quickly his thick-framed glasses wobble on his nose. "Thanks. Thank you so much."

I hand him a pen from the drawer and he scribbles his address on the napkin.

"Good luck with your girl problems, man," he says. "I'm sure it'll all work out."

"I hope so, Brian. I hope so."

"One more thing," the kid says. "I need advice."

"On what?"

"How'd you get this girl in the first place?"

I think back to the first time I saw Annie, the first time she walked through the doors of that YMCA. I remember the way her eyes sparkled when I called her name and that swimsuit—that toxic green thing—glowed like a pool of alien vomit. She looked beautiful.

I shrug toward Brian as the events of the last few weeks, hours, days creep into my mind—from our first kiss to our first date to the moment she admitted to being my girlfriend in front of Coach. I almost forget Brian's there.

"Any tips?" he asks again.

"Sometimes, I guess you just get lucky."

"Cool." Brian nods, gives a half wave. "Thanks again for the tickets. I'll hook you up with some extra egg rolls next time."

The smell of Chinese food has my stomach growling, but I don't tear into it like I would if Annie wasn't around. Instead, I dig through my cupboards until I find the girly, stupid wineglasses Chelsea gave me as a Christmas set for *special occasions*. I'll have to thank her later.

I pull out another bottle of wine and uncork it, letting it breathe while I pop open a beer for myself. Then, I haul the shrimp and noodles and chicken and broccoli onto plates, and bring the feast into the living room. Once there, I look around for candles.

I don't keep candles on hand, but I do keep matches on hand, and I look for something I can light. No genius ideas hit me, so I settle on the next best thing. Flicking on the television, I flip to the channel that plays the crackling Yule log all year long.

Is it romantic? Probably not. But I suck at romance, and this is the best I can do on short notice. Even so, I feel like our first night together as an official couple should be something special.

Hopefully it's the thought that counts.

Chapter 34

Cohen

"Wow!" Annie pauses in the living room entrance. One glance at the image on the television and she winks at me. "A fire? You didn't have to go through all that trouble."

"I'm sorry I didn't have real candles," I say, busy placing forks and spoons next to our feast. "So hopefully this will do the trick for..." I look up at her, losing my place mid-sentence. "Annie. You are stunning."

She's beautiful, too beautiful for words. Her brunette hair trails in loose, damp waves over her bare shoulders, her feet moving soundlessly across the carpet as she steps toward me.

She's once again wrapped in my robe, and the way it's draped in loose folds allows a generous view of her pale skin. Her cheeks, pink and rosy from the shower, glow under the flickers from the screen.

She laughs, a light, tinkling sound. "But I haven't put on any makeup. Or fixed my hair. Or anything."

"You look incredible." I realize that I've stopped mid-table-setting, and a napkin dangles from my finger. I tuck it unceremoniously under the plate. "I can't even... I don't know what to say."

I take quick steps across the room, one of my hands sneaking between the folds of the robe and coming to rest on the lower curve of her back. She smells just as good as she looks, warm and sensual and feminine, and I want more than anything to taste her mouth on mine.

"Wait, Cohen," she says, as my other hand comes to rest on her cheek. "I need to tell you something."

"Okay."

"I didn't really need to shower."

I blink, not expecting that one. "Okay."

"It's just—"

"You can stop right there. I know what's got you worried." I let my lips dust a kiss against her forehead. "Us being together doesn't change anything. Come to me when you're ready."

"I need to explain why."

"No, you don't owe me any explanation."

"I stayed with him because it was *easy*," she says, her lip quivering as she speaks. "My ex was the first boy, the first man, I'd ever been with, and I thought it meant that we were soul mates. It's stupid now, in retrospect—"

"Hey, it's not stupid. You thought you were in love."

"No, I knew he didn't love me. I just thought..." She blinks, tears frosting her eyes with a sparkle of sadness. "I thought that having sex with him would make him want me. Love me. I don't know, I was young and stupid, and maybe I still am, but... I just don't want that to happen with us. I don't want to ruin things."

"Me neither. Give yourself a break, Annie. We've only been dating three hours. I can have some patience."

"You're not upset that I don't want to have sex yet?"

"No, but I *am* hungry."

"Let's eat," she says on a light laugh. "But first things first."

I'm about to argue because really—I'm frigging starving. Tonight, I've played a hockey game, acquired a girlfriend, and had a raging case of lust that's not going away anytime soon. I need to stress eat some damn Kung Pao Chicken.

Then Annie drops the robe, folds of fabric bunching around her feet. She's a goddess standing there, perfect in her near-nakedness. Her face beams innocence, the rawness of her nerves fully exposed as she watches me, steps toward me in a lacy thing that hugs her gorgeous curves.

I can't do a thing except hold my breath.

"Now that we're dating, I can touch you whenever I want. Isn't that the deal?"

"Yes, but—"

"Good," she interrupts. "Because tonight is all about you. And I plan on making good on that promise. Returning the favor a little after last time."

"That's not necessary. I'm not keeping score, and even if I were—believe me, I had as much fun the other night as you did, if not more."

She gives me a patient smile while taking dainty steps across the room. She reaches across the table to grab my hand, and with a gentle touch, pulls me toward the bedroom.

"Annie, you don't have to—"

"You have been so patient," she says, giving me a light tap to lay on the bed, "and I can't tell you how much I appreciate it."

I fall backwards onto my comforter and stare up into the eyes of the most beautiful woman. Her eyes are soft, sweet, yet as her hands reach for my waist and tug down my shorts, a bit of fire dances beneath them.

My fingers lock through her damp hair, slide down her shoulders and caress the impossibly soft skin of her back. The only thing she's wearing is a thin swatch of lingerie, which means every curve of hers is perfectly defined against my hands.

I get a grip on her waist, my fingers clenching tight as I pull her against me. She grinds her hips hard as her lips crash to mine, and I'm not sure I can last longer than the count of five. If the way she feels against me is any indication, I am completely and utterly lost.

"Thank you for understanding," she murmurs in a tight voice. "For being patient, for trusting in me, for giving me time."

I try to gurgle a response, but she's too quick for me. Her hands press against my chest and she slithers lower, her beautifully soft skin a caress against my body. I grasp for her arms and try to pull her up, but she's stronger than she looks. She stops, halfway, and meets my gaze.

"Stop," she says, her voice quiet, yet firm. "Let me."

"Annie, you don't have—"

The second her mouth touches my skin, it's as if I can feel my eyes rolling to the back of my head. Her lips, her tongue—every stroke is a testament to perfection.

My hands run through her hair, graze her shoulders, but I can't say manage a word. I can only hold on, my mind a black abyss of pent up desire, infatuation for her. It's not until the moment she pushes me over the edge that I can finally formulate a word. *Annie.*

Her name spills from my lips as she catapults me beyond anything I've ever known before. I'm convinced my mind has shattered into a million pieces.

Pulling her against me in the aftermath, I savor the moment as our hearts race, her breathing quick as I fight my stunned silence to find words. I can't, so I squeeze her tighter and hold my lips to her forehead, breathing in the heavenly scent of her.

Thankfully, my senses eventually reset. As my energy returns, I roll her over onto her back in one motion, while simultaneously dusting her collarbone with kisses. If she thinks the night is ending here, she's sorely mistaken.

"Cohen, tonight is about you," Annie says, her nails gripping my shoulders with a delicious strength that bites into my skin. "I didn't expect anything in return. Let me—"

"No," I say with absolute finality. The smell of her—the shampoo, her lotion, the very essence of Annie—is driving me wild. I brush a hand against her forehead, pushing stray hairs away from her face. "Let *me*."

Chapter 35

Annie

"Good morning, Amanda," Claude says. "How are you?"

I roll my eyes, refraining from a smart retort. "Thanks for coming, Clyde."

He doesn't notice the name change, but Gran does, and she snorts into her elbow.

"Did you pay?" Gran demands.

She sticks her hand out to Claude and wiggles her finger until he produces a five-dollar bill and hands it over. Gran, bless her heart, is in charge of the money. She's vicious in her responsibilities. She tried to make the janitor pay before he entered the room, and he was just trying to empty the trash can.

"The really generous folks give twenty," Gran says. "You're generous, aren't you, Claude?"

"How much do swimsuits cost?" he grumbles, digging for another ten to add to the stack.

I give him a grateful smile and load up his plate with a tower of pancakes. My mother returns to the kitchen just as he leaves to take a seat.

"What did I miss?" My mother asks, as the room goes silent. She re-ties the apron around her waist. "What are you two talking about? Not Claude again, I hope."

"Nope," Gran says. "Clyde."

"Mother! You *know* his name."

"Sorry," Gran gives me raised eyebrows. "*Amanda* started it."

My mother gives a huff of frustration. "Let's go. The rush for breakfast will start any second."

Gran's roped the whole family and half of the community into helping with this event. Even Leigh had planned to help, up until Dominic surrendered to a stomach bug and she had to call in sick. Already, it's been a hit. We've earned enough money for the swimsuits and are well on our way to earning enough to donate a large chunk to the local summer camp.

"So, Annie..." My mother resumes conversation in a sweeter than normal voice that has me worried. "I got the phone bill in the mail the other day. Did your father call you?"

I freeze, just as one glop hits the surface and begins to sizzle. "Why?"

"I'm your mother. I'm allowed to be curious. What did he want?"

"We're having dinner tonight! What's the big deal?"

"Oh? Twice in one month? Must be a special occasion."

"Nope." I blow out a breath, trying for patience. It's tough this morning. "He's just my dad."

"I never did ask. How did your last dinner go with him?"

I won't lie to her, but I won't play this game either. I flip pancakes in silence until the awkwardness is too much for Gran to bear.

"So, are you dating that hunk yet?" Gran chirps. "He's a nice looking man."

It's been exactly one week since I started officially dating Cohen, and I haven't exactly spread the word yet. It's been a busy week so, in my defense, it's not like a lot happened between us. His practice schedule has been crazy with playoffs coming up, and my exam schedule is equally nuts thanks to upcoming graduation.

"Boyfriend?" My mom's voice goes shrill. "You have a boyfriend, Annie, and you didn't tell me?"

"Keep your voice *down!*"

"Is he here?" My mother fans her face. "For goodness' sake, Annie. Do you keep everything in your life a secret from me? A *boyfriend*?!"

"It's only been, like, one week," I say in a hushed voice. "It's nothing serious yet. I didn't tell you because I didn't want you guys to make a big deal out of it."

"A big deal?!" Mom's still talking in that weird-pitched voice.

"I'm not making a big deal about it. I'm just wondering why you insist on keeping me out of your life?"

"I'm not keeping you out of my life—it's just new!"

"Is he coming today?"

"Probably." I flip the rest of the pancakes onto a plate and face them. "If you guys can't mind your own business, I'm going to keep things from you. Like this. Because you go and do things like look at my phone bill to see who I'm talking to—this invasion of my privacy is completely unnecessary."

"It's just because we love you," my mother says. "We care about you."

"Speak for yourself," Gran says. "I love her as much as you, but I'm not peeping at her phone bill."

"Both of you!" I cross my arms and try to keep my voice low, just between us. No need to ruin a perfectly good breakfast for everyone else. "I'm an adult, and I have been for several years. I don't need you looking over my shoulder at *everything.*"

"But—"

"Mom, I know dad sucked as a husband, but he's still my dad. It's up to me if I want to have dinner with him or answer his phone calls."

Gran stays silent, eyes averted, and even my mom stills.

My mother's back stiffens and she gives a short nod. "Yes, of course. Sorry."

"Mom, no... I didn't mean to upset you!" I call after her as she turns to head deeper into the kitchen. "Wait a second."

My mom pushes through a set of double doors into a small back hallway. I have to speed up and literally corner her before she stops moving. It's not until I grasp her shoulders and manually spin her around to face me that I see why she's in such a hurry.

There are tears in her eyes, and although she's trying her best to hide them, they're there, bright and shining like bits of broken starlight.

"Mom?"

Her lip quivers, but she manages to hold it together. My mother is a tough woman. I've never doubted that for a second—I'm just not used to seeing her cry. It takes me a moment to adjust, to gather my thoughts, and in that time I watch her do the same.

"I hate that your father didn't try harder when we were together," she says finally, tremors coursing through her words. "Not for me, but for you. For our family."

"It's okay—"

"It's *not* okay. He missed everything. Your ballet recitals, your flute lessons... he missed our *family* vacation to Mexico. He stayed home to work that weekend, do you remember?"

Reluctant, I nod. A part of me had pushed those memories away, blanked out the worst ones in the hopes that he'd change. There was always the hope that he'd change. To a small degree, I suppose there still is. Otherwise, I wouldn't be going to dinner with him tonight.

"I still love your father. He's the father of my child—*our* child." My mother's voice is hoarse, raspy as she flicks her gaze over my shoulder to make sure we're still alone. "But I couldn't stand to watch him break your heart over and over again."

There's a sudden lump in my throat, and I'm finding it hard to speak.

"It wore me down, grated on me over and over again for years. Do you know what it's like when your husband says he'll be home for dinner... when he tells his daughter to expect him that evening, and then doesn't show?"

"Mom—"

"I was the one stuck watching you wait for him on the front curb. Watching as the sun set, and he still wasn't there. Watching as your smile faded just a little bit with each car that passed and wasn't *his*."

Her hands ball into fists, a tiny bit of a tremor rocking her body.

"Always waiting, always smiling—somehow, you kept a huge grin on your face every time this happened for so long. Too long. You were *so* optimistic, honey." A memory of a smile warms her cheeks for a moment, but the memory ages her. Lines her face with those lingering worries, missed dreams, lost hopes. "Nothing could fix the look in your eyes, though, when you finally gave in. When I made you come inside for dinner with one empty place setting."

My mother pauses for a moment to run a hand across her eyes. She gives one dainty sniff, as if banishing the urge to show any emotion, and continues with dry eyes.

"That's why I'm with Claude now," she says. "I need a companion, a friend, someone who is there for me. I'm not looking for more money, more work, more... *things*. I just want someone's time. Their presence, a listening ear, or a hug. That's all I've ever wanted."

My mom's never opened up to me about these things before, and I'd never considered the pain she went through. Double the pain, in fact. The pain of losing a husband while her daughter lost faith in her father. I'd been selfish thinking I'd had it the worst.

"But you were always there," I finally manage to say. "I always had you."

"We were supposed to be a family. If these things had happened once, twice, three times—I'd understand. I'm a forgiving person, Annie, but hundreds of times? I had nothing left to give."

My mother's shoulders sag, and she looks utterly run down. Completely exhausted, as if the memories of these years have returned in full force. I'm hurting for her and, even worse, I don't know what I said to dredge everything up from the past.

"That's why I looked through your phone records. I was trying to protect you from more disappointment. I shouldn't have done it, I *know*. You're a beautiful, successful adult." My mother's eyes well up again, and finally, one tear slides down her face. "But no matter how brilliant and self-sufficient you are, you're still my baby."

My own eyes are smarting. I mumble something nonsensical, but thankfully, my mom opens her arms and gifts me a hug that takes care of any words I want to say.

"I know he missed your last dinner," she whispers against my ear. "He called that night to see if you'd come home, and of course I was confused. I told him I thought you were with him. We just want you safe more than anything."

"I'm sorry I didn't tell you," I murmur against her shoulder. "I didn't want to call you because it felt like you'd *win* or something, and I guess... I guess I didn't want you to be right."

"Honey..." Her arms rest on my shoulders, her fingers playing with the tips of my hair in the most soothing way. "I'm not perfect. But I'll always be there if you need me."

"Thank you for everything, mom, really." I let the smallest of smiles inch over my face. "For what it's worth, I knew I could always count on you. Even if he didn't show up, you did. Every time. You still do."

The smile on my mom's face shines a light across those years of exhaustion, adding a luminosity to her skin and turning her age backward. "I love you, honey."

"I love you too," I mumble through a very weird gurgling noise that occurs as I try to swallow. "I'm also sorry I didn't tell you about my boyfriend."

"Speaking of boyfriends," Gran says, apparently having eavesdropped from behind the double doors. "Hello, yes, I'm here. And I came to announce there's one huge hunk of burnin' love out there, and I suspect he belongs to my granddaughter."

My mother laugh-snorts, which makes me laugh-snort. Like mother like daughter.

"Well, I'd better find Clyde—" My mother stops, horrified, a hand to her mouth. "Oh, you little rats!" She points to my grandmother, and then me. "Look what you've done! *Claude*! Claude. *Claude*!"

"*What*?" Claude storms into the kitchen. "Who's calling my name?"

"How are the pancakes?" I ask. "They taste okay?"

"I'd give them three out of five stars." He nods. "Good work, Amanda."

"Thanks, Clyde."

By the time he leaves, my mother's shoulders are shaking with laughter, and my Gran's gripping the sink so hard it's about to fall off. Maybe Claude is *just* what my mother needs after all.

"You ladies are the worst!" My mother gasps. "Stop it! And get cooking."

"Wait, mom..." I grab her hand before she can grab her spatula. "Would you like to meet my boyfriend?"

Chapter 36

Annie

"Mom, over there is..." I hesitate as Cohen walks over to the door of the church basement and opens it for a flood of big, buff, grouchy-looking men that can only be his fellow teammates. "A heckuva lot more people than I expected."

"Which one's yours?" My mother surveys the crowd with an eager eye. "How did you meet?"

"You uh, you might recognize him," I say. "We met at the—"

My words are drowned out as the group's rowdy chatter grows in volume. Thank goodness Gran's not out here, or she'd have a ball as money collector with this many men flooding into her zone. For everyone's safety, we left Gran in the kitchen.

"Hey, sweetheart," a familiar voice murmurs. "I missed you this week."

Despite my blatant surprise, Cohen eases a hand behind my back and dips his head to brush a kiss to my lips. Just chaste enough to not offend my mother, just spicy enough to send signals down south.

"Cohen," I say, once our lips have unlocked. "Meet my mother."

Straightening, he doesn't remove his left hand from my back as he extends the right one to greet my mother. I'm surprised to find that I adore this about him, the fact that he doesn't care who is watching as he holds me to his side. Compared to an ex-boyfriend who wouldn't hold my hand around others, it's a welcome relief to find a man who's not afraid of a little public affection.

"It's a pleasure to meet you, Mrs. Plymouth. Thank you so much for the invitation to come this morning. I hope you don't mind I've brought a few friends."

"A few?" My mother can't stop grinning like a crazy person. "A whole herd, more like."

Cohen laughs. "I mentioned the event to Coach, and he did the rest."

I double-blink as the man known to me only as Coach, turns at the sound of his title and makes his way toward us. His gaze lands on mine, as if we share a secret. Maybe we do, I think, remembering the vending machine.

"Annie, is it? I believe we met once." Our hands clasp, and he gives me the faintest of smiles. "After the last game?"

"Pleasure to see you again."

"We appreciate the invitation. The Stars like to support local fundraisers, and as a bonus, pancakes make for a great carbo load." He gestures around the room. "We're heading straight to practice after."

"Well, I should get cooking then," my mother says. "Please find seats, and we'll bring your breakfasts shortly."

"Oh, hey there, hockey boys!" Gran appears suddenly, completely unimpressed at the fact that an entire NHL team is standing before her. "Did you bring your money? We say five bucks a head, but I'm thinking twenty would really go a long way to support those kids."

"Twenty bucks, everyone," Coach bellows to the team. "Let's go, fork it over, people."

"Oh, wow." Gran beams up at him like he's George Clooney. "I didn't expect that to work, but this is great. It's going straight to charity."

"How'd you get involved with this?" Coach asks Cohen.

"It's for our bathing suits." Gran snatches the money from his hand before he can possibly think about retracting it. "We're all doing a synchronized swimming competition and needed matching uniforms. We've already covered those, though, so this is for the children. Annie's boyfriend didn't tell you?"

"Why, no, he didn't mention it." Coach turns to Cohen, his gaze somewhat mystified. "I wouldn't have forgotten a detail like that."

For the first time since I've known him, Cohen's at a loss for words, his face coloring, eyes staring hard back at Gran.

"He just mentioned this was a fundraiser for the YMCA," Coach continues. "But please, do tell."

"It's my fault!" I say again. "I forced Cohen to join."

"You are..." Coach turned to Cohen. "Helping out with a synchronized swimming class?"

"Oh, he's not teaching it," Gran says, waving a hand. "He's performing in it."

Cohen's eyes close, and he looks like he might die.

"It's my fault," I say, weaker this time. "Completely my fault."

"Annie Plymouth," Coach says, an amazed look on his face. "You are one incredible woman."

"Seriously," Gran says. "She's my granddaughter. Pretty incredible! You should see her twirl in the water."

"Cohen will have to give me the details of the show." Coach lifts an eyebrow at his star forward. "I'd really love to see *this*."

"I'll send you the formal invitation." Gran pipes up. "Venue is the YMCA. We'd love to have you there. I don't think retirement organizations for synchronized swimming fetch much of an audience. We don't even wear them skimpy bikinis that look so good on the beach volleyball ladies. My granddaughter said *no*."

"I'll be there," Coach says. "Can't wait."

One by one, the players file into the room behind us, and I steal a moment to pull Cohen off to the side. My insides are squeezing with nerves. "Cohen, why? You didn't have to bring your whole team here! I didn't *really* expect you to show."

"Of course I was going to show." Already, the blush is leaving his cheeks. "I told you I'd always be there, and I meant it."

"Yeah, but this is... silly." I offer an apologetic smile. "I understand if you'd prefer not to do the competition thing with us. It was a stupid idea in the first place; I don't need you to do random stuff to *prove* yourself to me. I trust you."

"You..." Cohen pauses, his eyes searching mine. "You trust me?"

The words had just sort of popped out of my mouth without me thinking them. As if they'd been floating in my subconscious, just waiting for the moment to surface. I hardly realized I'd said the words at all.

"Yes, of course I do. You can back out, I promise."

"Back out?" He shakes his head. "Nah. I don't care what anyone thinks."

"But—"

"Hey, Boxer." Cohen gestures for one of his friends to join us. "Come here."

A huge man with a chipped front tooth and a wide grin lumbers over to us. "What?"

"I'm part of a synchronized swimming team with Annie and her Gran." Cohen grins. "We're doing a competition."

Boxer nods, chews on the thought, and then crosses his arms. "And?"

"Exactly. Let's go eat, Annie." Cohen grabs my hand, pulling me toward the table, but I dig my feet in until he stops and returns to me. "Something wrong?"

"Yes. No. Thank you," I say, and then I sigh before continuing. "I wanted to be in love before we took things to the next level. I don't know why, it's just the way I felt, and... I don't know. It feels too soon for love, but dammit, I think I'm falling for you, Cohen."

The look on his face is priceless, one of shock and awe, and maybe a little bit of disbelief. He glances behind him, sees people, and tugs me into the nearest empty hallway. Easing me against the wall, my back presses against the cold blocks while our every step is muted by the rich red carpeting.

"Annie, I'm already falling for you."

"We haven't even slept together."

As he presses against me, it's clear how he's feeling—mind, body, heart. When he speaks, his voice is husky, low, dripping with want. "Do you have any doubt that it'll be perfect, too?"

Suddenly, the desire for him rips through my body, spins my stomach inside out, and I can't wait any longer. "I want you, Cohen, so badly. Now."

"Not now, sweetheart," he murmurs in my ear. "Tonight. Tell me you'll be mine tonight."

"Yes, of course," I say. "Before, if possible. What are you doing after this?"

"Goddammit." His eyes are burning with a fire in them, the desperation there reflected in my own. "I have practice."

"I have dinner with my dad tonight."

He curses again, but I giggle and put my finger to his lips to warn him against swearing in church. "Come over after dinner," he begs. "Please."

"Yes."

Pressing his lips to mine, he holds me so close I'm warm from the heat of his skin against mine. Every millimeter of his body is hard, his chest, his abs, his arms—one of them presses to the wall above my head, the other tipping my chin so he can ease deeper into the kiss.

Then that hand slides down the wall, skimming over my shoulder to caress my breast. I'm wearing a light, pretty summer dress and the fabric is thin enough that he groans when he makes contact.

"A-*hem*." This loud, forced throat clear sends my swirls of heat spiraling into a place of burning embarrassment as we break apart.

"Coach!" Cohen says, sliding his hands away from my chest, the look on his face like that of a child caught peeking early at Christmas gifts. "Hello."

"Hello, James."

"Enjoying the pancakes?" Cohen murmurs.

"I am, actually. I just needed to use the restroom." Coach raises his eyebrow again—he's getting alarmingly good at this motion—and crosses his arms. "I don't care what happens when I'm not looking, James, but I expect you to keep your damn head on straight for playoffs."

"Yes, sir," Cohen agrees. "Of course."

"We need you him, understand?" Coach directs this question toward me. "Can you help me out on this?"

"Yes, sir." I nod, not quite sure what to do with my hands. He continues to stare at me, so I add on a salute.

"Did you just salute me, Miss Plymouth?"

"Yes." I wince under his stare. "Sorry."

"After playoffs, he's all yours," Coach says, his gaze locked on mine. "Have him take you on a nice long vacation—Mexico, maybe?—and get your own damn room."

"Yes, sir," Cohen says.

"Now, if you'll excuse me," Coach says, pushing past us, "I still need to use the restroom."

"I'm really sorry," I tell Cohen. His eyes are as big as saucers. "That awkwardness was probably all my fault."

"I don't know what to think," Cohen says slowly. "I'm even wondering if he likes us."

"Likes us?!"

Cohen gives a mystified shake of his head, and then loops an arm around my shoulder. "I've never seen him smile before."

Chapter 37

Cohen

"What do you think they're talking about?" I ask, loading up with more pancakes while watching Annie out of the corner of my eye. "I can never read women."

"Beats me. Maybe books?" Ryan says. "Boxer?"

"Not a chance." Boxer shakes his head. "Doesn't matter. I'm gonna go eat."

Boxer strides to a seat at the team table, leaving me alone with Ryan Pierce. Ryan is the team captain of the Minnesota Stars and, though we've had our fair share of disagreements, we're forced to be civil over the fundraiser breakfast this morning. Annie's grandmother has roped all three of us back here to the buffet table, and each of us is too afraid of her to argue.

So here I am stuck with Ryan, piling more pancakes onto our plates while trying to decipher what Andi Peretti—fiancé to Ryan Pierce—is discussing with Annie. The man's obviously got some skill with women because he's managed to snag Andi Peretti. I've very briefly met her before, and she seems like a good egg. Second best, of course, to Annie.

I watch the women for a few seconds more, but I can't read either of their lips. Instead, I sneak a glance at Annie's grandmother and, to my surprise, she's turned with her back to us. I take the opportunity to dump a few of the pancakes into the trash can.

"Nice," Ryan says, and does the same.

This is probably the most we've ever talked. Ryan is the poster boy for a Minnesota *good guy*. I'm completely straight, and even I can admit the guy's got looks. He has that wholesome vibe the internet has fallen in love with, and even Coach can't seem to find anything wrong with him.

Now, on top of everything, he has the girl, too. Andi's without a doubt a great match for him—funny, smart, beautiful, and very cool.

Up until today, I've always stayed away from Ryan, thinking he was a bit of a kiss ass, but now I'm not so sure. A part of me wants to know his secrets, how he's managed to have it all.

I want my cake, and I want to eat it, too.

But I'm not Ryan; I'm not *that* guy. My face isn't pretty, and I don't love dressing up in suits and going to events and being in the public eye. I've got scars and tattoos, and I can't suck up to the coach if my life depends on it. It just doesn't *work* for me.

What's really sickening about the whole thing, though, is that he deserves it. Ryan is, without a doubt, a good dude. He stays out of trouble. He's never been caught up in the hazing crap between team-mates, and he hasn't had one too many drinks at the bar and then slurred to the media. He hasn't been traded across the country be-cause people were tired of cleaning up after him.

Unlike me.

"Pierce." I clear my throat and fork a bite of pancake into my mouth. "I need your advice."

"Never thought I'd see the day." Ryan turns to me, his eyes nar-rowing on mine. "What happened?"

"Well..."

"Never mind." He waves his hand, following my line of sight to land on Annie Plymouth. "*She* happened."

I swallow my food, and then nod.

"I don't want to hear your bedroom talk, James, sorry."

"It's not about that. It's about... everything else."

"Oh, *shit*." A slow smile spreads across Ryan's face. "Relationship talk."

"Yeah."

"Annie seems like a really great girl." Ryan glances back over toward the table. Andi and Annie have their heads lowered in a private chat, smiles and giggles making their way across the room. "I mean, Andi seems to really like her. Andi doesn't just sit down and talk with anyone."

"Annie is a nice girl. She's perfect."

"So, what's the problem?"

"Me."

"Right." Ryan nods. "You want to become less of an asshole in order to keep her?"

"Pretty much."

"I'm sorry, man. I don't know if I have advice." Ryan crosses his arms over his sweater. "I just got lucky with Andi."

"Andi's great, and she wouldn't be with you if you were screwing everything up. What's your secret?"

He pauses, biting his lip in thought. "I've never thought about it. Life with Andi is just *easy*."

"Do you buy her presents? Cook for her?" I wave a hand before me, more awkward than I've ever been in my life. "What sort of shit should I be doing to keep Annie?"

"Well, that's where you're going wrong." Ryan shoots me a somewhat mystified glance. "Just treat her like a normal human being. Annie's smart and capable. Listen when she talks, do what she asks—you know, within reason—and then there's the last thing. But that's self-explanatory."

"The last thing?"

"Great sex," Ryan says with a grin. "That helps, too."

"Yeah, well." I tip my plate into the trash can, so absorbed in the conversation I don't notice the scathing look from Annie's grandmother before it's too late. "Unfortunately, I can't do much on that end."

"What the hell are you talking about?" Ryan gives my shoulder a light punch, his eyebrows furrowing with annoyance. "Don't be a moron, James. It's not that hard. Don't be selfish. Just make her... I don't know, feel nice."

"That doesn't work if she doesn't want to have sex." I glare at him. "*Capisce?*"

Ryan's shocked into silence.

"That's what I thought," I murmur. "Hence my crawling to you and begging for advice."

"You haven't had *sex*?"

"She's not ready. I'm not going to fucking pressure her, asshole."

Ryan's silent for a long moment. "I assumed—"

"You assumed I wouldn't be with Annie if we weren't hooking up, didn't you?" I try to control my temper, but it's not working. My blood is starting to boil, and I have to remind myself that I came to *him* for advice. "You think I'm not good enough for Annie, that I'm interested in the easiest target. Well, it's not like that. Not anymore, at least."

"Look, I'm sorry." Ryan turns to face me, his eyes meeting mine. "I didn't realize."

"You didn't know better," I grumble. "It's fine."

"It's not fine." Ryan reaches out, extends a hand. "I owe you an apology. It was stupid of me to assume."

We shake, and it's enough to call a truce. For the first time, my respect inches up a few notches for the guy. If his apology means anything, maybe he's changing his tune about me, too. Maybe it's not too late for us to coexist on the Stars without intense mutual dislike.

"She's..." I take a breath and wait until the pancake line runs back down to zero. "She's got some trust issues. Her dad is a tool, I think."

"That sucks."

"Yeah, and I'm trying to be patient, but I don't know what else to do."

"Any signs of progress?"

I think about the last few weeks—the way she stood up to Coach last week at the vending machine, the way she's been staying over more and more. The way she kissed me this morning, and the things she's promised for tonight.

"Yeah."

Ryan turns toward me and studies me, scrutinizes me with an intensity that makes me a little weirded out. "I've gotta admit, James, I read you all wrong."

"Lots of people do."

"I think you're doing just fine," he says. "For the record."

"You're not so bad yourself," I tell him. "For a suck-up."

"Okay, asshole," Ryan says with a grin. "As far as Annie goes, just stay the course. Let her come to you, and you'll be fine."

"I hope so." I catch a glimpse of white hair speeding our way through the crowded room, and my pulse races a bit as I warn Ryan. "You should probably get going. Annie's Gran is headed over here, and she's going to tear us a new one when she finds our pancakes in the trash can."

Ryan claps my shoulder. Before he leaves, though, he turns and gives me one last, fleeting smile. "I'll make you a promise, James."

"Yeah?"

"If you stay the course, you won't be sorry," he says with a knowing glance toward Andi. "Let me tell you, buddy, it's all worth it."

Chapter 38

Annie

"Good, they're gone." Andi Peretti, fiancé to the Stars' captain Ryan Pierce, turns a bright set of eyes on me. "Now we can *really* talk. How long have you and Cohen been seeing each other?"

Andi sent the boys back up to the buffet table for more pancakes, and now, we're finally alone. A group of us—me, Cohen, Ryan, Andi, Boxer, and one or two others—have been sitting together for almost an hour. Time has flown by, and it's a little scary to think, but I could get used to hanging with this crowd.

"It's new. We're new." I glance over my shoulder at Cohen, who's flanked by Boxer and Ryan.

Andi claps her hands. "That is so exciting! How did he ask you out?"

I'm too distracted to answer. The boys at the pancake table are unabashedly watching us, and it makes my face heat up under their gazes. "What do you think they're talking about?" I ask Andi. "They won't stop staring."

Andi rolls her eyes. "Boxer's probably trying to convince them we're talking about our boobs or something."

I laugh, turning back to Andi. "You and Ryan are so sweet together."

She clasps her hands to her chest as if she's having a heart attack. "I *know*!" She stretches the word out, pausing for drama before returning her hands to the table. Holding up a ring, she flashes the engagement sparkles at me. "I love him! And he is *so* great. But we're old news, and I want to hear about you and Cohen."

"I'm not sure there's much to say." I bob my shoulders up and down. "Everything is so new."

"Yeah, but that's when the fun stuff happens. Tell me one thing—is the sex awesome or *what*? Like, is it all hockey guys? Because I didn't know what I was missing until I met Ryan." She fans herself. "Thank God he ordered pizza, or my life would be *boring*."

"I don't know—"

"Don't you dare hold out on me!"

I glance around, and then lean over the table, lowering my voice. "We haven't had sex yet."

"What?! I mean... I didn't see that one coming."

"I know, I'm sorry."

"What are you apologizing for? I actually think a little more highly of Cohen right now."

"I waited at first because I didn't want to be burned. You know, another notch on the bedpost." I hesitate, feeling odd opening up to an almost complete stranger, but something about Andi inspires confidence. "And now I *am* ready. So ready, I'm just... I'm nervous."

"Oh, honey." She reaches across the table and grabs my hand. "About what?"

"I don't want to ruin things," I say, a tightness in my chest lightening as the words gush out, the fears I've been holding inside for weeks. "I *want* to think that I could date casually, but I know myself too well. I can't *do* casual. I've only had one boyfriend, and we dated for several years."

"Wow," Andi says. "Why'd it end?"

"He was..." I hesitate, searching for my canned explanation that I give whenever anyone asks. "We weren't..."

I stopped again. Somehow, I couldn't bring myself to say that we *just hadn't worked out*. Maybe I'd never really come to terms with what had happened in my previous relationship. Maybe I'd never even stopped to think about it.

I suppose I'd always assumed that we just weren't a good fit. That maybe I wasn't cutting it for him, wasn't exciting or sexy or spontaneous enough to keep the fire alive. Not that there'd been more than a weak flame, even in the very beginning.

"Oh. One of *those*?"

"He was a *jerk*!" I explode. It feels great to finally say it. "You know, I never realized it until recently, I guess."

Andi grins. "Until you met Cohen?!"

I give a shy nod. "I thought it'd been my fault that things didn't work out, but I'm not so sure anymore."

"Honey, I can tell you it wasn't your fault. I mean, everyone has flaws, but this guy sounds like an asshole, and you haven't even told me his name yet!"

"And now I've got all these feelings for Cohen, and it's driving me insane! I've never had these..." I gesture toward my stomach. "These...."

"Butterflies?"

"Yes!"

"That's a good thing! Butterflies mean you're doing something right."

"But it makes no *sense*. He's a hockey player. I want to go to law school. What if I go somewhere out of state? What if he's traded? What if he sees some beautiful fan outside the rink and decides I'm too boring? What if—"

"Hold up, there, Nellie." Andi raises her hands up, giving the signal to put on the brakes. "That's a lot of *what-ifs*. I mean, look at me and Ryan. We have a cross country relationship, and it wasn't always easy."

"But you're perfect for each other."

"If Cohen's perfect for you, then you two will make things work." She taps her fingers against the table. "Look, I'm just *now* beginning to trust that things will work out, and we're engaged. We've dated for months. The thing is, Ryan and I love each other. We choose to work at it every day, every month, every year. Once two people make that a priority, everything else starts to become clear."

"How do I know if Cohen wants those same things?"

"Well, you have to become a mind reader."

I squint at her. "What?"

"I'm *kidding*," Andi teases with a grin. "You have to ask him. There's no magical way to know. It's awkward at first, but it gets better. Ryan and I have been talking for so long now that I just blurt out whatever I want. Try me! Ask a question about our future."

"Where do you want to live?"

"I'm working in LA now, so we're doing some back and forth. Once we're married, we'll get a house here. My dad's going to let us build a condo over his newest pizza shop, so we'll have two homes and figure it out from there."

"Do you have a wedding date?"

"August 8th."

"How many kids do you want?"

"He wants five, I want three," Andi says with a good-natured roll of her eyes. "We'll see how that ends up."

"You guys are so adorable."

"I know," she says, giving me a wink. "Doesn't it make you sick?"

"When did you know you loved him?"

She pauses from her rapid fire answers, her eyes taking on a hazy sort of look as she glances across the room at her fiancé. "I think I knew... well, I knew really soon after I met him. Even before I admitted it to myself. The way he talked to me, treated me, even those little touches. It wasn't a *bang* moment of epiphany, it was all of the little things adding up."

"How long did you wait to have sex?"

"Honey," Andi says with a shake of her head. "That's a personal decision. You have to go with whatever feels right to you."

She's blushing pink at the memories these questions have brought back, and it's heartwarming.

I'm trying to think of another question for her, but she beats me to the punch.

"Do you love him?" she asks. "If he asked you to marry him tomorrow, would you say yes?"

"It's way too soon for that." A tingling goes down my spine. "I can't answer that."

"That's what your head says," Andi tells me with a confident wink. "If you want my advice, listen to what your heart says."

"I'm not very good at hearing what my heart has to say. What if—"

"There you go on the what-ifs again. What if Ryan's traded to Tampa? What if Ryan sees a puck bunny with bigger boobs than mine? What if I get struck by lightning and die tomorrow? You can't know these things. If you ever want to dive into a relationship, you just have to do it."

"I'm not much of a diver. I'm more of a toe-dipper."

"And I'm a belly-flopper," Andi says with a laugh. "Awkward and slightly painful to watch. But that's the charm in it—we're all different. Plus, Cohen's crazy about you. He can't keep his hands off you, and he's been staring at you all day."

"Seriously?"

"Hey, Boxer," Andi says loudly, widening her eyes and giving me the signal that girl time is over. "How's it going?"

"Fine." He takes a seat next to us, maneuvering his big form onto the chair. He bumps into the table and sends all of the utensils flying. "What are you ladies talking about?"

"Books," Andi says without breaking stride. "What'd you think we were talking about?"

"Damn." Boxer stands, shaking his head. "Don't tell Ryan that."

"Why not?"

"He's always right," Boxer says with a grin. "And I can't stand it."

"Oh, Boxer," Andi says. "He's so lovable."

"What about Boxer?" Ryan asks, returning to the table. "What did you just tell him?"

"No comment," Andi says, standing and hooking her arm through her fiancé's. "I think it's time for us to be going. Nice talking to you, Annie. You have my number now—don't be afraid to use it."

I stand when she stretches out her arms and leans in for a hug. "Thank you for everything."

"You too," she says. "Good luck."

Before I can turn around to look for Cohen, he appears behind me with a cup of coffee. "Your grandmother is going to kill me."

"What? Why?" I look up, catching his gaze. "Oh, death by too much food? Yes, that's a real threat with Gran."

"She loves Boxer, though. He's a black hole."

"Yeah," I say. "I like your friends."

"They're not so bad." Cohen says with a quiet smile. "Anyway, I have to head to practice. Will I see you tonight after your dinner?"

"Yes, please," I say, giving him a lingering kiss. "I can't wait."

He brings a hand around to the nape of my neck and draws me toward him, brushing a kiss against my forehead. "I'm going to embarrass myself in front of your grandmother if you keep talking."

"Better get going then," I tell him, my hands coming to rest on his sturdy chest. "Don't be late on my account, or your coach will hate me."

Cohen takes my hand in his. "Let me walk you out."

"I'm going to stay and help clean up. I'll see you tonight."

"One more thing." He takes one step away and stops in place. "What were you and Andi talking about?"

"None of your business."

"Yes or no question."

"Mmm?"

"Were you talking about books?"

I make the zip-my-lips gesture. "I'll never tell."

Chapter 39

Cohen

"It's me," I call through the dark entryway. "Dad?"

There's no answer. Instead, the sound of the television draws me through the small, cluttered house toward the living room. I step over a cardboard box crumpled in a heap on the overflowing trash bin; the beer cans that were once inside are now long gone.

"Dad?"

No answer again. I know he's here, somewhere. He's either ignoring me, or he's lulled himself into a drunken stupor again. I take advantage of the quiet in the house to swing into the kitchen and pop open the fridge. *Let's see what the man's been eating.*

The shelves aren't empty, but it's not a pretty sight. Jar of pickles, leftover containers of pizza and Chinese... something growing in the back corner that looks like it was once a carrot.

Disgusting.

I slam the door shut and stomp my way into the living room.

My old man's there, eyes wide open, watching an infomercial on a new ab workout machine. Not that he needs it—he's thin as a rail, despite his horrendous nutritional routine.

"What the hell, dad?" I gesture to the living room. A pigsty would be an upgrade. "What happened to Becky?"

"The bitch tried to move my shit, so I sent her packing."

"I *pay* her to clean your shit," I say. "She was supposed to do your grocery shopping, your laundry, your dishes—you know, the things that make this place liveable for a human."

"Yeah, well, I prefer to be alone."

"You can't handle being alone."

"When's the last time you stopped by to check on me?" My dad looks up, but it's only to gesture toward the TV. "Change the channel, will you? I've been watching this idiot on the Bowflex for an hour. The batteries are out on the remote."

"If you hadn't sent Becky away, I bet she would've gotten you new batteries." I move toward the TV, turn it off with a punch of my finger. "She's the third maid I've hired this year and we're barely into spring."

"If you helped out a little more, you wouldn't need to hire someone."

I close my eyes and take a deep breath. This was a horrible idea, coming here. I'd thought, for a second, that because Annie's giving her dad his zillionth chance tonight, I should do the same for mine. I already have regrets.

"I was here two weeks ago."

"Two weeks." He snorts.

"I'm an adult, dad. So are you. I'm not your babysitter. I have a career, I have a life, I have a girlfriend—"

I didn't mean to say the last part, but it just spilled out. Somehow, without my realizing it, Annie's worked her way into my list of top priorities. Right next to *life* and *career*.

"Girlfriend? I thought you were smarter than that," he says. "*Women.*"

"Wo*man*," I correct him. "She's incredible."

"Is she nice-looking?"

My hands are balled into fists. "I shouldn't have come here in the first place. I came here to... you know what? Never mind."

"What did you come here for, son?" My dad's fumbling for the remote, even though there are no batteries in it. I can see the opening where they *should* be from here, since he hasn't bothered to insert the backing. "You don't enjoy my company."

"You know, you're right," I say, and it kills me to do so, but I'm fed up. My mom took off when I was little, and ever since I *could*, I've been taking care of the both of us. Meanwhile, he's taken the opportunity to slide deeper and deeper into this mess he's created. "But you're my dad. My only family, and I thought you should know that I've got a girlfriend."

"You don't *do* girlfriends. You're like me."

"No, dad, I'm not."

"'Course you are. When's the last time you spent more than a few weeks with one woman?"

"I'm not having this conversation with you. Annie's different. She's special, and—"

"Oh, for Pete's sake—you're in love."

"Yeah, dad, I am!" My voice rises, and I'm practically shouting. I haven't even bothered to admit it to myself yet, let alone Annie, but when the words tumble out, I know they're true. "I thought you might care to know. You don't, so I'll see you later."

"What about the batteries?" My dad calls as I turn to leave. "How the hell am I supposed to turn the television on from here?"

"I don't know what to do anymore." I stop in the doorway and turn, my shoulders sagging, the familiar ache in my stomach now a hard knot. "I've lived here, and I've moved out. I've hired help, and I've done it myself. You won't even talk to me about what's going on here, so I'm done."

"When do I meet this girlfriend of yours?"

"You're not. Not like this."

"You going to marry her?"

I'm silent. I don't have a good answer to this, and I'm not up for debating the point with my father of all people.

"Good," he says, mistaking my silence as a *no*. "You're not the marrying type. Me and you, kid. We know. We get it. Women will never stand by you. They take off the second things get tough."

"It's not your fault she left. Mom ran off. It happens."

"I'm just warning you to be careful," he growls. "Otherwise, the next thing you know you'll end up with a kid, a ruined marriage, and an empty house. Is that what you want?"

"Look, dad. I'm really sorry I ruined your life." I take a deep breath to still the frustration, the fury, the sadness at this broken man into something more manageable. "I didn't ask for mom to run away. I didn't ask to raise myself. I didn't ask to be born to a dad who never wanted a son. I have a choice with Annie, and I'm not going to let her go. I'm not letting her see you like this, either. So, figure your shit out, or we're done here."

"Buy me some damn batteries next time, will you?"

I turn to leave and barely make it outside before I slam the front door shut and pound my fist against it. Nothing I do, nothing I say seems to get through to him. I'm beginning to think it might never.

But I'm not introducing Annie to this—not now, not ever.

The thought of Annie sends a ripple of worry through my spine. She's supposed to meet her dad in half an hour, and if I book it home, shower quickly, and shove myself into some clothes, I'll be there in time. Just in case. Because I know what it's like.

Annie and I might never figure out our fathers, we might never have golden, sparkly relationships with them. But what we do have, and what we can have, is each other. For tonight, at least, and hopefully forever.

"Rosa?" I dial my phone as I fly through Minneapolis traffic. "So sorry. He's done it again. Do you have anyone who can stop by for a cleaning at his place? You have my credit card. Tomorrow's perfect."

I make it home, still a smelly mess from hockey practice. My knuckles are bruised, but that's from my father's door. I haul myself into the shower and make quick work of cleaning up, but I can't stop the words rumbling through my head. My dad's words.

Are you going to marry this girl?

I chew on it, picture what that might look like. Up until now, I'd never believed in marriage. It hadn't worked for my parents, nor Annie's, nor plenty of others. To me, it didn't seem like a ring and a sheet of paper proved a whole lot of love between two people.

But, as the shower cascades over my shoulders and down my back, I picture Annie. I picture the two of us, together, years down the road. A house, a family, kids.

And suddenly, it's not so damn scary anymore.

For once, I like the looks of my future.

Our future.

Chapter 40

Annie

"Another glass of tea, ma'am?"

I look up from where I've been staring into a piping hot mug. "Sure," I say with half a smile. I don't bother to correct him on the use *ma'am* this time. "Thank you."

"Can I get anything started for you, or..."

I sigh, frustrated for the waiter, for myself. Look, I get it. The server wants his table back because he needs to make tips for the night, but him asking me ten times isn't going to help anything. It's been almost thirty minutes, and I need a few more. Just in case.

Reaching into my purse, I pull out a twenty dollar bill and slip it under the centerpiece, a gently flickering candle that has been my main source of entertainment this evening.

"Give me a few more minutes, please," I say. "And I'll be out of your hair."

He has the grace to look a bit flushed, but it doesn't mask the pity in his eyes. I wonder how often this happens; a girl like me sitting alone at a restaurant, waiting for a man that'll never come.

I wonder if he's guessing that I'm on a first date, or maybe that my boyfriend has broken up with me and left me out to dry. I wonder if it'll ever cross his mind that maybe, the person I'm waiting for is the person who's supposed to love me the most.

I shake my head and set back to work on the sketch I've doodled on my napkin. Hearts, lightning bolts, a stormy sea. I let my hand draw whatever it wants. I'm hardly thinking about it, which is why I'm surprised to find myself drawing the name Annie James there. I've drawn it three times and just now noticed.

The image makes me smile and cringe all in one. For all I know, Cohen's idea of a relationship is a two-week fling. He never talks about marriage, or the future, or anything beyond the now. I suppose like Andi said, I have to ask him. At the same time, I'm scared to ask because I'm terrified I won't like his answers.

Another waitress stops by to refill my water glass. I've been so nervous, I've inhaled the liquid as if it's my lifeblood—my courage—and because of this, I've used the restroom twice already. Another ten minutes, and I'll leave. I'll have been here nearly an hour, and that's long enough. He could've called. He has a freaking phone.

I'm not sure if he's forgotten, or if he's busy. If he's run into a problem at work, or something else. I'm not sure I care all that much.

"Sorry you're still waiting," the woman pouring my water says. She's pretty and young—late twenties maybe, a bit older than me. Old enough to offer a soft smile filled with empathy. "If I were you, I'd be drinking wine."

"Been there, done that." I offer her a friendly smile. "It doesn't help."

"Well, if I can get you anything else, don't hesitate to let me know." She takes one step away, pauses, and then looks back. "For what it's worth, he's an idiot. Whoever it is."

I nod and watch as she leaves, grateful for the ripple of understanding in a sea full of onlookers. And in the sea full of prying eyes and hushed voices wondering who I am, there's sympathy for the girl who waits for the man who'll never show.

I want to tell these people that I'm hopeful. That this will be the time he'll show up, but I can't. In my heart, I doubt it's true; I've learned the hard way. I know he's not coming, yet here I sit, and here I wait.

"Excuse me, ma'am, can I please take your order?" It's the waiter again, and though his eyes are filled with sympathy, there's a brusqueness to his tone that's begging me to give up my spot. It's a high-end restaurant—my dad's choice—and there's a line waiting to be seated out the door.

"Oh, yes, um..." I look down at the menu, a sheepish blush blooming on my cheeks. "I haven't looked yet. Please, give me one second, and—"

"I recommend the salmon. The sweet potato fries are also excellent." It's clear that he's not moving until I order something. "If you're looking for something lighter, the chicken salad is *incredible*."

The way he says *incredible*, it's with as much enthusiasm as if he's suggesting I eat dirt. My brain's not working, and neither are my reading muscles. I wave a hand. "Sure, fine. Whatever you said first."

"Salmon and sweet potato fries? Excellent choice, ma'am."

"Can I please get it to go?" I say, the blush on my cheeks spreading to the back of my neck. "And I'll take the check with it. Thanks."

He nods, finally having the grace to look slightly uncomfortable, as he retreats toward the kitchen. I take the moment to examine my napkins, the drawings there. The stormy seas shifting a tiny boat on waves too big to hold it. The name Annie James—foreign looking, foreign sounding to me—surrounded by squiggles and boxes and rays of sunshine.

I draw a line through one of them, my pen tearing so hard at the napkin that it rips the paper. I'm about to go to work on destroying the rest of the fantastical names when a hand clenches on my wrist and halts me in my tracks.

"Annie James?" A deep, husky male voice says from behind me. "Now, I like the sound of *that*."

"Cohen?" I gasp, turning to face the sound, finding the man behind it who stops my heart. "What are you doing here?"

He stands tall, wears a gorgeous suit—the severe black and white giving his face angles that hadn't existed before. His chin is strong, his shoulders wide, his eyes swimming with complexity as he leans forward and pulls the loose curls tumbling over my shoulders to the side. There, he presses a kiss to my exposed neck sending instant shivers down my spine.

I can feel the eyes of other patrons—those who've been whispering and waiting all evening—collectively inhale a breath. The waiter is back then, asking if he can get Cohen something to eat, something to drink. Apparently, Cohen looks like money, and the waiter senses a tip.

"No, thanks," Cohen says. "In fact, you can cancel her order, too."

"But—"

"I'm taking her home with me, and you can have your damn table back."

"The salmon," the server says weakly. "The fries."

"It's okay." I rest a hand on Cohen's arm. "Let's go. I'll just pay the check, and we can leave."

"No, I have dinner plans for you," Cohen says. "This isn't the place for us, sweetheart."

Pulling a wallet out of his pocket, Cohen retracts a fifty and hands it to the waiter, who makes an effort to look surprised.

"Keep it, cancel the order," Cohen says. "Sound good?"

The waiter nods, but Cohen's already directed his attention toward me. Hooking an arm through mine, he guides me to my feet and marches us toward the front door. He's either oblivious to the stares around us, or he's ignoring them. He's supremely excellent at pretending we're the only two people in the entire room, and I try to do the same.

He's grabbed the napkin from the table and, just before we head outside, he takes one glance at it. With a boyish grin on his face, he stashes it in his pocket. "Annie James," he murmurs to himself, almost giddy. "I like the sound of *that*."

I don't know how he does it, but even when I feel like crying, the man can make me laugh. "I was just doodling."

"I think you're an artist."

Once we're outside, Cohen approaches a valet, hands over a tip, and the man points to Cohen's waiting vehicle. We climb into the car, and I look over, trying to find a way to thank him. I end up stuttering and mumbling some nonsense as we pull onto the street, but he merely shakes his head and rests a hand on my lap.

I'd told him the name of the restaurant at the pancake breakfast, so I understood how he'd gotten there. What I didn't understand, however, is how he'd known my father wouldn't show.

"Thank you for what you did back there," I mumble, my hands trembling in my lap. "How did you know he wouldn't be here?"

"I didn't. I *hoped* he would be there when I arrived."

"You showed up anyway?"

"Of course," he says, giving me a quick glance before fixing his stare on the road. "I told you I'd always show up."

"What if my dad had been there?"

"I would've left." He shrugs. "I was Plan B for tonight. I only wish I'd been there sooner, but I was... taking care of something."

"Something?"

"Nothing important. I came as soon as I could."

"Well, I *really* appreciate it. It's not your job to show up because my dad can't be bothered to."

"No," he says thoughtfully. "It's not my job."

"But you did it anyway."

"Because I care about you, Annie. I didn't show up tonight because it's my job." His fingers tense on the wheel, his lips a flat line as he explains. "I showed up because that's what a boyfriend does."

"Yes, but—"

"There are no *buts* about it," Cohen says, an edge to his voice now. Not at me, but at something else, something beneath the surface. "When you're hurt, I'm hurt, and when someone breaks you, it's my job to put you back together. I wish I could protect you from everything, but when I can't, I want to be there to scoop up the pieces."

I swallow the lump in my throat, move his hand into my lap and squeeze it tighter. It's the only thing I can do. It's the only thing I have to give him now, and thankfully, it's enough.

Chapter 41

Cohen

It took every inch of my self-control not to give the waiter a taste of my fist as he tried to usher Annie out of the stupid restaurant. I wanted so badly to knock him off the high horse he rode in on, but I didn't because Annie wouldn't have approved.

It takes even *more* self-control not to march over to Annie's dad's house and give him a piece of my mind. Who in their right mind leaves a woman so beautiful, so smart, so incredible, sitting alone at a restaurant for an hour? An entire frigging hour? Either that man is the most selfish bastard on the planet, or he's clueless. I don't know which is worse.

All I know is that walking into that restaurant and seeing Annie swirling a teabag through an empty mug, doodling on a napkin while wearing a dress fit for the red carpet, made me ache. It made me ache in a way I've never hurt before.

Even in my own, very un-perfect life, I've never hurt in a place that feels like it can't ever be healed. The only thing that can get rid of this dullness is Annie and the smile on her face.

When she touches my skin, her fingers grasping my own, the annoying pain in my stomach lessens. This type of pain is worse than the physical sort—I've been whacked enough with a hockey stick to know how bruises heal. I don't know how to handle the ones on the inside, the hurts that I can't see.

She looks beautiful, I think for the zillionth time. I unlock the door and watch her move into my apartment. Her dress is red, short enough to show off her gorgeous legs, long enough to leave mystery as to what's underneath, and with just enough of a dip in the neckline to give a hint of cleavage.

Over her shoulders is a black furry coat, and I feel underdressed in my suit and tie. She belongs among the sophisticated, the movie stars, and I'm just some hockey-playing oaf that someone shoved into fancy clothes.

The way she moves is unique, feminine in her cautious footsteps. Her hips sway as she slides the coat from her shoulder and sets it, along with her purse-thingy, onto the kitchen island.

The dress is strapless, and the sudden peek of skin, her delectable collarbone, begs for kisses. It's too stunning for words, so instead, I pause for a moment and simply observe.

"I know it's not the best time, but you are gorgeous." I shouldn't be thinking about getting her undressed at a time like this, but it's nature. I'm a man. She's beautiful. I think I love her. It's simple math.

My arms stretch forward of their own accord; my hands reaching for her exposed shoulders. Instead of flinching, or pulling away, she leans into me, her eyes closing as my hands trail down her arms. There's a thin bracelet circling her wrist, and I toy with it for a second before latching onto her fingers.

"Look, I know we talked about tonight," I say. "But don't worry, I'm not trying to start anything, it's just that you blow my mind. You're insanely beautiful, and—"

She raises to her tiptoes and cuts me off with a kiss. "Why are you dressed like that?"

"Like this?" I look down. I'm not actually sure, except that she'd told me the name of the restaurant, and I'd recognized it to be a pricey one. "Just in case you needed a substitute dinner date."

She gives a little giggle, the sound music to my ears. "We didn't stay long enough to eat."

"I didn't like the waiter."

"Me neither." Her smile is shy and slow to bloom. "I think you look great. Very handsome."

"The suit doesn't make me pretty enough to stand next to you."

"Good thing you're not pretty." She moves in, wrapping her arms around my waist. "You're tough. And manly. And sexy."

Her fingers sink into my skin as she hugs me tight. It goes on for too long, and even though I can feel myself wanting her, it's more than that. When she looks at me, it makes me feel something. Something incredible.

When she pulls away, the absence stings.

"I'm going to, uh..." she hesitates, stepping away from me. "Use the bathroom quickly. I'll be right back."

"Annie, wait—"

"One second!"

I don't really have a choice except to let her go. I'm anxious, wondering what made her pull away from everything good happening. A part of me wants to knock and ask if she's okay. But waiting outside the bathroom door is creepy, so I force myself to back away.

I retreat to my bedroom and prowl for the next few minutes. I alternate between wrestling my hair into submission, checking it out in the mirror, feeling like a douche, and then mussing it back up out of frustration.

Finally, I fall back onto my bed and close my eyes, trying not to think at all.

"Cohen?"

When she calls for me, it's soft, almost angelic, and sweet. I sit up and blink, then I blink for a second time because she's standing in the door looking like a picture of paradise. She's freed her face of makeup, and her hair, loose and curly, tumbles over her shoulders. She's wearing nothing but my robe, and I'm speechless all over again.

Pulling the material close, she leans against the doorframe. "Thank you for being there, even though it's not your job."

"You don't have to thank me."

She nods, running her tongue along her lips as she takes one step, and then another, and another into the room. With each footstep, she lets her fingers trail down the edges of the robe, inching it open to reveal nothing but skin underneath.

My breath is stuck in my chest, and even though I want to tell her she's beautiful, I can't. There just aren't the right letters, the right words, the right phrases to capture her essence. The way she moves, the things she says, the look in her eyes. A drop of dew on a chilled morning, hopeful and so very precious.

"We don't have to do this tonight." My voice is gruff. "Come here, let me hold you. Let's save this for a different time."

"No, Cohen, I have something to tell you."

She climbs onto the bed, the fluffy fabric surrounding her body falls open, exposing only a black lingerie set. Even so, I can't look anywhere except her face. As I stare, I fall deeper and deeper into those pools of golden honey until I'm wondering if I can ever pull myself out.

"I didn't let myself sleep with you because I was scared." Her lip trembles, but she doesn't cry. Quite the opposite. She guides me back until I'm leaned against the headboard and she's perched next to me. Folding herself into a sitting position, she rests her hands on her lap, legs tucked beneath her bottom. "I didn't want to be a notch on your bedpost."

"You were never going to be that."

"I know, but you have to understand why I might've feared it. The rumors, the articles, your glamorous life in Los Angeles. I'm not glittery and shiny; I'm normal. I thought you'd take me to bed once and then leave me alone. I hate being alone."

"I *always* knew you were different. I knew that before we began."

"Different, maybe. But you couldn't have known you liked me."

"I knew I liked you," I correct, a smile creeping onto my face despite her wide, searching eyes. "From the first moment I saw you in that suit. You were funny and sweet and so much more. Don't you understand? I always *liked* you, Annie, I just hadn't realized I loved you."

We both pause.

Well, *I* pause.

I've said it. It's out there—I love her. Of course I love her.

However, if I had been hoping for a reaction, I would've been sorely disappointed. Annie continues as if she hasn't heard me at all, shifting herself closer, but I'm hardly listening.

Now that I've realized—and admitted—I love Annie, I want to tell her again, and again, and again until she's convinced of it. I want to show her, make her feel its truth.

Annie's still talking, almost as if she hasn't heard me. Finally, my attention is drawn back to her face as her eyes close, releasing a tiny trickle of tears through her lashes and down her cheeks.

I make them vanish with a touch of my lips. "Why are you crying?"

"Listen." She's determined to speak, arranging herself next to me in a bundle of limbs all wrapped around each other. "Cohen, I *know* I've made you work hard to get me here, and I want you to know why."

"You don't need to explain."

"I was trying to protect my heart from you. I figured you'd inevitably disappear down the road."

I flinch, but I don't respond.

"You have to understand, I had to—have to—protect myself. Nobody's going to do it for me." She presses a hand to her heart, the tears streaking down faster, faster, a pitter patter against my comforter. "But I made one mistake."

"You didn't do anything wrong."

"Maybe you're right," she says finally. "But I *was* wrong. You see, I can't possibly protect my heart when I've already given it away."

I'm trembling. My hands are shaking. I'm not supposed to act like this, but I can't help it. She looks so fragile, and I need to touch her, hold her. Spindly arms wrap around her legs as she hugs them to her chest.

"I love you, too, Cohen," she whispers with a vengeance, finally returning my confession. "And I know it's crazy to say, but I also know it's true. I want to be with you tonight."

"Annie—"

"Please."

It's a whisper, a feather drifting through the air between us before my will breaks, and I have to touch her. My fingers make contact with her skin. Her shoulders, first, as I drag my finger down curves soft as silk, knocking the robe from her arms.

"You are everything I've ever wanted," I tell her. "Let me kiss you."

She leans in, eyes still closed, lips parted just a sliver. It's enough for me to taste the sweet flavor that is Annie Plymouth. I can't imagine ever wanting another flavor again.

"Are you sure you want this?" I ask. "Absolutely positive?"

Her eyes blink open, bright and sure. "Yes," she says. Then she gives the slightest shake of her head. "We've waited long enough."

"I can wait longer."

"No." Her answer is swift and firm. "I want you more than anything, Cohen James."

Chapter 42

Annie

His eyes are molten at my words, dark and thoughtful. There's a spark behind his green irises, a window into Cohen James that's newly opened as he pulls me onto his lap, curling my body to his chest.

Hands rake through my hair, soft and gentle at first, then faster, wilder. Our mouths connect in a tangle of heat as his hands fall still, grasping my hair tight. I can feel him against me as my legs wrap around his waist, and the sensation of him there, the anticipation for what's to come mounts with each passing second.

When I part my lips to let him deepen the kiss, he groans, the note of pleasure sending shivers down my skin. Neither of us have much patience; as sweet as this moment might be, the tension between us has been building up for days, weeks, months, and it's dangerous.

When the promises from our kiss becomes too much, Cohen presses a hand to my back and flips the two of us around, laying me on the bed as he hovers over me. The scent of him alone is enough to drive me crazy.

"Your clothes," I murmur. "Take them off."

He doesn't need to be asked twice, losing his shirt, his pants, and the rest of his items— save for his boxers—in a matter of seconds. "Your turn."

"Me?" The robe has fallen completely open, so I shrug it off. It's useless now, anyway. All that's left is a lingerie set that I'd worn specially for him. "What's left?"

He doesn't seem to notice the lingerie, except to frown because it's blocking his view of whatever's underneath. He fiddles with the hook of my bra for so long I wonder if he thinks it's a Rubix cube, before he finally curses and adds a little force. It comes off, finally, then the panties, and then I'm naked.

"God, Annie, you are... even more beautiful than I could've dreamed." He grits his teeth, scanning me with an intensity that has me feeling more exposed than ever. "So gorgeous. You're a masterpiece."

His eyes are so piercing in their stare that I can't help but bring up an arm to cover my breasts. I give him a playful smile, as if it's all an act, but he doesn't buy it.

"No, sweetheart. Let me see you." He reaches for my arm, rests his fingers there, before gently pulling it away. "You have nothing to be shy about."

"But you're staring."

"That's what you do with a work of art, honey," he says. "You admire it."

My default is to lean into a smart retort, but Cohen seems to sense that too, cutting off my sarcasm with a touch of his lips against my throat. It's hot, tender, and when his hand comes up to my stomach and presses there, it steals the words from my mouth.

He moves his head down, cupping my neck with one hand as he continues his rainbow of kisses across my chest. When he reaches my breasts, he gives them equal attention, massaging, teasing with his lips, his hand.

He stills there, pressing his other hand firmly against my core. Then, ever so gently, he slips one finger inside me while drawing my nipple into his mouth. The motions, together, bring out a moan that's like no sound I've ever made before.

He knows just how to move, to stroke, to touch, pulling me toward the edge of sanity. I need to touch him, but the way he's situated my hands, they're pinned to the bed and clenching at the sheets. Eventually, my hands find his shoulders, latching onto him as my body arches against him.

Cohen lifts his head to find my gaze, my ragged breaths making it hard to respond. "Are you sure you want this? I will wait for you."

"No," I tell him. "We can't wait a second longer."

He nods, makes quick work of removing his last article of clothing and securing a condom, and then he's back, perched over me. "I've wanted this moment for so long," he says. "God, I love you, Annie."

"I love you, too," I whisper, and then I slide my arms around his neck and hold on as he presses inside of me. I bite back a cry as his name spills from my lips; the sensation of having him, all of him, sends ricocheting streams of fire through my veins.

His eyes are closed, teeth biting his lower lip as he, too, savors each and every pinprick of pleasure from this first moment together. Then, he moves. Slowly at first, gentle, as his eyes flash open to watch my face.

I meet his gaze with a needy whisper, urging him onward as my hips press toward him of their own accord. My fingers are digging into his back, the intensity rising with each beat we have together. The beats combine, forming a melody so vibrant, so filled with passion it pulses with wicked desires.

Cohen drives us toward the grand finale with a desperate crescendo. My eyes close, unseeing in blind ecstasy as his touches blur into one incredible rush. Just before the climax, we find each other in the midst of chaos, my eyes on his, our fingers locked in a spell that can't be broken.

And when the waves of passion begin to subside, the adrenaline receding, we're left with the golden dust, the aftershock of a fantastical symphony, a piece of art, of pure magic. Through doubt and fears we've wound our way here, together, and as Cohen wraps me tight into his embrace, I know this is where I belong.

Chapter 43

Annie

"You had sex."

"What?" I turn to Leigh. "You're crazy."

"Right," she says. "I'm the crazy one."

It's been nearly a week since Cohen and I slept together, and the ensuing days have been incredible. We've spent every night together. I flunked my first exam in four years of college. Worth it.

As it turns out, I love when Cohen kisses me: my lips, my stomach, my breasts. I can't get enough of him. Now that the dam has been broken, our need for one another is uncontrollable—a wash of excitement, thrilling cuddles, tender kisses, and whispered secrets into the wee hours of the morning.

"I feel like I'm sixteen," I tell Leigh, letting the smile burst free. "All those emotions! It's insane. I think I slept about five hours total this week."

"And you are still walking?"

"Not *all* of it was sex!"

"Right." Leigh pulls me in for a one-armed squeeze. "I'm so happy for you. He seems like a great guy, honey. Really. When I mentioned my son was a huge fan and wanted to play hockey this year, Cohen brought him a new hockey stick and signed it. I mean, Dominic died. Cohen didn't have to do all of that."

I give her a dramatic swoon. "He is something else."

We're the only ones in the pool area. Leigh is twenty minutes early because her kids were driving her up the wall this morning, and I'm early because Cohen had to leave in the wee hours of the morning for practice, and I didn't want to wait a second longer than I had to before seeing him again.

I glance around, ensuring the area is Cohen-free before whispering in her ear. "I made him wait a long time."

"I'll say. Was it worth it?"

"Worth it?" My heart does a flutter. "Oh, it was magic."

"God, I'm jealous." Leigh moans, as if remembering something similar once upon a time. "Well, enjoy it, honey. You deserve it. Savor these moments."

"These moments?" The way she phrases it gives me pause. "What do you mean? Do you think it's all going to end?"

"No, I didn't mean that, I just meant..." She trails off, waiting for me to interrupt. "Forget I said it. Look, I'm just a bitter single mom whose husband left her for a new model. I'm an idiot for even giving my two cents."

"I value your two cents."

"Well, here it is." She squeezes my knee. "You two are adorable together, and I know you'll get through anything life throws your way. Do you love him?"

I flinch.

"Oh, Annie." Leigh's eyes soften, her voice a cloud of comfort. "You've got it bad."

I nod, a pit growing in my stomach. "I haven't even asked what he wants for the future," I say, my voice rising. "What if this is a fling, a game for him? I know he says it's not right now, but what if he gets bored and changes his mind?"

"He can play games with anyone. You're not a fling girl. He knows it, you know it—you can stop worrying about that."

"What if he wanted a challenge?"

"Do you really think that?"

I hesitate, letting myself feel, remembering Cohen's arms around me, his lips pressed to my neck. "No, I don't."

"That's the only thing that matters." Leigh reaches out and squeezes my hand. "Only you know what's right. If your heart is telling you this is right, then it is."

I'm spared a response at that moment because the man in question strides into the room, a clipboard at his side and no shirt over his chest. A chest that I know so well—a chest that I've rested my head on, pressed my lips against, felt its weight over my body.

His face lights up when he sees Leigh and me sitting there. "Good morning, sunshine," he says to me. "Hello, Leigh."

While he turns to adjust the towel around his waist, Leigh hooks her arm through mine and lowers her voice. "You've got nothing to worry about."

"You think?"

"He's smitten."

Chapter 44

Annie

"It's time to practice the big twirl. The ultimate twirl. The only reason we have this stud here is for this stinkin' twirl." Gran gestures toward the group of old women—and me. And to everyone's amazement, Cohen is in the water, too. "Did you watch the video I mailed you, Mr. James?"

"How'd you get my email?" Cohen looks at Gran. "No, sorry. I didn't see it come through."

"Not email, you goon," Gran says. "Through the mailboxes. I sent you a VHS."

"A VHS? Why would you send me a VHS?"

"Because I recorded the Olympics twenty years ago, and we only had VCRs at that time. You were supposed to watch it and learn the moves."

"We're not going to be able to do that, Gran," I say. "First, because neither of us have a VCR. Secondly, because this isn't the Olympics."

"Fine." Gran expels a long, loud breath. "I suppose that's fine. I came up with an alternate plan just in case."

"Let's stick with the original plan," Lottie says. "Charlie Hubert will be there, and I want to look good for him. He's been asking if I'll help with his laundry for weeks, and I think this might be my big chance to move our relationship to the next level."

"Once he sees you in that swimsuit," Gran says. "He'll be drooling all over you. Original plan it is. Pay attention, Annie and Cohen. I'm only demonstrating once."

Cohen and I watch as Gran spirals through the water, splashing more than she's twirling.

"Got it?" When she finishes, she extends one hand and puts it firmly on my butt. "Cohen, you'll have to support her like this while you twirl."

"I can do that," he says. "I like this class."

"Of course you do," Gran says. "You get to touch—"

"Gran!" I say. "We get it! Let's practice."

"Like this?" he asks cheerily, looking at Gran as he takes a healthy squeeze of my rear end. "Am I doing it right?"

"A little too right," Gran says. "Looks like you've had some practice."

I close my eyes, wishing suddenly for the water to swallow me whole. I thought I'd been doing Gran a favor today by staying late after swimming lessons to practice. The synchronized swim team had rented the pool for an hour extra, and it was the first and last time we'd get a full rehearsal before the event.

"Move it along, folks. Let's see the twirl." Gran gestures for Cohen to lift me up, spin me in a circle, and then throw me back into the water. "It'll be beautiful. So beautiful."

"He's throwing me across the pool," I argue. "It's hardly beautiful."

"But there's a twirl," Gran says. "Like a flower."

I'm rolling my eyes when Cohen latches on firmly. As instructed, he lifts me near his shoulder, turns in a circle, and then drops me into the water. It's a good thing I'm wearing floaties and have a smoking hot swimming instructor next to me, or I'd be panicking.

Also, the water is only four feet deep, so that helps to keep the panic at bay. In fact, it's almost exciting. I'm barely terrified of drowning. Proudly, I plant my feet on the floor and propel myself up through the surface of the water with a broad grin on my face.

We've done it. We've completed the twirl.

My smile turns slightly dimmer when I realize the room is silent. Shouldn't people be clapping? I mean, the twirl wasn't *horrible*. Maybe it wasn't as beautiful as a flower, but still. It's an accomplishment.

Suddenly, it hits me that not one person is staring at my face. Not a single person.

I take one look down—at my very bare chest—and shriek.

I don't even feel embarrassed. There's no *time* for embarrassed. Somehow, when Cohen tossed me from his shoulder, he snapped the string of my suit, and the whole top vanished. It must have landed three feet away because it's bobbing like a sad little fish in the distance.

I lunge toward it like a crazed woman while Gran grins at her friends.

"She got those from me," Gran says proudly, nodding in my direction. "Nice, huh?"

Cohen clears his throat and leaps to attention, fishing the top of my suit from the water before I can get to it. My arms are too busy trying to control the whole nude-in-public situation.

"Here, so sorry," Cohen says, stepping close, shielding me as much as possible from the audience of curious women behind him. "Let me help."

"You can't help," I hiss. "It's broken!"

He glances down, the realization dawning on his face as he sees one triangle in one hand, and the other drifting away in the pool. "Oh, *no*. I owe you a new suit."

"Ya think?"

"Good thing I brought you a backup," Gran says. "That bright green beauty from the first day of class is in the locker—go get it. We'll practice once more before Cohen has to leave."

I swipe the single triangle from Cohen's hand with one last glare around the room, then pull myself out and stomp carefully toward the exit.

"I'll help her." Cohen jumps out after me, grabbing a towel on his way, and follows without a word. "Here, let me cover you up."

"You couldn't have waited a few hours to get home?" I say under my breath, once we're out of the pool area. "You had to undress me in front of my elders?"

"It was an accident. I owe you big time."

"Yes, you do."

"How can I make it up to you?"

"Come to my mom's wedding with me."

"What?" Now Cohen's mouth is hanging open, and I'm pretty sure mine is too.

"Nothing. Sorry, I'm going to go change." I try to move past him and forget my invitation, but he blocks my progress. I try again. "*Excuse* me."

"Do you want me to be your date to the wedding?"

I inhale a shaky breath. "I hadn't meant to ask you standing here, like this, but... I've been thinking about it. Unless—"

"I would love to come."

"It's not too soon?"

"Are you kidding?" He looks pointedly at my chest, now covered by the towel. "I've been dreaming of getting you on a cruise ship since you mentioned it."

"Really?"

Cohen reaches forward and drapes an arm across my shoulders. He curls me into his body, giving me a kiss that melts my bikini bottoms right off. Nearly.

Until Gran whistles, and Cohen steps backward as if he's been burned.

"I'll go change," I say, slipping away from him and into the locker room. "But I didn't forget about your offer of a new bathing suit. You're taking me shopping."

"Shopping?"

"Shopping."

Chapter 45

Cohen

I don't know how she does it, but Annie Plymouth makes that strange little swimsuit shine like a ballroom gown. Or something. She looks freaking incredible in a suit that'd normally make me nauseous, like a Tilt-a-Whirl or one of those Funhouse mirrors.

There's a bit of guilt over breaking her bathing suit, but at the same time, I can't seem to make the feeling stick. Because it got me an invitation to her mother's wedding, and the thought of being there with her, on a cruise ship, has me grinning like a lunatic.

Annie's already mentioned that she's the maid of honor, and thinking about seeing her in a dress like that has me all worked up in a way that's inappropriate at a synchronized swimming routine. For retired women. I try *not* to visualize taking that dress off her, kissing every inch of her skin under the Caribbean sun, but it's hard. In so many ways.

"Okay," Annie's Gran calls. "I think we can wrap up for today. Can I get a picture with the group?"

"Sorry," I say gruffly. "Gotta go. Coach wants me early to practice."

"But—" Gran says. "Pictures!"

"Sorry," I whisper to Annie. "I've gotta go."

"No picture?" she asks.

256

"You don't want me in a picture. Trust me."

Annie takes one look down, turns a bright pink that brings out the neon in her ruffles, and nods. "Hey, Gran, let's take the picture later. In our costumes."

"Fine," she says. "I suppose it's better to have matching suits anyway. See you, Cohen."

I pull myself out of the pool and wrap a towel around my waist before turning to wave at the ladies, who all finger-wave back. Then I give eyeballs at Annie until she climbs out of the pool and walks me to the door.

"So," I begin. "When can I see you?"

"What are you doing tonight?" She gives me a playful smile. "I'm free if you are."

"That's what I like to hear." I let my hand rest on her shoulder, and my fingers develop a mind of their own. Sliding down her arm, to her wrist, then a quick hop over to her hip. "Sweetheart, I have twenty minutes to kill if you want to meet me in the showers."

"Later," she says. "I promise."

I groan. "Are you sure?"

She leans in, presses her body against mine, and it doesn't do anything to help with the situation in my pants. "I'm sure."

"You're cruel, and I love you."

"I love you, too."

With a devilish grin, she disappears into the locker room and leaves me alone with my daydreams. I can't seem to think straight, and all I'm sure of is that tonight is seeming too far away.

Chapter 46

Annie

"This is going to take like, twenty minutes, right?" Cohen asks, casting a skeptical gaze around the mall. "When I said I'd buy you a new bathing suit, I meant that I'd give you my credit card. Not that I'd go shopping *with* you. I'm not much of a shopper."

"Come on! It's fun. And, we're celebrating."

"What are we celebrating?"

"Me! You!" I smile as Cohen pulls me into his arms, my sunny yellow dress billowing around my knees as he wraps me in a hug. "I passed the class. *Your* class."

Cohen gives me a peck on the forehead. "Yeah, but don't you think that sleeping with the teacher gives you a leg up?"

"Ah." I wink. "Sure does."

Cohen trails off, and I can see him thinking about legs bent up in suggestive ways. I let him think it through for a long minute, mostly because I enjoy being pressed against his chest where he's got me in a hug.

We're at the mall, now, in search of a new swimsuit that I can bring to my mother's wedding festivities. I'm not a huge shopping queen, but Cohen offered to take me after our swimming class. He came out of the locker room this morning wearing these black jeans that round out every part of his lower half, and a white tee that's simple, soft, and just sexy enough to turn every woman's head we pass. I changed my mind. With the right company, the mall's not so bad.

Especially when Cohen is completely oblivious to all the neck-cricking and sideways glances from other women. Holding my hand, ducking me into dark corners for stolen kisses—Cohen knows how to make a girl feel special. It's almost dangerous.

I graduated from swimming lessons today, much to my mother's approval. Gran was there, too, as Cohen handed out those stupid certificates, and yes, she'd worn her *Go! Annie!* socks. Even though the whole thing was silly, it'd felt good to graduate. Me, Leigh, and Jason.

I'd even treaded water for a minute and swam up and down the stupid pool because I didn't intend to pass only as the teacher's pet. Sure, I swam doggy paddle, and yes, I looked like a drowning bird, but I'd done it.

I'm basically Michael Phelps.

Minus the abs.

Minus the ability to eat ten thousand calories per day and not balloon like an elephant.

"Okay, so where are we going for swimsuits?" Cohen breaks my train of thought. "Is there like... a women's swimsuit store?"

"Here." I pull him into one of the large department stores and weave him through the shoes, the jackets, the bras and pajamas until finally, we reach the summer section. "*Tada!*"

Cohen looks at the wall full of swimsuits, agog at the plethora of options. He takes them all in, shakes his head, and finally turns his stare on me. "All of these perfectly functional options, and yet somehow, you managed to select the two worst swimsuits to wear to class?"

"The green ruffles suit was all Mom!"

"And the burlap sack?"

"Yeah," I say with a grin. "That one was me. Told Gran to make me look like the biggest, ugliest spinster ever so that you wouldn't want to get involved with me."

"And how did that work out?"

"Well..."

"Oh, come on," he says, pulling me into his arms and backing me into a clothing rack. "You know exactly how well that went, judging by the smile you had on your face this morning."

I can't help the blush that creeps up my neck, or the wobbliness in my legs at the memory of this morning. A shower that was worthy of folktales. We've been dating for several weeks now, and each week is somehow better than the last. If things keep progressing at this rate, I'll be a puddle of bliss by autumn.

Now that we're finally together, it's almost an obsession. I don't think we've gone out with friends in over a month. The couch, the bed, the shower—now, they've seen plenty of action, not all of it romantic. Last night we'd watched a movie and hadn't even fooled around. Much. Until this morning. However, judging by the way he's stumbling around and playing with my hair, the morning is already forgotten, and he's ready to go again.

"Grab a suit."

"What?" I glance up at him. "I haven't gotten the chance to look yet."

"Grab a suit. Any suit."

Cautiously, I extend a hand and reach for the nearest one. I hold it up, waggle my fingers, and raise my shoulders. Turns out to be a maternity suit. "What now?" I ask, curiosity piqued. "What do you want me to do with *this*?"

Cohen clearly doesn't care what sort of suit it is, as he gives me the thumbs up. "Come with me."

He pulls me toward the fitting room, casting a shifty-eyed glance around the place before we sneak into it. There's no front desk attendant, no one stocking clothes, no one else in the changing area. It's a complete ghost town, which must be a bonus to shopping on a beautiful Saturday afternoon.

It's all peace and quiet until Cohen pulls me to him, lowers his head to mine, and whispers in my ear. I'm turning hot and bothered as we crash into one of the fitting rooms.

"All morning through lessons," Cohen says. "I couldn't keep my hands off you, let alone my eyes."

"I was wearing that horrible old suit."

"I wasn't looking at the suit." He locks the door behind us, guides me onto the seat in the corner. "Let me kiss you, sweetheart."

"Like I'm going to say *no* to that."

Cohen unzips my sweatshirt to reveal a thin black camisole. There's no bra underneath which, in my defense, isn't on purpose. I'd forgotten to bring an extra to change into after swimming, leaving me to go without. Cohen doesn't seem to mind this development for obvious reasons.

Letting his hand linger at the tiny spaghetti straps, he lowers one before tiptoeing his fingers across my collarbone to the other. He slides that one down, too, until my breasts spill over the edges. His hand inches lower, little by little, until he's moving in a way that has me closing my eyes and leaning against the wall for support.

After a morning spent at the pool, forced to keep our hands off one another, the tension has built up, zipping between us with the ache for more. I've never done more than kiss in public—a peck on the cheek with my ex, maybe, so this is new to me. There's something thrilling about Cohen needing me now, here, and I can feel the logical, practical side of Annie disappearing like magic.

"Are you doing okay?" he asks, his voice gentle in my ear. "Because I don't want to stop."

"Yeah," I mumble. "I'm great. Carry on."

Fortunately, Cohen's become an expert at unbuttoning my jeans and getting them over my hips. He leaves the lacey black panties on as he spins me, wrapping a hand around my waist and pressing into me as I rest a hand against the wall.

I catch a view of the both of us, entangled, in the mirror—and it's perfect. When his eyes meet mine, an intensity runs through me, and I shudder, my senses more in tune with my body than ever before.

His fingers play over the fabric as he whispers all sorts of suggestions into my ear, the mere sound of his voice sending shocks of pleasure racing across my skin. His fingers continue their dance across the silky fabric, teasing, toying, and I'm surprised to find the low murmurs of delight are sounds coming from me.

"Cohen," I whisper, as one of his fingers slides underneath the fabric. "I don't think we should do this here."

"But you're so ready, sweetheart." He groans, his finger circling my opening. "I'll make sure we're quiet."

"Yeah, but..." I trail off as he begins with the small swirls, the ones he knows drive me crazy. My hands curl into fists, and there's no chance of arguing now. I'm past the point of return, past the point of caring that we're in the mall, past the point of worrying whether or not people hear us, until—

"How's that working out for you in there?" A woman calls through the door with a strong Midwestern drawl. "Need a different size, honey?"

I glance at Cohen in a panic, yanking my undies up and giving him a light shove away. "Uh, yeah!" I call. "I mean, *no*. Everything fits... uh, perfectly. Thank you."

I wave wildly for Cohen to jump on the bench; if the attendant cares to peek under the stall, she'll definitely see a set of large male feet. I'm pretty sure this is a women's dressing room, but then again, I was too distracted to check.

"Great!" she chirps back. "Well, I'll be waiting right here. My name is Sharon, so just holler if I can help you with anything, dear."

"Aw, hell, Sharon," Cohen murmurs.

I glare at Cohen, trying to make him evaporate outside with my mind, but it doesn't work. He capitalizes on my silence, brushing a hand low, tenderly over my bare stomach that sends erotic thrills straight to my core. For a brief moment, I wonder if we can be extra *extra* quiet—no doubt, he'd make the risk worth it.

Then Sharon ruins everything. Freaking Sharon. She starts humming *Yankee Doodle* just outside of the stall, and this brings back logical Annie with the force of a typhoon.

I can't get arrested for having sex in a department store dressing room. I want to be a lawyer. To graduate from college. I can't risk these achievements, not even if Cohen's promising amazing orgasms in the meantime.

"Let's go," I mouth to Cohen, peeling his hands off my lady parts. "I'll run out first. You can do the walk of shame later."

"But—" He trails a hand down my back. "You haven't gotten your suit for the cruise yet."

"We'll find a different store. Unless you want to get yourself ten more weeks of community service at the YMCA because of Sharon."

"Will you be there again?" He raises an eyebrow, reluctantly pulling me to my feet. "Because that doesn't sound like a half bad punishment."

"Come on." I haul him to his feet and cautiously open the door. Sharon's temporarily distracted by another customer, and I wave for Cohen to follow. "I have another idea."

Chapter 47

Annie

Two hours later, I've got three swimsuits, a sundress, and no orgasms.

The rest of our shopping trip was relatively uneventful which, I suppose, is better than getting caught in the dressing room. Cohen tried to sneak into the stall at Victoria's Secret, but they run a tight ship over there and made him wait outside of the dressing rooms. *Busted.*

After a late lunch, we started home, but I changed my mind and instructed Cohen to take a detour. We arrived at the lake a few minutes ago, parked, and wandered near the beach. I guided us to this lake for a particular reason, and when he looks over at me, I can see he understands why.

"This is where you fell through the ice."

"I haven't been back here for awhile. But I guess..." I trail off. "I just wanted to show you. I thought maybe if I jumped in again, it'd prove something to myself. Maybe I wouldn't be so terrified of water anymore. It's stupid, I know."

"It's not stupid. Plus, you're an expert swimmer now."

"Fast track to the Olympics."

"Thank you for bringing me here." Cohen stares out at the lake as he speaks, softly and unhurried. "It's beautiful."

I step to him, unable to resist the image of him against the horizon. He's more gorgeous than any sunset I've ever seen, and I hook my finger over the edge of his pants to pull him in for a kiss. My fingers walk up his arm, decorated with ink, before sliding around his neck.

"I think..." I give a one-shouldered shrug. "I think I brought you here because you take away all my fears. When I'm with you, it's *easy* not to be scared."

"I'll always be here for you." Cohen brings both of his hands up to my face as he steps back from me, watching my eyes for a long moment. "I love you."

"Always?"

"Always."

"How can you say that?" I can feel the overwhelming urge to spill my guts cropping up whether I want to or not. Words topple into one another until I can hardly understand myself. "I'm not trying to pressure you, but I have to ask. To know. What do you want for the future?"

"The future?"

"Do you see yourself in Minnesota? What about marriage, kids? I'm not talking now, but down the line. Years away."

"I haven't thought much about it," he says, slow and a bit unsteady. "I just know that I want you. Isn't that enough?"

"It is..."

"But?"

"But I can't *help* that I think about these things. I know it's early on, but when you promise you'll be there forever, it makes me scared. What is *always* for you? A lifetime?"

"I don't know the answers, Annie. I *do* know that I'm not scared to say I want to be with you. If that means marriage, or kids, or whatever... we'll figure that all out in time."

"Right, of course. I just—"

"No, Annie, I'm sorry." Cohen runs his hand through his hair and reaches for me. "I don't know how to say what I feel for you. I love you, and I want to be with you. I've just never been with a woman who makes me *want* to think about the future. It's new to me still, but that doesn't mean I don't want it."

I can only manage a nod. It's enough and it isn't, all at once.

"Come here." He pulls me into a hug, his fingers running soothing lines through my hair. "Look, everyone's gotta jump into the unknown sometime. I would rather do it with you than anyone else. I'll think about it, I promise."

I hold onto him like a lifejacket, pressing a kiss to his lips in the hope that he'll understand how wonderful he is. That he'll understand how much he means to me, to my heart, to my life. I am starting to picture him in the future and, as terrifying as that might be, it's also exciting.

"Speaking of jumping in..." I back away, sliding my pants down around my ankles. I have one of my new swimsuits on underneath, and as it's nearly sunset, the private little beach is deserted. "I'm going to go for it."

"Can I help you?" Cohen's eyes are on my legs. "Er—go with you, I mean?"

I straighten myself and pull off my shirt. The breeze is warm, but my skin shivers with goose bumps. I shake my head. "I have to do this for myself."

Then I begin my march to the end of the rickety old fishing dock with my chin tilted high. I don't stop my forward progression for a second because if I do, I'll be running back to the car.

Timing my breaths with my footsteps, I watch the end of the dock get nearer and nearer still with every pace.

Three more steps, and then two.

Then one.

I close my eyes, suck in oxygen, and take a flying leap.

There's a splash. Sudden darkness. A brief flirtation with panic, and then my feet hit the cool sandy bottom of the lake. I press my toes into the sand, little tornadoes swirling across my skin as I propel myself upward.

"Seriously?" I spit out water as I break through the surface. The water's up to my chest. "I remember it being deeper than this."

Cohen's face is a mask of concern, but at the look of surprise on my own face, he throws his head back and laughs. I grin, too, before a shiver rocks my body and the wind suddenly feels cold.

"Come up here," Cohen says. "I've got a blanket to wrap you up in. Let's get you warm, Michael Phelps."

I drag myself out of the water, elated at the lack of fear I felt when underwater. I still don't *love* swimming, and my doggy paddle leaves a lot to be desired, but something is different, and this gives me a boost of confidence. Enough confidence to pull Cohen in for a kiss, clutching his shirt with my hand as his tongue slips past my lips and searches for more.

"Jesus, Annie," he says, eyes widening. "You need to jump into lakes more often."

I grin back. "I guess so."

Maybe it's adrenaline speaking, but I can't seem to stop.

"Cohen," I whisper, stealing a glance of the abandoned lake. "I want you. Here, now."

We're on a small beach, tucked into a cove of trees only accessible through a tiny path. We will be able to hear anyone coming from a mile away, thanks to the crackling of sticks and the quiet of the isolated area. There's only the ripple of water, the stream of sunlight, the lapping of the water on the shore to keep us company.

Cohen doesn't need asking twice. He doesn't give me a chance to change my mind or doubt the urge. Instead he takes control and reaches out, lifting me so that my legs wrap around his torso, and I cling to him like I'll never let go.

I'm soaking wet from the lake, but he doesn't care. One of his hands is pressed against my back, the other holding me up from the bottom. Without letting go, he eases to his knees and shifts the blanket open in one motion, laying me down with a gentleness I hadn't expected from the hockey star.

"You are..." He presses a kiss against my lips. "The sweetest thing."

"I was going for sexy, but I'll take it."

"The sexy is always there." His eyes darken, flanked by the green of the trees around him. "The sweet's what's in here." He brings a hand to my chest, presses it to there. My fingers surround his, pressing his hand as close to me as possible.

I close my eyes and savor the touch. As sweet as it is, it's not enough. "Kiss me, please."

He obeys, cradling his arms on either side of me as he presses his weight against my body. It's delicious, feeling every long, hard curve of him, and when his lips meet mine, it's as if time stands still. The warmth of his body battles the chill away as he curls me close enough to feel his heartbeat.

The kiss is furious, desperate, our lips fused together as the scent of him mixes with the outdoors. A hint of spring freshness swirls with the all-male scent of Cohen, a heady cocktail of passion.

Cohen reaches for my bikini bottoms, running his hands along the edges. He starts to tug at them, but I rest a hand against his wrist.

"Don't break these, too," I say. "I need them for the cruise."

He stills for a moment, his face breaking into a grin. "But I happened to enjoy swimsuit shopping."

With a roll of his eyes and a shake of his head, he slides them off without harm. We're laughing under the last bright rays of the sun, the mood light and breezy, brimming with the joys of spring. The air is cool, our bodies are warm, and between the two of us is a fire that can't be tamed.

Cohen tucks the blanket edges around my body as he pulls his shirt off with one hand, balancing above me with the other. It's a feat in itself, and the ripples of his chest, the strain of his arm holding the weight of his body is all muscle.

I let my hands reach for him, caress over his soft, bare skin. He might be a man who skates for a living, throwing people into walls and all that other sporty stuff, but when he's here, with me, it's different. There's a quiet confidence, a gentle edge to each and every movement.

His hands trail over my body, finding each and every sensitive area and spending time there. When his hands reach my breasts, my hips raise to him, my breath coming in pants. He pauses for a moment, reaching down, dipping a finger inside me and feeling my need.

"Be patient, sweetheart," he murmurs, leaving me wanting as he continues a treasure trail of kisses across my stomach. "Not yet."

Patient is a foreign word at the moment. I'm not in the mood to go slow, to be patient—I've figured out what I want, and I want it now. Him. Cohen. Everything. So, I reach down to fumble with the button of his jeans while our lips find each other in the tangle of heat.

"Okay," he groans, standing for just long enough to free himself from the burden of pants. "Patience is overrated."

He is stunning. I knew this, I *know* this, but every time I see him it's a small miracle all over again. By the time he's eased himself back onto me, I've found my voice. "Remind me why someone like *you* is hanging around with someone like me?" I breathe. "You're gorgeous, and you could have anyone—yet you're here, fooling around with me by the lake."

"We're not fooling around," he says, pressing himself to me. There are no more layers between us, save for the condom he's pulled out of nowhere, and the thrilling threat of what's next is heavy in the air. "I love you."

I already forgot the question. Instead, I'm focused on the feel of him situated between my thighs. Heat curls in my stomach, the sensation of him against me not enough to satisfy my cravings. He moves slowly, teasing and taunting to maddening levels as he gently nudges against my opening.

"I'm here because I love you," he says. "And I want to be with you. It's simple."

His words propel us onward, and I hold him even tighter, so tight my fingers dig into the skin of his back. The angle of my hips against his silences him as we press chest to chest, skin to skin, core to core as his eyes close in pleasure, in anticipation.

Then, Cohen's eyes flick open, a jungle reflected there as the sun slips behind the trees, the sunlight streaking across us in shadowed beams to stand guard against the chill of the air. With it comes the glow of mystery, hope, the end to another day. Behind him, branches sway from the trees, twisting over the water, the gentle waves crashing against the rocky ledges.

"You're the only person who fits me," Cohen says, easing between my thighs, his voice heavy with lust. "In every way, Annie. I can't get enough of you."

With those words, he pushes into me, hissing with the satisfaction of the moment, the tipping point after a day spent burning with desire for each other—looking, touching, exchanging secrets and whispers.

My fingernails dig into his shoulders before he even starts to move. He fills me in a way I'd never imagined possible. When he brings a hand up, presses it to my lower stomach, his thumb hovering just on the edge, rubbing small circles, I close my eyes and focus on staying here, in the moment.

Then he moves, and my eyes flicker open. It's no longer a tender, sensual moment—it's everything I've asked for. Intensity, passion. He fists a hand through my hair, crashes his lips to mine. I raise my hips, asking him, needing him, and he delivers.

We move in sync, the end arriving fast this time, circling us, swirling, just on the verge of taking flight. One of his hands reaches behind my head and angles it to deepen the kiss, his other hand holding my back as he thrusts.

Then, everything fades, and all that's left is us, rushing toward blackness. It swallows me whole as Cohen drives us to a wild frenzy, my hands gripping him as he clutches me to his chest. We hold each other for dear life as we spiral into a shimmering abyss, caught somewhere in between the light of the sun and the incoming moon as evening sets.

When I return back to reality, my breath is quick and sharp, while Cohen's is stilled, calm. His eyes are closed as if resisting the return to reality. I wait patiently, unable to wipe the grin off my face, until he scoops me into his arms and rolls to the side, cradling my head to his chest.

"Wow," he says.

"Excellent."

He drapes an arm across my waist, and it's like this that we fall asleep. We doze on and off, covering one another with the blanket until sometime under the setting sun, Cohen shuffles me into some clothes and carries me to the car.

When I wake the next morning, it takes some time for me to remember if last night—if Cohen, and everything we shared—was a dream. But Cohen's still there next to me, an arm draped over my waist.

Lucky for me, he's real.

Chapter 48

Cohen

The heat from our time at the lake extends for several weeks. Weeks filled with sleepless nights, lazy mornings, and sleepovers that rock my world.

I haven't felt this incredible since I believed in Santa Claus. These past few months with Annie, however, have peeled back layers to reveal a level of excitement I didn't know I possessed. A thrill for being alive that has been keeping me out of trouble everywhere... except when Annie's involved. Together, we've managed to find plenty of trouble.

Until tonight.

The biggest game of the season. The *one game* Coach asked me to give my all. To keep my head on straight and to leave any distraction at the door.

Somehow, I failed, and we lost.

We lost the biggest game of the season, and it's all my fault.

I should've finished it off when I had the chance. Slammed the cross from Pierce into the back of the net when I'd first received the pass, but instead, I tried to be fancy. I tried to dance my way around the defender and, instead of sinking the puck into the back of the net, I hit the frigging post.

Thank God Annie's not here. Thank God my dad decided years ago that he never cared to see me play. Thank God for small miracles. I know Annie's watching from home on TV. She's called three times since the buzzer rang, and I can't bring myself to answer.

It's been a few weeks since our night at the lake and, in recent games, it hasn't bothered me so much to win or lose. It *sucks* to lose, but at the end of the night, I know I'm going home to Annie. And there's something comforting about that, and it makes losing a little more bearable.

Tonight, however, things are different. It's *my* fault we lost, and Ryan Pierce can't even look at me. I don't know what the hell I was thinking trying to dink around out there when I had a shot—a wide open goal—and I missed it.

We're all in the locker room as Coach talks to us, winds us down, offers quiet words to keep our heads held high. *What else can he say?* This was the go hard or go home game, and we're going home with a two to one loss in overtime.

"We had our chance, but it wasn't our night," Coach says. "It was a great season. Shower, change, and put on a decent face when you leave the locker room. We'll be back next year. Understood, Pierce? James?"

I don't look up.

"Did you hear me, James?" Coach repeats. "You fucked up, we get it. But so did everyone else. It's not your fault we lost."

The pity only makes it worse. Sure, everyone makes mistakes but, unlike everyone else's mistakes, mine was the big one. The one that'll be remembered for weeks to come.

"Get in the showers," Coach yells. As the guys scatter, he strides across the room to me. "What the hell did I just tell you?"

I bring my head up, though I can feel my eyes blazing.

"Watch yourself, James," he says. "Don't screw things up now."

"Too late for that."

"Don't feel sorry for yourself." Coach crosses his arms. "Stand up. Get dressed. Go home."

I can't stand Coach's sudden sympathetic attitude, so I shift my ass off the bench and haul myself to the shower. It's silent in there save for the patter of water, the occasional cough, the grumblings of the losing team.

I don't look at anyone. *Yeah*, I feel sorry for myself. I let the team down, let down anyone watching the game. I can't even bring myself to see Annie tonight, and we had plans. It's not fair to her—she doesn't deserve to date the team loser.

The water turns scathing hot all of a sudden, like locker room showers sometimes do, and I don't bother to change it back. I scrub myself until my skin's red and raw, and then I climb out, towel off, and shove myself into some acceptable clothes.

Annie's called twice more, but I can't bear to listen to her messages, can't text her back. I know what she'll say: she'll try to talk me into coming over so she can calm me down. She won't say the loss is my fault, but we'll both know it, and that makes my stomach churn.

I've always been a screw up in one form or another. It's no *wonder* my dad has no interest in watching me play; I can hardly expect him to be excited when I'm putting on shitty performances like this one. Maybe he's right. Maybe I'm not cut out for the finer things in life.

Things like Annie.

My phone rings again, her name popping up on the screen. I silence it with a swipe of my thumb and sweep out of the room like a storm cloud. I'm brooding, moody, pathetic, and I don't care a bit.

The team's going to grab some food. I *should* join them, but I'd be a major buzzkill. Best if I'm alone tonight. With the mood I'm in, it'll be better this way.

I make it outside, past the herd of folks waiting for a glimpse of players, and lower my head, desperate not to be seen. The worst possible thing that could happen now is a reporter catching me like this, asking questions, prodding me like an injured animal. Because I'll lash out, and I don't want that recorded.

"Excuse me, Mr. James?"

I keep moving. *Reporter.* Figures.

"Mr. James? Sir? Cohen?"

"What?" I'm still walking.

"Quick question." The woman hurrying after me is pretty enough with brunette hair and crisp, piercing eyes. She reminds me of a hungry little bird. There's a falseness to her voice that has me cringing with each breath. "Tough loss tonight?"

"Obviously," I growl. Not only is she a reporter, but she's Captain Obvious. Just lovely.

A cameraman scurries behind her, just in time to catch the start of the next question. I finally slow down my pace, rolling my eyes as I turn to face them both, digging my manners up from the darkest corners of my person. Coach will not be happy if I screw this one up.

"You played well tonight," she says. "Really unfortunate about the missed opportunity off of Pierce's pass—"

"Oh, really?" My voice is dry, eyes shifting for signs of an exit. This woman and the cameraman have me cornered. "I hadn't noticed."

She fumbles her response for a moment, and I almost apologize. Then, she starts waving a tiny pad of paper around, offers me a wink, and starts the next question. I immediately forget about apologizing.

"So, Mr. James, where are you off to so fast?" she asks, looking down at her paper for a brief pause. "Rumor on the street is that you're in a brand new relationship. Are congrats in order?"

I raise an eyebrow, refusing to drag Annie into this mess. "That's the best you've got?"

Her jaw tenses as she balances the notebook and begins to write, reading the words aloud as she does so. "Can't score on the ice, but I'm hearing confirmation you've scored a woman. Are you exclusive?"

I glare at the cameraman first, since the reporters gaze is too penetrating. The man doesn't offer me a lick of help, so I look into the birdy eyes of the woman. "I'm in a relationship."

"Congratulations. Can I assume we'll be seeing some sort of ring?"

"Ring?" Coach has approached from behind me, noted the camera, and now steps into the shot. The reporter's excited to see him, especially since he seems keen to comment on *my* relationship. "I don't think James is the marrying type."

I remember the distinct *clink* of the puck against the post. Annie's missed calls, which now number into the double digits. My need to be alone tonight.

Coach has a point. Whether or not I love Annie, I'm not the marrying type. I've disappointment my dad for long enough—I can't bring the burden on Annie, too.

"I've gotta go." I move away as Coach claps me on the back hard enough to signal my time to shine is up.

"Pleasure chatting, James," the reporter says. "Better luck next year."

The interview continues, a distant buzz against my ears as I hightail it to the door, drag myself into my car, and begin to drive. Somewhere. Anywhere. Away.

Chapter 49

Annie

Not the marrying type?

Cohen had nodded after his coach had said this, and that nod was like a stab to the gut. For me, for him, for both of us. He'd ignored my calls all night. I'd called no less than thirteen times since the game ended, and it's now after midnight. I can feel him pulling away, distancing himself from me like a physical pain.

Clearly, he's not planning to call me back.

I'm sitting on my couch, watching the replays of the playoffs, as Sarah comes out to join me.

"Still here?" She plops down next to me, still in her volleyball clothes from a co-ed game earlier this evening, with a bowl of ice cream in hand. "Tough loss, huh?"

"Yeah."

"You're not moaning about that interview, are you?"

"I'm not *moaning.*"

"Look." Sarah pauses to dig a spoonful of cookie dough out from underneath a hunk of chocolate chip. "He's a professional athlete. The game's got his blood pumping, and I'm sure he's pissed at himself for missing a goal that could've stopped overtime in its tracks."

"Yeah, but—"

"Then some stupid reporter shoves a camera in his face, and his coach pulls that douche-canoe move? Focus on the positives. Cohen *said* he was in an exclusive relationship."

"True," I agree.

"He's nuts about you." She shrugs. "Give him a break. It's a tough night for him, so you'll just have to be patient. He'll come out of it on his own."

"I don't know what to think—he won't return my calls."

"Look." Sarah shifts to face me, setting the spoon down for a moment. "Cohen worked his ass off to get you to trust him, didn't he? Spent weeks just trying to get you to agree to go on a *date* with him."

"I suppose."

Sarah stands, polishes off the bowl and dumps it into the sink. "Don't you think he deserves a little bit of the same effort?"

"What?" I stand too, following Sarah into the kitchen. "Do you think I'm not *trying*? I am trying. Maybe I'm just not *good* at relationships."

"Maybe he's not either, but you two are going to have to figure it out." She leans against the counter, searching my face with her gaze. "If you want to be with him, show him that. He's fought for you—now go fight for him." She rinses her hands, letting her gaze fall from my face. "I love you, girlfriend, but as far as I'm concerned, Cohen has proven that he loves you—that he'll show up. Make sure he knows the same thing is true in return."

"How? What can I do if he's not answering my calls?"

"I have to shower. I smell like a rhinoceros. Think about it."

"But—"

She pauses at the bathroom door, then offers a sympathetic smile. "You know what to do, babe. I'll see you tomorrow."

Chapter 50

Cohen

I crash through the door, slamming it shut so hard the wall rattles. I don't have a lot of self-control right now, which is why I've come to the place where it all began. I should've gone straight home, but I didn't. I came to face my father.

I take loud steps toward the living room as the bumble of television chatter filters down the hallway. The channel changes from a sports network—*a sports network?*—to some stupid late night sitcom as I round the corner.

My dad doesn't bother to look over from his place on the La-Z-Boy. Raising a beer to his lips, he takes a sip and watches a dumb joke that gets a round of applause from the laugh track. The way he's focused on the screen sets off alarm bells. Nobody can watch a sitcom with that much interest.

And then, it hits me.

He watched the game—and he doesn't want me to know it.

"Are you proud?" I move across the room, standing directly in front of the television so he has no choice but to stare at my stomach instead. "You saw everything, didn't you?"

He takes another long, lazy pull of his Bud Light before giving a disinterested smack of his lips. "Why are you here?"

I pace around the room, his low drawl getting on my nerves. He didn't ask me to stop over—he never calls, texts, emails. I'm still wondering why the hell I'm here when he begins to speak.

"Cornered you at the end there, didn't they?" He takes a moment to swallow. "Great interview, son."

I can't look at him. If they'd aired that clip and Annie had been watching... it couldn't have made her feel great. *Not marriage material.* I shake my head, cringing at the replay in my mind.

A year or two ago, I wouldn't have shied away from that reputation. I might've even flaunted it, been proud of my independence, my desire to stay single and live a life free from those ties.

Then Annie arrived in the picture, and now I don't know what to think anymore. Tying myself to Annie for a lifetime sounds pretty good, actually, and I'm beginning to wonder if I had my priorities all wrong before.

"I knew you had it in you, kid." My dad, for once, sounds almost proud. "Women. They always leave. Better if you don't get attached to some girl."

"Annie's not *some girl*," I snarl.

"You think she'll stay with you after you admitted to the world you don't want to get married?"

"I didn't *say* that. Coach put words into my mouth. We were both upset."

"What does it matter? She'll misinterpret it, just like women always do."

I'm silent. Not because I agree with him, but because I can see how Annie might've taken the interview to mean something it didn't. I have to find her, set the record straight before it's too late.

"Don't blame your shit on me, Cohen." My dad stands suddenly, tall, thinner than he used to be, soft around the middle. "I can see what's going through your mind. This is all your old man's fault for turning you off marriage. You'd *never* be in this situation if it weren't for me—that's what you're thinking, isn't it?"

I remain quiet, fuming, because a part of me is thinking *exactly* that.

"Don't let me stop you, Cohen. You want to marry the girl? Marry her. Invite me or don't. It's your life."

It takes a second for me to process, to figure out why the hell I'm still standing here. My dad hasn't changed in twenty years—why should I expect him to offer me advice now?

"Maybe you're right," I tell him, softer now. "Maybe I shouldn't get married. Because Annie is perfect, and I don't deserve her."

"Get out of my house, kid. I'm sick of you dumping your problems on me. I've got enough of my own without you coming to whine at me."

I wait for a long moment, offering up one final chance for him to change his mind, to offer me a snippet of hope, a bit of wisdom from his fifty odd years on this planet. But there's nothing. I'm drained, emotionally and physically, and he's pissed. Nothing good will come of me standing around.

"I'm sorry I came here." I turn, leaving him to return to his armchair in peace.

I make my way to the front door, noticing along the way that Rosa, bless her heart, has sent one of her cleaning ladies to brighten this place up. There are flowers near the door—not that my dad will ever notice—and I make a mental reminder to send her a massive tip.

This time, when I slide into my car, I point the wheel toward home. I need to think, to cool down, to figure out what to do. My dad might be a jerk, but he has one point. I went to his house to yell and moan about my problems, but it didn't solve anything. I wanted to dump my crap on him, but it didn't work. The problems that need solving aren't at my dad's house.

I couldn't admit it before, but I can see it now. I'm terrified to face Annie Plymouth. I'm terrified of the fact that I love her more than I love the game, my career, life itself. I'm terrified because I can see myself spending a lifetime with her, and here I was, looking for a way out.

My fingers grip the steering wheel tight at this realization, the yellow lines of the freeway licking the underbelly of my car as I fly toward my condo. The way I see it, I have two choices. I can go home, sulk, and make my dad proud. I can give up on love and turn into a single, bitter old man with only a beer koozie to keep me warm at night.

Or, I can turn my car around, go find Annie, and tell her what I should've told her weeks ago.

Chapter 51

Annie

He's not here.

Or, if he is home, he's not opening the door.

My heart sinks, inch by inch, until it's descended to the pit of blackness in my stomach. I'd thought *for sure* that he'd come home after the game. He's probably frustrated, sad, annoyed—exhausted from the ups and downs of the day. Where would he go to nurse these wounds if not home?

I knock again, but there's no answer. The thought that he's inside, listening and ignoring me, sets my pulse on fire. He wouldn't hide from me, right? Surely he knows that the outcome of some stupid game doesn't change how I feel about him.

I lean my ear against the door, but there are no signs of movement inside, no sounds, either. The water isn't running, nor is there a stray light shining from underneath the door.

Sinking to the floor, I clutch my phone in my hands and consider my options. I could call him again, but I think I've made it clear I'd like to talk to him. If he wants to find me, he has my number.

As I scroll through my phone, I catch sight of Andi Peretti's number. I'd forgotten she added her digits and, in a flash of worry, I press *dial*.

"Hello?" She sounds peppy and chirpy, like usual, over the ambient noises of a cocktail bar behind her. "Who is this?"

"Hi, sorry, this is Annie. From the pancake breakfast?"

"How are you? Sorry, I hadn't saved your number yet. Tough loss tonight, huh?"

"Yeah."

"I'm currently trying to convince Ryan that the world hasn't ended because their team didn't slam the little black thingy into a patch of fishing net. You doing the same with Cohen?"

"Unfortunately, I'm not."

"What's wrong?"

"It's Cohen. Do you know where he is?"

"Oh, *no*. I thought he would be with you. He ducked out right after the game."

"Yeah, I haven't seen him. I'm at his condo... well, outside of it. He's not home, and I'm worried about him."

"I'm going to call around and see if I can find anything out. Ryan will help, too. I'm sorry, hon."

"It's fine. I just want..." I swallow. "If he wants to be alone, I get it. I just want to know he's somewhere safe."

"Keep your phone handy. I'll text you the second I get a bite."

By the time I hang up, my hands are shaking. I let the phone drop to the floor and sink my head onto my hands. I can't stop the thoughts from coming, from wondering if I pushed him too far at the lake, tried to move things too fast, too serious, too quick.

Why did I have to bring up marriage? Why couldn't I just *relax* and enjoy what we had? My lip quivers, heart speeding, bursting with pinpricks of regret, wishing to go back and change things. Wishing to be *normal*, wishing I could just let myself feel, wishing to let myself simply *be*. In love, happy, together with Cohen.

The first tear slips from my eye and skids down my cheek.

I don't wipe it away.

When the rest of the tears arrive, I let them fall.

Chapter 52

Cohen

She's not here, not anywhere.

I'm at her apartment, but her car is gone and nobody's answering the door. Raising a hand, I give one final knock as a last ditch effort. I can't call her since I left the phone in the car in my haste to see her.

One last knock, just to be safe.

To my surprise the door flies open this time.

"What in the world are you doing here?" Sarah, Annie's roommate, is dressed in a robe with a towel wrapped around her hair. She's got a cookie in hand, and her face is pinched in frustration, as if I've interrupted something. "I had to get out of the shower mid-rinse just to find *you* here?"

I glance at the cookie, push the confusion away, and meet her eyes. "I'm looking for Annie."

"Well, duh!" Sarah takes a bite and chomps away. "She's looking for *you*! Go find her, idiot! Sorry, you're not an idiot. But *honestly*, she called you a hundred times. You couldn't have picked up once?"

"Oh, I *am* an idiot." I agree, her words a startling breath of fresh air. If Annie's looking for me, too, maybe all is not lost. "One more thing."

She wipes crumbs off her hands. "Yeah?"

"Do I still have a chance with her?"

She closes her eyes, gives a shake of her head. "You both are the most frustrating people I've ever known."

With that, she slams the door.

I pound on it again.

She opens it with a roll of her eyes. "*What?*"

"What'd you mean by that?"

"Go talk to your girlfriend, Cohen!" She steps forward, narrowing her gaze at me. "Don't screw this up—she loves you."

"I love her, too."

"I know, that's why I called you an idiot. Now go away and be in love."

I jog to my car, fingers itching to call Annie. But I don't lift the phone from the cup holder because I need the time to think. To figure out what I can say to make everything right. To convince her that I'm more in love than I'd ever thought possible.

Whipping up to my condo, my tires screech as I fly into the parking garage. Snatching my phone, I put the car into park, and jog toward the entrance. It takes all of a minute, but the motions feel like years.

I come to an abrupt stop when I push through the door to the hallway. She's there, curled against the door of my condo like a forgotten puppy. Big eyes filled with glittering tears meet mine, and my heart stutters as my breath gets caught in my throat. The picture cracks my soul in two.

"Cohen." She stands carefully, like a fawn finding her shaky balance, and blinks. Her eyelashes flutter, sending a cascade of the tears down her cheeks. "I need to talk to you."

Chapter 53

Annie

I can't tell what's going through his mind as he strides down the hall toward me. His eyes are dark and murky, yet his footsteps are clear and purposeful. There's a lick of anger on his face fading into something uncertain, cautious even, as he nears me.

At the same time, my phone *pings* with a message from Andi, probably alerting me on Cohen's movements. I swipe it to the side—to reply later—and focus my attention toward the figure striding toward me.

"Cohen," I say, swallowing, wiping away the last of the salty droplets sliding down my cheeks. "I need to talk to you."

Without a word, he unlocks the door and ushers me in from the hallway. I walk in slowly, wondering if he's too upset to speak, or merely annoyed to find me camping outside of his apartment. His lips are pressed tight together, his face a wall of stone.

A sliver of stubborn rises through me, starting at my core and blooming until I'm feeling thin tendrils of frustration at myself—at my goose bumps, my wobbly legs, my insecurities. I might be a woman in love, but I'm here for a reason, and I'm not leaving until Cohen's heard what I have to say.

"Annie." Cohen's back is to me as he closes the door. He leaves his hands pressed against it when he starts speaking. "I'm sorry—"

"No," I interrupt. "Stop."

"I should've—"

"*Stop.*" My voice comes out loud, breaking with emotion. "Please, just let me say what I've come to say."

Cohen's gaze lands on me, his eyes surprisingly bright, if a bit distant, as if he's already hardened himself to whatever's coming next. A sigh sinks from his chest, stealing the last ounce of energy from his face. "I'm all yours."

As much as I want to reach for him, touch his hand, whisper a word of reassurance in his ear, I can't do it. I can't avoid the problem like I did with the lake, the water, for *years*.

If I've learned anything these last few weeks, it's that love, much like fear, isn't something that vanishes on its own. It doesn't disappear when shoved behind a wall or swept under the rug. It lingers, out of sight, growing in silence.

When flowers grow, they bloom into beauty and joy and love. But when it's fear, regrets, missed opportunities—it grows into a chokehold strangling all brightness. For Cohen and me, there are no short cuts. There's no way over the walls between us. There are no ways under or around it. If we're going to make this work, we'll have to go through it.

"I realized something, tonight," I tell him, my fingers wrestling before my body. "I came here to tell you I loved you."

"Annie—"

"Wait, *please.*" I step backward, needing the extra distance to gather my thoughts. "I wanted to apologize. For pushing you too far, too fast, too serious. At the lake, maybe I shouldn't have asked about marriage. We haven't even known each other a year. We have time to figure those things out, I'm sure."

He absorbs my words, the expression on his face hard as slate. As per my instructions, he stays quiet, unmoving save for a twitch of his fingers.

"But I was sitting out there, crying in your hallway, and I decided that I'm not *really* here to apologize." I'm not shaky, but my voice cracks from the effort. "I'm here because I love you, and I am not going to let you give up on us. If, of course, you love me back."

He shifts, moving his arms to cross his chest. Still no reaction on his face. "I do love you."

I nod, buoyed by this confirmation. "I thought that we could never find love. We're too different." I shake my head, a new wave of tears pricking at my eyes. "But I was wrong. Completely and utterly wrong."

"I know," he says, finally offering an upward curve of his lips. "And I'm glad."

"But this time, *you're* wrong," I tell him, gaining momentum. "You've been avoiding me all night. Not answering my calls. We'd made plans to meet up after your game, Cohen. I wanted to see you, win *or* lose."

"I'm sorry."

"Don't apologize! Just stop pushing me away. You have to let me in—*especially* now."

I'm moving toward him, my hands reaching, grasping his arms. I can't appreciate the sturdiness of him, the maleness in his unwavering stance. I can only latch onto his warmth.

"I don't care if you score a million goals or zero goals. That doesn't change how I feel about you. I don't care that your coach thinks you're not marriage material—he's wrong, too."

"You're not upset about that?"

"Of course not!" He looks surprised by this, so I continue. "What were you supposed to say?"

He exhales a breath, the first fissure in his stony face showing. I can't tell if it's a look of relief, or a look of disappointment. My palms turn slick with the uncertainty.

"Look, I'm not asking for you to say anything back. But I am here because I'm *not*, I can't, let you put up shields to guard yourself from this..." I stop, swallow. "From something this special, this sweet, this... *right* without a fight. You helped to take my walls down, now let me do the same for you."

Tears stream down my face, and my entire body is weak. I'm on the verge of collapsing against him, a wave of exhaustion hitting me hard after spilling the contents of my heart. If I've read this all wrong, if Cohen tells me he's no longer interested, I will be broken.

However, before I let myself give in to the tiredness, Cohen gathers me in his arms. He dries my eyes with a touch of his sleeve before resting his cheek against my forehead, his scent bringing me home.

After resting like this for a long moment, he presses his thumb to my chin and tilts my head back until I'm looking into those portals of green.

"I came here tonight to tell you that I'll marry you. Tonight, to-morrow, whenever." Cohen kisses me with a motion so tender, so gentle, it brings a stifled sob to my throat. "I love you, Annie, and I want to be with you forever."

I clutch to him, holding him as his words sink in. "Cohen, we don't... we don't have to get married anytime soon. That's not what this is about."

"Oh, thank God," he breathes over my shoulder as he lifts me into a hug, my feet lifting from the floor, a light laugh on his lips. "I'm not ready for that yet. But if you wanted it, I'd do it for you."

"I know, Cohen, but we can get there, together. Just like we got here together."

"Can I take you to bed?"

"Please."

My legs wrap around his waist as he connects us with a kiss. There's an urgency between us that's never been there before. We've made love in sweet and tender ways, in the throes of passionate lust, but it's never been like this. Never so raw, so emotional.

He peels off my clothes as the moon streams through the white curtains of his bedroom, then lays me open on the bed there. As he slides out of his pants, his shirt, I watch every movement, every motion in unbridled anticipation.

When he climbs onto the bed, my arms are wide, begging for him to fill the gap, the emptiness against my chest.

His eyes darken as he drinks me in, his hand searching lower, lower, until he finds me ready. "God, Annie, I love you more than anything."

"I love you, too."

With a groan of primal pleasure, he pushes inside, and the sensation is too much. Too much of everything good, of everything soulful and sweet. When he moves, I can barely hold onto him as my back arches, my hips rising to meet him, matching him beat for beat.

The silver of starlight dances across the deep green of his eyes, the pale scar across his eyebrow. My hands twist through moon-drenched hair as he brushes his lips to my neck, my collarbone, my mouth.

His hand presses firm to my stomach, then slides round to my back, lifting me, holding me until we're both rushing toward the deepest depths of pleasure.

We rise together, a cry escaping from one, or both of us, as we reach the climax. My nails dig into his back as he holds me to his chest, hearts beating in sync with one another, as if to separate would be to perish.

Cohen eases us down, back to the mattress as the waves subside. Pulling me into his arms, he caresses every inch of my skin, presses light kisses against my neck.

I shiver, a jolt of happiness trembling down my spine.

"I need to hold you tonight," he whispers against my ear. "Don't leave."

In answer, I snuggle closer to him.

"When I promised you I'd show up," he says, his lips pressed to my temple, "I meant it."

"I know, Cohen."

"I'm going to show up to love you. I'll hold you when you cry and laugh when you're giddy. And I'm going to show up to marry you. I'll show up for kids, too, if that's what you want. I promise I'll be there as long as you'll have me."

I roll to face him, eyes smarting. "I'm going to show up, too," I say, pressing a kiss to his forehead. "I promise."

We curl together, wrapped in the warmth from our bodies. A new level of comfort has settled over us. Despite this, I can't seem to fall asleep. My eyes are glued open, even as I hear Cohen's breathing begin to even a half an hour later.

"Cohen," I whisper, giving him a nudge to the ribs. "You awake?"

"Mmm."

"Remember, a little while ago, when you promised you'd show up for anything?"

"Yeah."

"Great." I roll to him, caressing his naked back with the tips of my fingers. "Gran bought you a Speedo for the competition. How do you feel about wearing it?"

His eyes flash open. "*No.*"

"I love you, too."

Epilogue

Annie

"Put that away."

"Can you believe this was what... seven years ago?" I hold up the photo and sigh wistfully, giving my husband a wink. "You'd never do something like this for me *now*. You were so romantic back then, weren't you?"

Cohen grins, handsome as ever, and slides an arm around my neck while he glances at the photo. He shifts uncomfortably at the sight of us holding participation medals during our synchronized swimming days which, considering we'd come in last, was more of a prize than we'd expected.

He presses a kiss to my forehead, runs a hand over my stomach, and shakes his head. "Whatever you want, honey. Just no more Speedos."

We're standing next to a table on the pool deck of a Caribbean cruise ship. I'd say we are celebrating my birthday, but the *real* reason we're here is because my mother and Claude are renewing their vows. Again.

"Where's Bre?" I ask, tucking myself under his arm. "Is she with Gran?"

"Here! Here!" A small voice shouts. A bundle of energy arrives in a flurry, pitching herself into her dad's legs. She's got jade green eyes, just like him, and a smile that melts my heart. "Can we go swimming? Dad. *Dad?!* Mom. Can you swim with me?"

Cohen lifts her up and gives her a huge smooch to a set of chubby cheeks. "In a minute, sweetheart."

"Oh, now *that's* a pip of a photo." Gran appears behind Bre and looks over our shoulder at the old synchronized swimming snapshot. "I remember those days. We won, didn't we?"

"Sort of," I say with a grin. "We won best dressed. We got last place in the competition."

Gran winks at Cohen. "They probably liked your suit."

He turns red, looks at me over Bre's head, and uses our now-perfected signal for escape.

"Why don't you take Bre swimming for a minute," I say, watching relief flood into his eyes. "Me and Gran will hunt down some snacks."

Cohen doesn't need asking twice. Setting Bre on her feet, holding her hand, the two make their way to the side of the pool. Cohen slides in first, then turns and opens his arms. Bre's standing on the edge, knees positively shaking with excitement. Luckily for her, she inherited her father's lack of fear for dangerous things.

Cohen's arms are wide, but Bre's already taking off, flying through the air before he's completely ready. She plops into the water, her little four-year-old body tucked into a compact cannon ball.

Laughing, Cohen reaches for her and pulls her to the surface. Blinking water from huge, bright green eyes, Bre looks for a moment like she's going to cry. Then, she throws her head back and laughs, giggles, and wraps her arms around her dad.

"Aren't they cute," Gran says. "Do you think I can recruit her to be on my synchronized swimming team in a few years?"

I raise my eyebrow at Gran. "Already?"

"Just think. We could have three generations at once. Do you think Cohen would participate again?"

I cross my arms, knowing he'd hate being asked. Which is why I *wouldn't* ask him because I also know he'd do just about anything for me, for us, for our family. He'd proven that to me since the day we'd met.

We'd waited until I was twenty-five to get married and, just over a year later, Bre arrived. She hadn't exactly been planned, but she'd come when she'd been ready—and now, four years later, she still does exactly as she pleases.

I'd finished law school and now work part time as a lawyer. The part time is because Baby James #2 is well on his way, and I'm taking extra time off to enjoy my family. I rest a hand over my growing stomach, wondering what it'll be like when we have four little feet to chase instead of two.

My eyes rove over the crystal blue waters of the Caribbean, the upscale dining area next to the pool, the palm trees waving on the nearest shore in the summer breeze. My gaze lands on the two loves of my life as they splash around in the pool, singing silly songs and giggling over secrets.

Cohen's eyes land on me from across the deck, and my eyes are torn away from that sculpted body I've come to know so well, catching his piercing stare. His eyes soften like butter, and hold there as he smiles. Then his gaze travels down, lower and lower, before dragging it back to my face. Nearly seven years together have taught me to read his every expression, and I know *exactly* what he's thinking.

Mr. Cohen James wants some time alone. My theories come to fruition when, after a few more flying leaps from Bre, Cohen ushers her out of the pool and brings her back to Gran and me.

Water ripples down Cohen's shoulders, over his slim, rock-hard abs, and I can't wait to get my fingers on them. The man turns more and more handsome with age, and every day we spend together is another day I fall deeper in love.

"Say, I've been wondering, grandson-in-law," Gran wheedles. "Are you up for another synchronized swimming competition?"

"Sorry, Gran," he says. "I don't think so."

"But you were such a hit at the first one!"

"I'll tell you what," Cohen says, lifting Bre to his chest. "If you watch Bre here for the next hour or two, I'll do whatever you tell me. Within reason."

"Really?" Gran narrows her eyes between us "Wait a second. I know what's going on here."

"I'm so tired." I fake a yawn, rest a hand over my mouth, and arch my back as if in pain. "Cohen's going to walk me to bed."

"Well, okay then." Gran sticks out her hand to Bre. "I can't be without my partner in crime, anyway. Let's go, kiddo. I hear they've got cheese sticks down at the buffet. Let's go find them."

Once they're gone, Cohen turns to me. "I hope you don't mind I stole you away, but I have plans for you."

"Mind?" I turn to him, raise an eyebrow, and sink into his embrace. "*Mind*? Sweep me away anytime you like."

We haven't made it off the pool deck yet, and already his hands have planted firmly around my waist. They slide around my body as he guides me into the hallway.

We're walking awkwardly, our limbs entangled, the sound of our laughter like two teens sneaking off under the bleachers. He gives the elastic of my bikini bottoms a playful snap as we hurry toward our room.

Cohen doesn't care we're not at our room yet. He takes a brief break in the privacy of an abandoned corner of the hallway, far from prying eyes. Circling his hands around my waist, he issues a spicy kiss against my neck that sends ripples of anticipation prickling across my skin.

When he leans in closer, whispering a few naughty suggestions in my ear, I'm tingling from head to toe, needing him right then and there. "Where's our room?" I say more urgently. "Let's go. Quickly."

"That's what I thought," he murmurs in a low, husky voice, with a smirk on his lips as he pulls back. He gives me a squeeze, then urges us onward. "Not far now."

"Oh, there you are! Amanda!" Claude rushes toward us. "I am supposed to give you a present from your mother."

"Thanks, Clyde," I tell him as he arrives in a swimsuit severely lacking in square footage. "Can we do this later, maybe? At the party?"

"The party?"

"My birthday party." I'm trying to focus, but it's difficult. Cohen's taken me as a hostage, holding me in front of his body. "That's, uh... there's a party later."

"Oh, yeah, sure," he says, eyeing the pair of us and getting the picture. "I'm going to get some sun, then."

A few more steps down the hall have us tangled up in another embrace, one of my legs wrapping around Cohen as he takes a firm grip of my rear end. For balance, he claims. We're desperately close to our room, but now that we have a daughter, we've got precious few minutes of alone time, and neither of us want to waste a second.

Until a throat clears behind us. *That* hasn't happened in years, and I'm breathing heavily, my face pink as I turn to find my mother.

"Hello, birthday girl and Cohen." My mother gives us a stiff nod. We never *nod* at each other—clearly, she's uncomfortable. "Have you seen Claude?"

"He was just looking for Amanda," Cohen says. "We sent him up to the deck."

"Oh, well, he forgot his sunscreen, and he's burning. I'll find him and... I suppose I'll see you later tonight at the party?"

"Yep," I say. "Gran's up there with Bre, too. They're looking for cheese sticks."

"Well, I could use some cheese sticks, so..." My mother blushes and waves her hand at us. "Carry on."

Cohen's eyes close as my mother vanishes, and our journey is resumed. "If we have one more interruption," he begins. "I'm going to—"

"Do you have a minute, Annie?" This time, the voice is hesitant. Unsure and questioning, which is new, coming from my father. "I have... uh—oh, I'm sorry. You're obviously busy."

I untangle myself from Cohen's embrace. "Hey, dad," I say. "What's up?"

"I'm going to..." Cohen points down the hallway. "Uh, take a shower."

"Don't let me bother you," my dad says. "I can talk to you a different time, Annie."

"No, this is fine," I say with a bright smile, giving a hint of it to Cohen as I tell him I'll be there in a second. "What's up?"

My dad has started to come around in recent years, thanks in a large part to the appearance of his granddaughter. He's been at three of her four birthday parties, and at least one of her dance recitals. It's definite progress.

Getting him to come on this trip was a bit of a stretch but, to my surprise, he made it work. If only Bre knew the power she'd brought to this world. She'd been the cause of our family's shaky steps to reunite.

My mother and father are able to be in the same room together these days, and they've even held a civil conversation. To see how far we'd come as a family had eased an ache in my heart that'd been there for years.

"I brought a present for your birthday, and I was going to give it to you tonight." He coughs, clears his throat, and I can tell this is difficult for him. "But I wanted to do it personally, in private, and explain."

"Aw, dad. I told everybody not to bring presents. Everyone being here on the cruise is plenty."

"It's a selfish gift," he says, offering a handsome smile my way. "It's as much for me as it is for you. Will you open it now?"

"Oh, uh, sure." I accept the beautifully wrapped box—probably the work of his assistant—and pull the ribbons back. Carefully, I peel open the shiny blue wrapping paper, tucking it under my arm as I reveal the box inside. "Thank you, dad! We can definitely use a camera."

"It's not—not about that." A pinch of pain masks my dad's face. "I know you have your cell phones and what not, but my assistant said this one is top of the line."

"You shouldn't have spent so much, dad."

"It's not the camera that's the point," he continues quickly. "I just want... I know I missed out on a lot of your life, your childhood, the years that really matter, and I still haven't forgiven myself for that."

I'm shaking my head, trying to tell him it's okay, but the lump in my throat prevents me from speaking.

"I don't want to miss Bre's life, or her brother's." He nods toward me, offers a smile. "I want to be a part of their lives, and I've been working on it. I promise to be there, to show up to every ceremony I can get to, but in case there's a moment I miss, capture it with this. My point is that I'm sorry, Annie. Your daughter is lucky to have a great mom, but also to have a great father."

"Cohen is wonderful," I say, blinking back tears. Must be pregnancy hormones. Or just regular hormones. "Thank you, dad. This is so sweet. We all love you. Bre's lucky to have you as her Gramps."

My father opens his arms, and I sink into them. It's familiar now, these last few years having brought us closer together than ever before. I am in no hurry to move, or to rush this embrace, so I wait until my dad runs his hand through my hair and steps back.

"I should let you get back to..." He waves a hand. "Whatever you were doing."

"Thank you, dad. This is really special." I hold up the camera as he picks up the wrapping paper that's fallen to the floor. "We'll use it, I promise."

He nods, then turns and wanders down the hall. I watch as he goes, taking a moment to calm my breath. I never thought the day would come that my dad—and my mom—would brave the confines of a cruise ship together. Of all the birthday gifts I could've received, that one took the cake.

** **

Cohen

"Finally!" I'm laying on the bed, having rinsed off quickly and stripped down to my boxers. "I thought you'd gotten lost."

Counting the seconds until my wife walked through that door felt *excruciating*. Somehow, everyone had felt the need to interrupt our precious time alone. As much as I loved Annie's family, I wanted to make good on the birthday promises I'd whispered into my wife's ear ten minutes before.

As Annie closes the door behind her, there's a softness to her movements, a gentleness that doesn't reflect the urgency of moments before.

"Annie?" I sit up. "Everything okay?"

She turns to face me, the most beautiful woman in the world. Her hair cascades around her shoulders, teased by the sea breeze. She's got a flower-patterned dress-thing on that whips around knees, a set of sexy legs peeking out from underneath.

But on her face is a single tear, streaking down pink-tipped cheeks. One of her hands is holding a box, the other is resting on her stomach. I want more than anything to rip the box out of her hands, leaving it to crash to the floor, as I take her on the bed.

That tear, however, is troublesome. As always, when she hurts, I do too, so I push away my burning desire to have her, and I ease the box—a camera?—from her hand, before gently guiding her to the bed.

"What's wrong, sweetheart?" As she lays on the bed, I let my hands trail over her skin, making ribbons of goose bumps as I move, just how she likes. "What did your dad say to you?"

"He wanted us to know that he's determined to be an even bigger part of Bre's life, our life," she says with a shaky breath. "The camera's so we can capture moments when he's not around."

I don't point out that we have cell phone cameras that capture those moments just fine. As I've learned over the last five years as a husband—I'm a male, and males don't understand sentimental gifts. But since it's so emotional to Annie, I murmur something that sounds like, "that's nice."

"I know, I'm being silly. Blame it on my crazy hormones and my uncooperative tear ducts."

"No, you're perfect," I tell her, meaning it as I lean in to kiss the tears from her cheeks. "It was thoughtful of him. He's already been around a lot more since Bre was born."

"*You're* perfect, you know that?" She hooks a hand around my neck as I'm leaned in, and holds on tight. She doesn't let me go, even as she crashes her lips to mine in a possessive way that has me instantly at attention. "I'm so glad I didn't know how to swim."

"Christ, me too. I want you so badly, honey. Let me..." I ease her swimsuit bottoms off, running my hands up and down her legs, teasing her with promises of more. "Happy birthday, baby. Just relax, let me make you feel extra special."

She sighs, and it's a beautiful sound as her eyes close. "Your hands are magic. Can you just... never mind."

"What?"

"My feet are killing me."

"Say no more." I pull one of her feet into my lap, massaging the pale skin and dainty toes while imagining what's to come next. "How's this?"

"Ah..." she says, her voice breathy. "—mazing."

"Good. Just relax." I'm twitching and alert, needy for her in so many ways, but I can be patient. Take my time to ease her stresses, make her body writhe from the tips of her toes to the edges of pleasure. "Relax, birthday girl."

I massage one foot first, my eyes closed as I focus on each and every movement, turning myself on more and more with each touch of my wife's skin. I move up to her calves, rubbing there, and then switch to the other foot.

It's not until I've reached her calf on the second leg that I realize I haven't heard anything in a long while. No moan of pleasure, no groans of happiness or cries for more. I've been too wrapped up in my own fantasies of undressing her slowly, taking my sweet time kissing every inch of her body, nearly bursting from the anticipation.

That's when I realize we have a problem.

She's snoring.

I hide a smile as I lay her feet back on the bed. Standing, I move to the side, pushing flyaway hairs back from her face, her full lips poised for a kiss. I issue one, gentle and soft, meant not to wake her, before I retrieve a blanket from the chair and cover her up to her neck.

Struggling to remain silent, I slide under the blanket and pull her body against mine. She shifts and, in a sleepy voice, murmurs an *I love you* against my neck.

My heart is melted as I hold her tight, brush my lips to her cheek, and whisper, "Sweet dreams, birthday girl."

The End

Author's Note

Thank you so much for reading, and I hope you enjoyed the story! If you'd like to be kept posted on the release date for the next book in the series—another standalone coming soon!—please sign up for *Love Letters from Lily* at LilyKateAuthor.com or find me on Facebook.

***

***

Lastly, if you happened to enjoy the story and can spare five minutes out of your day, honest reviews at the retailer of your choice are always welcome and appreciated.
Thank you so much in advance!

***

Stay tuned for *Hangry Girl*, releasing on October 24th, 2017!

Don't miss out!

Click the button below and you can sign up to receive emails whenever Lily Kate publishes a new book. There's no charge and no obligation.

https://books2read.com/r/B-A-BSTD-OBIO

BOOKS 2 READ

Connecting independent readers to independent writers.

Did you love *Birthday Girl*? Then you should read *Hangry Girl* by Lily Kate!

COVER REVEAL - Coming soon!
A contemporary sports romance

Ladies & Gents,

I sold my soul for a **hamburger**.

And I have no regrets. When a girl is trapped indefinitely in an elevator with a smoking hot burger and an empty stomach, even the strongest of women will crumble.

The story goes like this: Bradley Hamilton, former professional hockey player and the most frustrating human alive, offered me half of his hamburger in exchange for a date. I took him up on the offer—while under duress—and now I'm stuck with the consequences. Specifically, the scorching kiss at the end of our date that has me drooling for more.

However, there's one whopper of a problem. This man has been a thorn in my side for the last twenty years—ever since he moved next door and became my older brother's best friend. We've gone head to head for years, and now, he's trying to buy out my restaurant in order to plop one of his big fat gyms there instead.

I refuse to let him ruin my business. Unfortunately, Bradley Hamilton is like an order of french fries: you just can't have one. It appears our lips are addicted to kissing. He's alarmingly handsome. Deliciously confident. And worst of all? Underneath that salty exterior he's starting to show signs of sweet.

Brad Hamilton is my guilty pleasure, my cheat meal, my greatest craving.

Which is why he'll be one habit that's hard to kick.

Also by Lily Kate

Minnesota Ice
Boss Girl
Birthday Girl

The Girls
Hangry Girl

CPSIA information can be obtained
at www.ICGtesting.com
Printed in the USA
BVOW08s1131201117
500905BV00008B/822/P

9 781635 761276